Fervent

USA *TODAY* BESTSELLING AUTHOR
CLAUDIA BURGOA

MW00764389

Copyright © 2017 by Claudia Burgoa
Cover Design by Hang Le
Edited by: Paulina Burgoa
Ellie Mclove
Virginia Tesy Carey
Marla Esposito

All rights reserved.

By payment of the required fees, you have been granted the non-exclusive, non-transferable right to access and read the text of this e-book on your personal e-reader.

No part of this text may be reproduced, transmitted, downloaded, distributed, decompiled, reverse engineered, stored into or introduced into any information storage and retrieval system and retrieval system, in any form or by any means, whether electronic, photocopying, mechanical or otherwise known or hereinafter invented, without the express written permission of the publisher.

Except by a reviewer who may quote brief passages for review purposes.

This book is a work of fiction. Names, characters, brands, organizations, media, places, events, storylines and incidents are the product of the author's imagination or are used fictitiously.

Any resemblance to any person, living or dead, business establishments, events, locales or any events or occurrences, is purely coincidental.

The author acknowledges the trademarked status and trademark owners of various products, brands, and-or restaurants referenced in this work of fiction, of which have been used without permission. The use of these trademarks is not authorized with or sponsored by the trademark owners.

Sign up for my newsletter *to receive updates about upcoming books and exclusive excerpts.*

www.claudiayburgoa.com

 Created with Vellum

For all the women who dream and work hard to become their own heroes.
Never stop.

love,
Claudia
xo

"I love those who can smile in trouble, who can gather strength from distress, and grow brave by reflection. 'Tis the business of little minds to shrink, but they whose heart is firm, and whose conscience approves their conduct, will pursue their principles unto death." – Leonardo da Vinci

1

LUNA

"**I**f you had only one word to describe yourself, what would it be?"

"Hazel, focus on work only. How do you compensate for your weaknesses?" Scott Everhart, the CEO of Everhart Enterprises, overlaps the questions.

"Dedicated." I turn my head slightly to the left of my computer screen, smiling to Hazel Beesley. According to my research, she's his right hand. She's also been featured in several business magazines as one of the most powerful women under thirty. While investigating the company, we didn't find much about their personal lives. However, Lucas and I gathered that if I get on her good side, I get the job. "Loyal would be the second one."

I turn to Scott, straightening my back. "My strengths and flaws aren't what define me or my work. It's the dedication and enthusiasm that I bring to the table while balancing my best assets and the challenges that the job brings."

I wish I had flown to New York for this interview. It would be easier for me to read their body language in person. From where I sit — in my grandmother's kitchen—it's impossible to get an idea if they are interested or not. Multitasking is proving to be harder than I thought. I'm keeping one eye on the screen and the other one at the entrance of the kitchen to ensure that my dear abuelita stays away. Nothing ruins a job interview like the lovely woman offering me food saying I'm too skinny and with my narrow hips and tiny ass, I'm never going to find a man.

After she reminds me that I'm alone, I'll politely tell her that she's wrong. My ass is huge, my hips are fine, and I don't need a man. The conversation is not fit for this important job interview.

"Describe a time when you were asked to do something you weren't trained to do. How did you handle it?" Scott asks a question I wasn't ready to answer yet—or ever.

Well, I handled it as best as I could. My boss didn't agree. I almost got fired, but they put me on probation for a couple of months instead. I was in therapy for a year because I hate killing people and using my gun. I fight them every time I want to go under-cover . . . They don't need to know any of that though, or that I'm an FBI agent. I perk up, flashing my best smile.

"There have been several times where I've had to steer away from my comfort zone. I guess the most recent was when my boss had a car accident." I pause to add a little suspense, skipping the gory details attached to my last case, I continue, "I had to step into his shoes. It was a different role for me, but I took charge during the difficult moments, and in the end, everything worked out as we planned."

"Difficult moments?" Hazel enunciates those words.

I nod. "We had a meeting with a potential client." I reach for my glass of water and take a few sips. "Negotiating contracts when there's a better choice within the price range for the client is challenging. I had to find a way to convince them that even though my offer wasn't as attractive, it was the right one in the long run."

"That's the attitude we want for this position," Hazel says with an approving smile.

If only she knew what I'm talking about. It happened a couple of months ago in the interrogation room. The better offer was twenty years in jail versus dying at the hands of a Colombian cartel. But I smile at her since I can't release that kind of information. Patiently, I wait for the next question. If I play my cards right, these two might give me what I need.

"My goal is to bring a new business approach to the company while following the philosophy of Everhart Enterprises." I take my pen and draw a squiggly line through that statement, making sure I don't repeat those words during the rest of the interview.

"If we offer you the job, how soon can you start?" Scott inquires after a long pause.

How about now? They don't know how important it is for me to start with my investigation. If I could, I'd have arrived weeks ago. However, my supervisor is an asshole who is setting me up to fail.

Who tells an asset to go and get her own shit? My boss. And I'll show him that I can find a job and do my work at the same time.

"It depends. As I said at the beginning of the interview, my dream is to live in New York. Though moving has to be right. I love my current job, but I would like to find just the right position where I can move forward," I lie and feel a little sorry about the situation. The reminder that my job is to catch pedophiles and save children dissipates the guilt. For now, they have to think that I'm the best out there and they are lucky to get me, even though the only business transactions I've made in my life are when I go shopping. I know about balancing my checkbook, but I don't do it often. And my knowledge about marketing is that I know those suckers know how to sell me cute clothing.

"How soon are you planning to make a decision?" I pull out my phone checking on the calendar.

"We need someone who can start within a week," Hazel responds. "Are you sure you can move to New York that fast?"

"A friend of a friend is subletting me his apartment," I lie because Lucas, my brother, hasn't confirmed anything about housing.

Luna: *Is the apartment available?*

Lucas: *What apartment?*

Luna: *I'm moving to New York. Remember?*

"New York is my dream city, I want to live there. At least for a few years."

"What about your other job?" Hazel narrows her gaze, waiting for me to slip. Or is it to make sure I'm reliable? She seems to be obsessed with plans and long-term commitments.

"I have some vacation time accumulated." I come up with the best plan to move into my new job ASAP. That is if they are going to give it to me. Please, hire me now! "If you offer me the job, I can start as early as next week. That gives me plenty of time to pack and say my goodbyes—while still giving my two-week notice."

Lucas: *You can't move.*

Luna: *It isn't optional.*

Lucas: *I'm still in denial. Also, I'm working on your situation.*

"Do you have any questions for us?" Scott asks.

"Can you tell me more about the day-to-day responsibilities of this job?" I click on my recorder and continue texting my brother.

He doesn't get it, does he? I don't choose my assignments. If he and my father don't like them, it doesn't matter.

Luna: *Well, my situation is that I am moving to New York soon. Is the apartment available?*

Lucas: *The place is yours for at least six months.*

Luna: *Thank you. You can always come visit.*

Lucas: *Have you told Abue about it?*

Luna: *Once I have secured a job and the transfer, I'll make sure our father is the one who takes the bullet. :D*

"What is the typical career path for someone in this role?" I continue with my questions toward my interviewers.

Lucas: *You're evil and smart.*

I learned from his past experiences. A few years back my brother moved temporarily to San Francisco. He told Abuela that he was leaving weeks before it happened. Worst idea ever. Every day she brought her best guilt-trip game. She played the *I'm going to die before you're back* card more often than she drank her *café con leche.* She drinks at least ten cups a day—it keeps her younger. I love her dearly. She's like a mother to me, but I can't handle those guilt-trips.

It won't be long before my grandmother takes the train to New York to drag me back. Moving from Alexandria to that city is going to give her a heart attack. I choose to miss the melodramatic display. I don't know how long I'm staying in Manhattan, but I'll make sure to take the train at least once a month on the weekends, unlike Lucas who never came to visit us. She almost disowned him.

How can he put his job before family?

Family comes first.

We should remain together.

To her, we have to be so close that we should live in the same city or neighborhood. She'll love me the most if I live next door. But I can't move out of the house until I marry a good Mexican man. A hot Latino is acceptable too. That's what good girls do. She thinks I'm still a virgin because no granddaughter of hers will be deflowered before she marries.

Sex, grandma, it's called sex.

I stare at the monitor, listening to Hazel Beesley speak about the incredible career track ahead of me. About all the benefits and opportunities within the company. They sound great, but I don't care much about the business world.

Luna: *I'm not evil. I just choose not to face the telenovela scene.*

Lucas: *Change your phone number and, your name, and perhaps she won't find you.*

Luna: *She'll send the hellhounds.*

"What are the next steps in the interview process?" I ask, hoping that they haven't noticed that I'm only half-listening to the conversation.

"We have a few other candidates to interview today," Scott answers promptly. "Our board will get together afterward, and we will be making a decision as early as Friday."

"Once we make that decision, we will want to move fast. Please, call me if you need help with the logistics of your move," Hazel continues.

Those words grab my attention. Moving fast is something we agreed on one hundred percent. I reach for my pen to write down Hazel's cell number when I hear the door. Damn it. I needed just a few more minutes.

"*Mijita, estas preparando el almuerzo?*" My grandma and her timing. Is she serious? Sorry, but I can't prepare lunch and find a job at the same time, Abue. She enters in the kitchen with my abuelo right behind her. He gives me a slight shrug. Yeah, I know he did his best to stall her. "*Me da gusto que ya dejaste ese trabajo en la policia? Porque eso es solo para hombres.*"

My face falls, what the hell is wrong with my grandmother. I cross my fingers, hoping that they don't know Spanish or that their knowledge of the Spanish language is limited to the basics. If not, my cover has been compromised before it even began.

How can she ask about my job? At least she didn't say the FBI. But damn she's back with her lecture that what I do is only for men. Her old-school attitude irritates me. I might stay in New York forever.

"Well, that's all for now." Hazel is the first one to speak after the embarrassing silence created by the intruders in the kitchen.

"Yes, I think that's all we needed to know." Scott's jaw sets and nods once toward Hazel who shakes her head slightly. I serve the screen a charming smile, hoping they have no idea what Grandma said. "Have a good lunch, Miss Galvez."

"Thank you for your time." I huff turning off the video call.

My stomach churns. It's either hunger or my gut telling me that I flunked the interview. Going to my browser, I pull up my daily horoscope.

Under today's outspoken moon, uttering out the first thing that comes to mind is an unsafe action. Unless, of course, you've got an ingenious idea.

Oh, God. I didn't say anything stupid, but it was stupid to have the interview at home. *Carajo!* Why didn't I read this before I scheduled the time?

Luna: *I need to continue my search.*

Lucas: *For what?*

Luna: *A job.*

Lucas: *I thought you already had it. Not that I want you to leave.*

Luna: *Well, my horoscope said so, and Abue entered the kitchen right when I was about to end the interview.*

Lucas: *You have to stop reading that shit! You're so smart. I just don't get why you base 99% of your decisions on what those sites say.*

Luna: *I love you, but this time it's not a hypothesis. She mentioned my job with the police.*

Lucas: *Fuck! Get something along the lines of your quirks, like a tarot reading or . . . Shit, you're fucked.*

Yep, shit and fuck are just about right. But his stupid comments about my quirks aren't welcomed. I love my brother, but he's never going to understand it. If Mom were here, she'd agree with me.

"What would you like me to prepare for lunch?" I rise from my seat, taking off my blazer and my button-down blouse, leaving me in a sleeveless sundress.

"That's more like you, Luna," Abue says, taking the clothing, I discard and folding them neatly. "You should find a husband. Men pay more attention if you wear those pretty dresses. I need some grandbabies to spoil."

"My mission in life." I kiss her on the cheek and march to the fridge.

You can only teach so many tricks to an old dog, but to my abuelita, there's nothing I can teach her. She knows it all. At least that's what she says.

2

HARRISON

"Not yet!"

It will happen any second now, I murmur.

"Are they ready to deploy?" I continue mumbling shit, watching. Waiting for what feels like fucking forever. "Everyone awaits, sir. All units are ready for your instructions. What is your take on this mission? This doesn't look good, when the explosion—"

"Shut the fuck up, Everhart," a voice comes through my earpiece. I adjust it and recognize Mason Bradley's voice bitching at me. "This isn't a fucking game with action figures."

"Or a video game," Anderson Hawkins, who is on the ground waiting for our informant, states. "I swear to God, I have no idea how I've been putting up with your shit for years."

"Because I've saved your ass a few dozen times," I remind him.

"You want me to kick his ass?" Tiago, who stands next to me, asks in a mocking tone.

"By now, you all should understand that I hate to be on standby." Tiago, Hawk, and I have been brothers since the Army. Then, we moved to the Rangers, and now we all work for the same high intelligence, private security company.

"I need some action," I mumble through the communicator, my

right index finger set on the trigger, my eye trained on the area where Hawk and Bradley wait. "This wait is killing me."

"No, you don't want action," Hawk mumbles back. "If the operation doesn't run smoothly, I will kill you after my woman kills me. She threatened me with bodily harm if I came home with a scratch."

"You're whipped, man," Tiago says.

We laugh. Aspen, his fiancée, is a foot shorter than him and looks so sweet. However, she can stand up to the guy and make him do whatever she wants.

"But he's right, Everhart. You have to chill. Imagine the nine o'clock headlines," Tiago paints the tragic picture. "'Terrorists taking over Manhattan' or 'A group of former Rangers lost their shit and terrorized New York.' My mama isn't gonna like that."

Tiago kicks me with his heavy boots in the ribs. "If you upset my mama, I'll have to bury you alive. You get me?"

I gasp. "Got it." I rub the side of my body. "Not that you can take me down, fucker."

I try to settle, but it's fucking impossible. I wouldn't care to wait in the middle of the Khash Desert in Afghanistan surrounded by terrorists—or to go through caves searching for the Taliban leaders. We've lived through danger. If we are careful, this could be nothing. I'm sure that's going to be the result. This isn't our first job together. They know that I hate lying on the ground watching the action play out from afar. They also know I will wait for as long as it's needed without saying shit. I understand that not every mission means jumping out of an airplane in the middle of a jungle shooting up shit and killing the enemy. Sometimes, like today, I come along to watch the backs of other security details.

What neither one took into consideration when they set up this mission is that, unlike the rest of our operations, this one is at home. My home. Today, I'm only a few blocks from my family. My loved ones are within a thirty-mile radius. What if something goes wrong? I can't lose any of them. Shit, I swore to protect them just as I protected my country for years.

My friends, partners, and brothers in blood weren't here on that tragic Tuesday when the sky lit up, and the towers burned to the ground. Nine-eleven is a day that we all remember. I not only remember it, but I also relive it. The scenes are ingrained in my mind, seared with pain and tears. I saw the flames from the street corner as I was on my way to meet my dad. I wanted to discuss my plans to change duties within his company. My life had been set up for me. I would work for him. One day, when he retired, I would take over Everhart Enterprises.

"Son, we're trapped," he told me over the phone. My chest constricted with his words. My stomach churned. It felt as if an entire battalion had punched me in the gut and left me breathless. He gave me so many instructions at once. I still remember each word, each plea, each piece of advice.

"Take care of your brothers, Harry." Mom implored.

Completely numb, I assured my parents I'd take care of my brothers. I sounded the same way I did when Hunter was only two years old, and Fitz was five; and Scott and I were assigned to babysit them by ourselves. I had no fucking idea what I would do without my parents, but I pretended that everything would work out without them by my side.

"We'll be okay," I promised as I watched from the buildings only a few miles away as the raging fire continued to consume the lives of so many people. "I'll always look after them."

They ordered me to call Scott and help him come back from Boston. They reminded me that Fitz had a weekly appointment with the allergist on Thursdays. That Hunter would need me more than anyone else.

"We will always watch over you and your brothers," Mom promised.

"We love you," they said in unison before hanging up.

"I love you" were the last words I ever heard from them.

"Are we there yet, boss?" I joke, trying to erase those memories and breaking the fucking tension. I regret not sending my family out of town. Everything would be easier to handle if I knew they were safe.

"It's almost over," Tiago informs me as I clean the sweat from my forehead.

We're on top of one of the tallest buildings in front of Central Park in the middle of August at noon watching, waiting. I'm sweating like a fucking pig.

"Can I complain about the fucking weather?"

"Tiago, you have permission to shoot him if he talks again," Mason Bradley, our fearless leader, barks. My ear buzzes after his loud voice comes through. I pull out the communicator for a second, moving the binoculars toward him. His trademark scowl is directed at where he knows I hide. His mouth continues to move.

I place the earpiece back, and I hear shit that makes no sense. ". . . fucking, Everhart, I swear I'd make the rest of your life miserable."

"The asphalt is melting," I complain waiting for his comeback. However, that's when I spot him. My eyes move to the guy with cropped dark hair and a dark camouflage jacket. He marches to Hawk. "Our informant is approaching, Hawk."

Hawk nods once, training his eyes on the man. The moment that they shake hands, I set the timer.

"We have three minutes," I call through the communicator. "Bradley, do your hacker thing. According to your intel, Kassi's people might be onto us. Though I was bitching earlier about the lack of action, honestly, I would like to avoid Armageddon."

Camo-boy sets a black portfolio in front of him. Moving my sight to the left, I spot Bradley tapping his computer urgently.

"Two minutes left," I warn him. "Can you fucking rush it, geek?"

Bradley's eyes fixate on his work but the corner of his lip tugs. He tilts his head, his black hair shining against the glare of the sun, and I almost miss the red fucking dot on his shoulder.

"Fuck!" I move my sight, searching for whoever is pointing a laser at his head.

"What are you doing?" Tiago asks as I stand up and pull out my binoculars, searching for the man who might kill the boss.

"Got you fuckers." I pick up my M24, point at his head, and pull the trigger. Then move the gun, shooting at the guy aiming at Hawk.

"Tiago, send a few men to the building right across the street to clean the area. Bradley, hurry. They are onto us."

"Done." Bradley jumps out of the seat nodding our way.

Tiago and I wait a few minutes, keeping an eye on Hawk and Bradley while they disappear through the crowd without leaving a trace.

"Thank you, gentlemen. This was another successful mission," Bradley announces through the communicator. "The plane is waiting for us. Everhart, are you coming with us? You don't have to be in Seattle until Wednesday. Everything else can be handled remotely. The Brussels project starts mid-September."

Adjusting my jaw, I rotate my neck to loosen the tension. What the fuck happened to "I will buy part of the company so I could do whatever the fuck I wanted?" But I get it. There are jobs that we have to do ourselves. "I'll take the offer of staying home for a few days. Call me if you need me though."

While I gather my equipment, Tiago speaks. "I'll take Brussels and any other shitty job you have for the next couple of months."

I secure my gun, close the case, and stand up glaring at him. "What do you want?"

He takes a deep breath and looks at me. "My sister needs help."

Wiping my forehead, I take a few seconds to think about that sentence. "Wait, fucker. You have a sister?" Wiggling my eyebrows, I grin. "Is she hot?"

"What part of she's my sister, and you don't mess with her, don't you get?"

"Just a minute. I've known you for almost twenty years, and just now you happen to mention a sister?"

He nods once. "Half-sister." His brows furrow as his eyes divert toward the horizon. "I love my mama, but the family shit is a mess, and I keep it as far as possible from my life."

"Is it safe to assume that your father is alive?" He nods at my question. "So, you have a sister that you just learned about?"

"Look, I'm not going to give you the dirt. Luna . . ." He rolls his eyes. "That's my sister's name, is moving to New York. This is the first time she's working undercover outside the DC area. We just don't feel—"

"Wait a minute." I lift my index finger. "Undercover? What is she? CIA, FBI . . ."

He exhales heavily. "She's an FBI agent in the human trafficking department. My sister is a chameleon and can blend in easily. However, she could use a well-known guy to help her navigate the social life in the Big Apple while keeping her safe."

I let out a guffaw. Shaking my head, I crouch to finish picking up my shit. "I get you, brother. If Hazel, who is like a sister to me, were in her shoes, I'd call you to give me a hand. But are you fucking serious? You want me to babysit?"

"Human fucking trafficking," Tiago growls at me. "It's my understanding that she's trying to find the root. The main fucking guy of one of those cells. You know what's going to happen to her if she gets caught?"

I run a hand through my hair, let out a breath, and nod. They'll torture her until they break her and then they might kill her . . . Or they might let her live, and she'll be reliving the hell they put her through for the rest of her life.

"My old man and I don't see eye to eye," he continues. "But I care for my sister." He stops, closing his eyes as he breathes a couple of times, his rough expression is drawn in agony. His eyes open, staring at me in a pleading way I've never seen before today. "I trust her. But if I can help to keep her safe…we can't lose Luna. You get me?"

Placing my hand on top of his shoulder, I squeeze it. "Luna will be safe, brother. I'll be whatever she needs and make sure she's safe. As long as you're my bitch for the next one hundred years." I laugh, moving toward the elevator. "Gotta meet the family for lunch, you want to join?"

"Nah, I'm flying to Florida to check on my momma. I'll contact you when I get more intel on Luna's assignment."

Harrison: *On my way to Juanes.*

Hazel: *You're joining us for lunch? What happened to the job?*

Harrison: *I told you it'd be quick.*

Hazel: *Hooray, you didn't die today!*

Harrison: *Order me a shot of Patron if you arrive first, bumble bee.*

Hazel: *I won't be the first. I'm in the middle of a meeting. Your brother is slaving me. We need help!*

Scott: *I'll order a bottle of Don Julio to celebrate. Jensen is waiting for us in the car. We'll be there before you.*

Scott: *And we are in the process of hiring a few new employees. Stop complaining, buttercup.*

3

HARRISON

The beauty of my job—what seems like a fucked-up day can change within minutes, and no one around me would know what could've happened if the operation was unsuccessful. That's part of what I do. I make sure the world doesn't know about potential threats. In some cases, ignorance is bliss. Now, I'm just a civilian walking through a typical New York day. The streets are humming. Blue skies, no wind, and despite the traffic fumes, it feels like a fine summer day. I swerve to the left to avoid the delivery guy while crossing the street. I pass the street musician and nod at him. I drop some change in the violin case and salute him while enjoying the chords of what sounds like Vivaldi's, "Four Seasons." That piece was one of Mom's favorites and the one she'd set on our CD-player before she went to bed. My chest loosens with the crescendo coming out of the violin. It reminds me of my mother's sweet voice and sunshine. The magical chords erase the two men I just killed. I've watched death before—seen the rivers of blood and desperate screams during battle. It doesn't get easier with time, but I've learned to cope and accept that by taking one life, I'm saving hundreds or even thousands of others.

The day I enlisted in the Army I wanted revenge. These days I pull the trigger to avoid another attack like the one that took away my parents and changed my family forever.

"Everhart!" The excited female voice comes from the other side of the street.

Turning to my left, I spot her. Hazel is across the street. She's waving at me, her chestnut hair pulled back from her face, wearing a dress and Converse sneakers. I cross the street. Once I am right in front of her, I smirk and hug her.

"Why don't you just buy normal shoes, shorty?" I twirl her twice, being careful with the crowd walking around us. "You look ridiculous wearing formal clothing and sneakers."

"That's a nice hug," she says with an unusually nasal voice. She kisses my cheek as I set her down.

"Where are Fitz and Hunter?"

She rolls her eyes. "They decided to hop on a plane and go to Boston."

I smile at her and tilt my head toward the entrance of the restaurant. "What's with you and that voice? You sick?"

"A vicious ear infection and strep." Hazel waves hello to the hostess and continues her way to the end of the room.

Pulling out my phone, I text Fitz.

Harrison: *What happened with the contingency plan? I never said go to Boston.*

Fitz: *Hunter was too tense to stay at home waiting for your call. He's doing much better. But shit, you dropped a text saying get the helicopter ready because all hell might break loose, and you can't expect for him to stay cool.*

Harrison: *Well, it's safe to come back whenever.*

Fitz: *We're working, don't worry about us. But next time keep your shit away from us, please. The contingency shit doesn't fly well with Hunt.*

I scowl at my phone as I continue following Hazel. Does he think I wouldn't keep him safe? Ungrateful fucker. He has to trust me. We had a contingency plan in case something went wrong with my mission. There's a helicopter waiting for my family above the building where the offices of Everhart Enterprises are. That's the reason why Scott had Hazel in his office. She's more than a family friend; she's the little sister we never had and love to annoy. We're also very protective of her.

Hazel dashes through the tables. I follow her looking around the restaurant, getting a head count. The place seems to be at full capacity. Thankfully, Scott sits by the left-hand corner of the room close to the emergency exit. Next to him, there's a group of businessmen wearing gray suits like his. When he spots me, I tilt my head, arching my brow toward the men.

"Who wears it best?" I ask, squeezing his shoulder and taking the shot of tequila in front of him.

He laughs, standing up to meet me with a hug and a pat on the shoulder. "Shut up, asshole. I'm glad you're back."

"To our favorite hero," Hazel proposes a toast, "and tacos." She sets the shot glass on the table, close to Scott, without drinking any of it.

My eyes widen. What the fuck? "Who knocked you up?"

"You," she answers with a straight face.

"Bumblebee?" I cross my arms, drinking two more shots of tequila.

Who am I going to kill?

"I'm serious."

She smirks, smacking her lips. "No one that I know of."

"Then why aren't you celebrating with us?"

"I have to abstain for two reasons. One, I'm taking antibiotics and two, Grandpa will kill me. He's a hard-ass boss, unlike him," she points at Scott, "who loves me so much he'd let me drink at my office."

"Drinking while working is not allowed." Scott's jaw hardens, and he hands her a glass of water. "Or while you're sick. Once you recover, I'll take you on vacations, and you can drink your weight in alcohol."

"She's still working for you?" I glare at him. "Aren't you hiring a new person?"

"He thinks he owns me," Hazel says, laughing at him. "Scotty doesn't understand that I own his ass."

Scott lifts his hand, signaling the waiter to come over. "You can say whatever you want. The deal was you'd work for me for as long as I need you, buttercup. Technically, I own you." He smirks at her. "Because I'll always make sure to need you."

"Ugh." She rolls her eyes.

Hazel transferred from Duke University to Columbia. Scott helped with the transition under the condition that she'd work for our company. He needs help and someone who he can trust when he's absent.

"Okay, enough about work." She turns her palm up and wiggles her fingers. "You have to pay your debt."

My brother pulls out a fifty-dollar bill from his wallet and hands it to her.

"Thank you, kind sir."

"What did you bet?" I raise an eyebrow.

"That you'd assume I was pregnant."

"Well, I don't see another valid reason to avoid alcohol while celebrating." Hazel always celebrates with me.

She takes a chip out of the basket, dips it in guacamole, and stares at me. "To get knocked up, I need a boyfriend—or to get laid." She shakes her head. "I'd have to find a man first and fall in love." She bites her chip smirking at me as she chews.

"Well, you do that." I dust my arms pretending I'm repelling something—love. "I think you should save the money you won today."

Hazel and I have our own bet going on—to see which one of us avoids falling in love the longest. "In fact, I'll find you a man. And it won't be Anderson. He's getting married soon."

"If I wanted, I'd find myself a man, thank you very much." Her snarky tone is replaced by annoyance. She rolls her eyes and grabs her purse, but my brother hands her a tissue and then hand sanitizer.

Thank you, she mouths at him.

"Today I'm not in the mood, Harry." Her voice is dry. The humor disappears.

"Too bad." I try to lighten up her mood. "I was thinking about starting a manhunt this weekend."

She glares at me.

"Stop this childish shit, Harrison. No one is falling in love and leave her the fuck alone. She's not feeling well." Scott who behaves like a sixty-year-old man sometimes uses his badass voice to warn me.

"Love isn't childish." She scowls at me and glares at Scott. "One day you're going to eat those words, Scotty. You'll fall so madly in love you won't be able to breathe unless she's right next to you. Her touch will be the only thing that will make you feel alive."

She turns to the waiter, ordering an assorted plate of tacos to share and more guacamole. Once he's gone, Hazel's head angles toward Scott and she gives him an *I got you* smirk. "I'm going to make sure I have front seats to the show. Seeing you fall in love is going to be fun. Watching you bend forward, backward, and every-where to make her happy will be the cherry on top. I can't wait, Scotty-boy."

I can't help but laugh at her scenario and my brother's mumbling. If there's a person who can shut down my brother and make him squirm, it's Hazel. She doesn't own him, but she can pretty much do anything she wants with him. They are complete opposites. He's tall, dark, sullen, and quiet. She's petite, sunny, and noisy. He hates love. She's a romantic at heart. And relationship meddling is her hobby. She's set on finding love for my brothers and me. Someone to spend the rest of our lives with because we deserve a happily-ever-after. I have no idea if that will work for me—ever, but some days I would like to have what my baby brother has.

He has a woman who loves him, and he loves. Even after a rough start, there's nothing one won't do for the other. Seeing how happy she makes him—just when she smiles in his direction—makes me want it. As I look at Hazel, I wonder if something between her and I could work. But there's no spark, no chemistry between us. I love her the same way I love my brothers. There's no way I could take it to the next level.

"Hazel, leave the heartless tin man alone," I chide but laugh again, rolling my eyes at his dark frown. He's planning my death.

"He's lying, Scott." Her hand reaches his and she gently squeezes it. She then leans closer to him, and I wish the noise level were lower so I could hear what she's whispering. The crease on his forehead is gone and the faint smile he only gives her appears for two seconds. "You have the biggest heart of the Everhart guys."

"Now, tell me what your next mission is." She turns around and questions me, a smile stamped on her face and her inquisitive mind ready to interrogate me.

"I'm going to be out of town for the next couple of weeks." I'm vague about my whereabouts, but I try to update them as they worry about me. "Though after that, you'll see me every day."

"Why? Are you old and ready to retire, Grandpa?" she smirks.

I think she's either not as sick as she says or she's trying hard to keep up with me.

"I'm only twelve years older than you, child. But my next job is in town, nothing dangerous," I specify when Scott's jaw begins to clench.

"Babysitting, I'll be around to make your life a living hell."

"Ha, it's the other way around, my friend."

The lightness of this moment makes everything that happened before dissipate. There's nothing better than being with the people I love the most. They erase the images of the smoke, the screams, the violence.

4

LUNA

The flight attendant announces that we'll be landing at JFK in only a few minutes. I stare out the window, glad to see the body of water and tiny buildings getting closer by the second. A feverish shiver runs down my spine. This isn't my first undercover assignment, but the first where I'm with a new team. Though I've been working for the chance to be away from my family, now that it's happening the jitters are eating me alive.

Things haven't worked as I planned. The job I wanted didn't happen. Hazel and Scott called to inform me that my background check came back with an interesting set of training skills. And if I wanted a job in the field, they knew a guy who could use them.

"Unfortunately, your badassery background is not for us, but thank you for applying." Hazel hung up the phone.

Bitch. I don't like her, not one bit. If I ever see her in New York, I'll make sure to use my badassery skills and kick her butt. Snobbish bitch.

Though they ruined my first option, I got a job nonetheless. Following my brother's advice, I searched for a job at a yoga studio where I could teach and also practice Reiki. It's so much easier than holding an executive position. Three emails, one long phone conversation, and two signed contracts later, it was confirmed. I have a job. This isn't anything but good news. The planets aligned. The stars shined. At least that's what I thought until today. Until this moment, when we're about to land and I happen to open the Astrology Daily app.

Mars and the sun enter your career sector. As they meet, they point to a real rush of activity and attention to your career or reputation. You're not content to simply think about or plan out these matters—you want to exploit every opportunity and take charge now!

This is the time to ask for a better position. But beware, people will make more and more demands on your time. It'll lead to a loss of control of your priorities. Keep your eye on the prize. Find a way to regain normalcy. Nevertheless, you refuse to give up; you know a solution is near and a great adventure ahead will once again inspire your heart and soul.

Watch for blind impulsiveness.

Luna: *This might not work out as well as I thought.*

Lucas: *Why?*

Luna: *Let me read my daily horoscope on the two other apps.*

Lucas: *No, no, and no. You can't possibly come to that conclusion based on those crazy apps.*

Lucas: *Luna, you're not seventeen anymore. Why the fuck are you still reading that shit?*

My brother doesn't understand why I follow my daily horoscope diligently. They center me when I feel lost. It's the idea of finding answers to questions only a mother would know how to respond to.

Like . . . *Don't worry, the job is yours. It'll be fine, maybe hectic at the beginning, but you got this. Be careful, things usually settle after you've been there for several days.*

At least, that's what I believe Mom would say if she were with me. I imagine her voice was sweet, calm, and loving. Lucas tells me the best stories about her. She made everyone around her feel as if they were special, loved. I wouldn't know. Mom died when I was only a few months old. I don't remember her. I recall her scent by recreating it. I use scented oils and the notes she left behind. Mom had many journals filled with so much love and knowledge. I also have letters she left. Of anyone, I think I know her best. She talks to me through her old words. Everyone misses her, except me. What's there to miss?

Though I yearn for the person, I never met, and the conversations I missed—the milestones we never had. She didn't hear me talk, or see me walk. I didn't go to mommy and me playdates. There was no one to hold my hand and kiss my boo-boos when I fell off my bike. She wasn't there when I had my first crush, nor to console me when the idiot broke my heart because he chose Ana instead of me.

We didn't have much time together, but I know that she loved me. Often, I console myself with the old pictures of her holding me. Her green eyes stare at the pink bundle in her arms as if I was the most precious, little thing in the world. Her sun and her moon, Lucas says that's what she used to call me.

Astrology is a prediction that doesn't always come true. But like the journals of my mother, it gives me something to believe in, to hold on to when there's so much turbulence around me. Having such a pragmatic career, I shouldn't base my life in the perhaps factor—the notion of coincidence—but there's something flattering about thinking that my entire destiny reflects on the stars. My fate is written by a cosmic energy that's close to my mother. It all sounds crazy if I voice it, that's why I don't say it out loud. Only a few know that I read my daily horoscope from at least three different apps. I doubt anyone will ever understand that I allow myself to believe in magic.

Luna: *It's a gorgeous Monday morning in New York. I won't allow you to tamper with what can be a wonderful, yet hectic day.*

Lucas: *You just told me you're heading to your impending doom.*

Luna: *No, I said this might not work as well as I thought.*

Luna: *My horoscope says that people will demand more of me. I just know what to expect. What happened with Abue?*

Lucas: *Dear Papa didn't tell her that you moved out. He said that you went on vacation. Good luck.*

Luna: *I adore our father, but sometimes I don't like him.*

Lucas: *Aren't you glad I got you a new phone number? She will* *find a way to communicate, though. Maybe you should deactivate your Facebook account.*

Luna: *I'm thrilled about this new venture but . . . I'll miss you guys.*

Lucas: *It's temporary, while we work through the shit going around. I think this is the best for you, we'll keep an eye on you.*

Lucas: *Now don't get mad, but I'm emailing you a second set of instructions. Tiago's got your back.*

Luna: *Santiago? The guy who hates Dad's guts, the FBI, and thinks he's above the law?*

Luna: *Nope. I won't take shit from him when it comes to my job.*

Lucas: *He's well connected. We're adding a layer to your cover.*

Luna: *What's the layer?*

Lucas: *I'll send you an email once you're settled in to your new place.*

Luna: *Next time I see you, I'll kick your ass.*

Lucas: *You are welcome to try. Just know that we're doing this because we love you. We want you to be safe and have a good back up plan. We need to keep an eye on you.*

I chuckle wondering how he'll keep an eye on me. They continue treating me like the baby of the house. Neither Dad nor my brothers look at me as the thirty-one-year-old woman who can do the same as they can. I set my hands flat on the tray table taking a few breaths and feeling the stress slide down my back. Following the flight attendant's instructions and gather everything together and put it in my purse. Now, I have to prepare for whatever my brothers decided to set up.

5

HARRISON

Two weeks later . . .

New York, hello my cruel mistress, I'm back. This is my city. The place I was born in and grew up in. The urban jungle I love because it has everything I always need a few blocks away. Though, I hate the crowded streets and the foul stench in the atmosphere. And the heat. Thank fuck summer is almost over. It's the worst time of the year to be in this forsaken place, because of the heat. But also because that's when we have more visitors. Tourists choose to vacation here from June through August. They are all sweating, yet smiling at their phones while they take thousands of selfies to share with their loved ones.

This is nasty, people. Why would you enjoy being here? Between perfume and the stench of the sewer, I'm gagging. Once I am out of the subway, I move along through the thick crowd. I'm several inches to a foot taller than everyone else. I see the bright shop signs, the towering skyscrapers, the accident that just happened between a cab and a limousine down on 53rd Street. At noon, the smell of the sewage and different food carts accompany me along the way until I am right in front of the high-rise where Tiago sent me to meet his sister.

Walking through the rotating door, I make my way to the elevators.

"Sir." One of the rent-a-cops who works there stops me, his eyes take me in from head to toe. "We need to see your ID."

Dropping my chin, I analyze today's attire. Black clothing, a thick armor vest with lots of compartments. A few scars on my face and dried blood on my left hand. I chuckle. This man must think I am about to blow up the building. That's not the case. This is my work uniform, and things sometimes get messy. We had a little incident in McAllen. Maybe I should've gone home to clean myself up before coming here.

At least he's doing his job. Not that his "Sir, can I see your ID" would stop me if I planned on blowing up the building. I could've deactivated the CCTV, shot him as I entered, and gotten rid of every undercover cop. That's it, new plan. We need to find Tiago's sister a more secure hideout. Why would she be undercover and staying at a safe house? I have to look for answers and fast.

Giving in, I pull out my wallet and show him my identification. His back straightens and his eyes open wide.

"My apologies, sir." He squares his shoulders, moving to the side. "Have a nice day."

I smile, shaking my head. He should be fired. My fake FBI badge is easy to detect for an agent of the bureau. Maybe he's just a security cop.. Making my way to the elevator bank, I take off my jacket. The air conditioning isn't working well. What the fuck? The FBI should do some maintenance in their safe house.

Harrison: *I arrived. What's her apartment number?*

Tiago: *22nd floor, apartment C*

Harrison: *Do you understand that releasing information as if this was a scavenger hunt is shitty?*

Tiago: *Just got that intel from my brother. Shall I remind you that we were off the grid?*

Harrison: *You have a brother? Fuck, what else is there to know? Is there a wife, children . . . What are you hiding? Years trusting my back to your skinny ass and you haven't told me about this shit.*

Tiago: *There's nothing else really. I have a brother and a sister. Same father, different mother. But if you want, we can organize a slumber party. Have a pillow fight in our pajamas and tell each other secrets.*

Harrison: *Fucker, you owe me.*

He doesn't answer, and I poke the elevator button one more time. I pull my phone out to check on my family. Hunter is out of town with his girlfriend, Fitz went to Japan to close on a deal, and Scott and I plan on having dinner later tonight. Hazel has been too busy to respond to my emails or my texts.

Harrison: *How's everything, bee? I'm home and ready to party. Are you available tonight?*

Hazel: *Hey, I missed you. Tonight isn't good. We can talk after you have dinner with Scott.*

Harrison: *What happened?*

Hazel: *I'm not sure what you're talking about.*

Harrison: *Hazel!*

Hazel: *It's complicated, but everything is okay now.*

I hold my breath. My gut clenches, worry freezing every muscle in my body.

Harrison: *Hey, what's going on with Hazel?*

Scott: *She's fine. I'll tell you later tonight. I'm going into a meeting.*

Harrison: *Why didn't you call me?*

Scott: *If she needed you, she'd have called you.*

What's his fucking deal? I'll find out later. Shoving my phone back into my pocket, I step into the elevator. My phone buzzes, a sequence of multiple texts appearing at once.

Bradley: *Enjoy the ride.*

What the hell?

Hawk: *Revenge tastes better when served HOT.*

"Hold it, please." A honey-like, melodious voice calls out to me.

Any other day, I would use my manners and stop the doors. Not today.

Bradley: *Place your bets, gentlemen.*

Hawk: *One hundred says he's going to complain in five.*

Bradley: *Have fun, Everhart.*

"Are you deaf?" I lift my gaze, finding a woman using her hands while speaking to me. Hundreds of bangles adorn her arms, jingling as they clash against one another. Too much bling, sweetheart. She's smiling. I swear rainbows ooze from her pores.

My gaze narrows, trying to understand whatever she's doing with her hands. Wait, is she signing? I laugh, watching her ridiculous display. "No. Perfect hearing."

She tilts her head to the side, her light-brown eyes framed with long eyelashes study me. They contrast perfectly with her olive skin and long, black, curly locks. My eyes relish her body. Working the flouncy, short dress, showing those long, toned, tanned legs. Chains and charms encircle her ankle. Going through security at the airport must be a pain in the ass with all those clingy things.

"Ah." She nods once as if everything has become clear as the crystal hanging from her neck. "You're one of those."

"One of—" The elevator moves at a faster speed than usual heading up, then changing directions. What's going on?

Honey eyes look up to the panel, her index finger tapping the twenty-second floor. Where is she going? "Weird. It's not illuminating the floors. Where are you going?"

Bradley: *The timer is on.*

Harrison: *What the fuck?*

Hawk: *Smile for the camera, sweetheart.*

I look up at the CCTV camera, flipping a finger. *Fuckers,* I mouth.

"Nowhere, sweetheart. We are going nowhere," I blurt, switching my attention back to my phone.

Harrison: *There's a civilian here. Let her out and try this some other time.*

Hawk: *No. This is perfect.*

Bradley: *She's bright, loud, and radiates sunshine. Just the way you hate them.*

Hawk: *Can you hear it? ". . . kumbaya my Lord, kumbaya."*

Those outside our circle wouldn't understand our relationship. We are coworkers, friends, and brothers. We know our strengths as well as our weaknesses. It is true that I hate the heat, bright shit, and women who smile too much. Why are they so happy? What's their agenda? Why fake that life is wonderful when it sucks?

Like this woman whose eyes are trying to suck me into her happy world. All those colorful charms and crystals she wears. They remind me of those kaleidoscopes Mom created for us to play with while she was in her art studio. This woman must be as disorganized as Mom.

Flaky.

Chaotic.

A convoluted mess.

I loved Mom dearly, but like my father, her disorganization drove me crazy.

"What do you mean we are going nowhere?" She frowns, chewing her lip. "Today is supposed to be a perfect day. One of those easy days where I can relax and smell the roses."

She pulls a spritzer out of her purse and sprays a couple of times around her. "This is as close as you can get to flowers?" I ask her, sarcastically. She gives me a *don't judge me* glare.

"Lilacs and lavender—New York stinks." She scrunches her nose a second time.

The corner of my mouth pulls slightly. At least we agree on something.

"How do you conclude that today is going to be easy?"

She pulls out her phone, smiling as she rolls her eyes. "Mine is going to be easy. I'm not sure about yours." A few taps on the screen and then her attention is back on me. "When were you born?"

"Excuse me?" My brows knit together. Tipping my head, I observe her.

"Well, if I ask what your zodiac sign is, would you know?"

"Why would I care?"

"Typical. Not many men care about it." She squares her shoulders. Her glossy lips don't drop the smile, even when her eyes narrow in frustration. "Let me tell you, horoscopes are essential to coexist."

She's crazy. Certifiable.

Harrison: *Get me the fuck out of here.*

Bradley: *Giving up so early in the game?*

Harrison: *Don't you have a wife and children to go torture, Bradley? Hawk, isn't your fiancée organizing a wedding?*

Fuckers. Scratching my chin, I watch her, estimating the time we would be stuck in the elevator. Yes. I could do it. Especially if I compared these next hours with the fifty miles, I walked through the jungle carrying my equipment and Tiago—who was wounded—to the plane where Wings waited. Could I stand Miss Sunshine? The light humor that her eyes carry doesn't fade with the fucking heat. She watches me intently. Analyzing me.

"Are you always this . . . joyful?" I ask, curious about her.

She moves her head to the side, twisting those lips again. Judging me? Maybe not. She's hard to read. Her beautiful features are enchanting, her mood confuses the fuck out of me. It's not every day that I find myself trapped in an elevator with a woman who looks like she's as happy as a unicorn flying along the rainbow.

"Why are you so mad at the world?" She sighs, arching her eyebrow.

"Am I?" I cross my arms, deepening my frown. Perhaps this will switch her attitude.

"You tell me," she retorts, and there it is again, the edges of those heart-shaped lips tugging freely to the sky.

Is it legal to be that happy all the time?

Her smile shines like the stars in the sky. She's the brightest one in the galaxy, and there is nothing that can dim it. Happiness flows through her, warming her skin like the rays of an early summer sun. Being near her lightens my insides, giving me serenity unlike any I experienced before.

She creates a warmth in my soul.

"You're smiling." She waves her index finger around my face. She's so close I can almost feel it caressing my jaw.

Yes, touch me.

Wait. What the hell is wrong with me?

Scrunching my face, I glare at her and take a step back.

Personal space, lady.

"*Alacrán.*"

"What?"

"You're a typical *alacrán.*" She sucks in her upper lip, resting the top of her tongue on top of it.

Fuck, I want to nibble on that lip so bad my mouth waters. It has been too long since I . . . fuck. We stare at each other for several beats. I try to decipher her end game. The tactic of this façade. There's nothing other than sunshine, rainbows, and flowers.

"That's Spanish for scorpion." She breaks the connection between us, moving her eyes to the elevator's panel.

"What?" I don't comprehend what she's getting into with her fixation with a poisonous insect.

"Zodiac signs," she growls. I chuckle as she wiggles her nose in annoyance. "Yours is Scorpio."

She's so cute.

"Scorpions can't hide their emotions," she explains, poking several buttons including the fire alarm. Nothing works. "This situation is easy to fix. We call the superintendent of the building, and in a few minutes we'll be out."

I pinch the bridge of my nose closing my eyes. That's not the solution. Unless I give in and ask the assholes to let us out, we will be here all day. I won't. I plan on staying here all day if necessary. At least until they get tired.

"Yes?" A voice booms from the intercom. Bradley. That fucker is going to pay.

"Your elevator broke down. It's in a loop going up and down, sir," she explains, her voice isn't that of a damsel in distress, but one of a woman taking charge of the situation. "How long is it going to take for your technician to fix it? I have to deliver some proofs to a client. Now."

She sighs, tossing her head for dramatic effect. "A new client. The repercussions of losing him are . . . my livelihood is in your hands."

I lean closer, whispering in her ear, "That's a little over the top. Acting lessons?"

She smiles, closing the gap between us, her breath caressing my skin. "Telenovelas," she whispers, the word travels through my system like thick honey covering every inch of my body with a coat of sweetness.

"Hours in front of the television and living with my Mexican grandparents," she clarifies, taking a step back. My body already misses hers, her gaze connects once again with mine. "They're full of drama."

"What floor are you going to, Miss?" Hawk asks through the intercom. I want to pull out my gun and shoot that thing. It interrupted us. We have all day, maybe all night, to get to know each other. If this ride ends I won't have the pleasure to taste those lips, run my mouth down her body.

"Twenty-second." Our eyes don't leave each other. I feel my lips copying hers. Why am I staring at her like an idiot?

"You should do that more often." She moves toward me, her lips kissing my cheek. All at once my body jolts with a surge of electricity running through it. The combination of her voice still ringing inside my head and the touch of her lips send a rush through my blood. My heart drills my chest, hard. It's trying to come outside. "Smile. It's good for your soul."

The doors open, and I freeze in place. I watch her turn around, swaying those curvy hips. The clinking noise of her bracelets hypnotizes me.

Fuck, what's her name? I am about to step out to follow her when the doors close.

"You thought we would let you go?" Bradly cackles. "In your dreams, *sweetheart.*"

I slam my head on the metal wall. Fuck. I didn't care about the heat. Only her name, her number, her lips.

Those angel eyes.

6

LUNA

My heart picks up its pace as I swing open the door to my temporary apartment. The paper I left between the door and the frame didn't fall. The shoe I placed right in front of the entrance is now a couple of feet away from where I stand. I hold my breath searching for my hair accessories inside my tote bag. I pull out a metal chopstick. My eyes scan the living room and the kitchen. I swear, if whoever broke in is still here, they are not leaving in one piece. I might have to call Tiago to take care of the body.

I slip off my shoes. A prickle climbs the back of my neck as I hear some noise outside the apartment. Someone is lurking around. I order my body to wait instead of reacting, but it's hard to remain still when my heart hammers fast against my ribs. I only have two hands and two chopsticks handy, and there could be two intruders . . . or more. Who could possibly be here? Only my boss, my brothers, and my father know where I am. And why would they care to find me when I'm here only to gather information?

I take a few steps toward the bedroom. From the corner of my eye, I see the doorknob turning slowly. I move toward the wall, pressing my back against it. Then I slide slowly, my hand gripping the metallic stick like a knife. I lift my hand as the door flies open and I charge toward the intruder.

"Luna, stop!"

I freeze.

The mention of my name makes me reconsider my next move. Though, I leave the sharp edge of the fake chopstick on the neck of the intruder, almost cutting through the skin. The pale-blue-eyed guy from the elevator stares at me. He stands tall, his broad, muscular frame blocking the doorway. His muscles seem to gape from his fitted black shirt. With all that dry blood on his ripped forearms and bruises around his face, he screams trouble. I just thought he was yet another agent.

"Who sent you?"

His breathing is shallow. His hands lift up in the air, his eyes move to the back of the room. "What the fuck, Tiago?" His voice is loud, rough.

"Tiago?" I sigh, rolling my eyes.

Without lowering the chopstick against his skin, I crank my neck slightly and see my oldest brother coming out of my room. *The other intruder.* "What are you doing here, Santiago Federico?"

"She's your sister, isn't she?" the man in front of me questions my brother, who gives him a sharp nod.

"I'm going to lower my hands and take a step back," the man in front of me warns me.

"What are you two doing here?" I ask one more time, stepping away . . . I angle my head, narrowing my gaze. "Who are you?"

"Luna, this is Harrison. Harrison, meet Luna."

I snap my head toward my brother, narrowing my eyes. "What are you two doing in my apartment?"

"The FBI is failing." Harrison ignores me. "This building isn't safe for her. I suggest we move her to a more secure area."

"Her is here, and she can hear you." I put the sharp edge of my weapon under his chin again. "I think your horoscope said something about shutting up or you might die a slow death."

He rolls his eyes, grabbing my wrist with both hands and trying to snatch the chopstick. I tilt my head, swing my left foot under his knees and using my free hand, push him on the chest. His eyes widen as he loses his balance and falls. My brother laughs when I put my foot on top of his throat.

Harrison grabs my ankle with both hands. We stare at each other waiting for the next move. I'm ready for him to pull it. My next move is kicking him in the nose. But we remain still for several seconds. He smiles at me. My heart skips a couple of beats as his dimples deepen.

"You're wrong. My horoscope mentioned something about meeting the girl of my dreams." He winks at me.

"Sweet talking me won't distract me. Don't move," I advise, pushing my foot closer to his neck.

Turning my attention to my older brother, I cross my arms. "Explain, and this better be good."

Tiago scrubs his face. "Lucas asked me to look after you. He's concerned about your safety. Harrison here can get you where you want to be."

"Where's that?"

"He can get you close to Gia Dominguez, among other people," he explains.

She's one of the New York socialites I'm supposed to be watching. There's a rumor that she's dating a wealthy man twice her age, Juan Carlos Medina. According to our informants, he's the biggest human trafficker in South America.

"How close?" I stare down at Harrison who is distracted looking at my legs. "Hey, I'm talking to you. I won't let you move from this position until you answer all my questions."

He smirks. "Who said I want to move from heaven?" He runs his callused hand up my leg while he uses the other to hold my foot. "Best view I've had in a long time. No underwear is the best underwear."

My face heats as I understand what he's staring at from his position. I fight to take my leg from his grasp. In two strides, Tiago is on the floor, choking his friend.

"My sister is off limits."

Harrison doesn't waver. He crosses his arms, and I want to smack that smile off his lips. "I see the similarity between the two of you. You like blood and threatening my manhood. In my defense, she's wearing underwear." He winks once again.

I press my thighs together, fighting the butterflies fluttering inside my stomach. Why is this guy getting to me?

"Everhart, I need you to help me, but if you fool around with Luna I swear—"

"Wait." I turn to face Harrison. "Any relation to Scott Everhart?"

He glances my way with a cocky grin. "Maybe . . . it all depends on what you want from him."

"His girlfriend is friends with Gia." I turn to my brother. If I didn't want to kill him, I'd kiss him. "You're right, Tiago. He might be useful."

"Big guy, do me a favor and move away from me," Harrison says, pushing my brother off himself and sitting up.

His light brown hair is a bit messier than before, and I want to shove my fingers through it and . . . nope.

Stay away from the hot mercenary.

My brother insists he's working with a high intelligence security company. All I know is that they charge millions for what they do while going above the law. But if this guy is related to Scott, I might be able to complete my mission faster. Waiting for Gia to appear at the yoga studio has been pointless.

"Do you know Hazel?"

"Whoa," he says, holding his hands up and narrowing his gaze. "Hazel is off limits." His voice is rough, the warning loud and clear.

"She's friends with Gia," I explain her importance. "The company where she works might have a few accounts that need to be investigated."

"Our clients go through a thorough background process." His voice comes out defensive. "If you need any information about them, you come to me. Not Hazel or my brother. I'm your man."

"I still need to make connections, expand my social circle." Not that I have a social circle here, or anywhere.

Does my large family count?

He shakes his head. "We know Gia. There's no friendship between her family and mine. You can use me, but we will not involve her. Though . . ." he looks around my apartment and sighs, placing his palms on top of his thighs, "this apartment isn't safe. We have to move you."

"Do we have a safe house in New York?" Tiago asks, watching his friend get off the ground.

"No," Harrison responds. "We have a rule. We keep our activity to a minimum in this area. But these are extenuating circumstances, aren't they?"

Tiago shrugs. His brown eyes soften as he looks at me. I smile at him. Even when he drives me crazy and only texts me once a month, I love him.

Harrison shakes his head. "Pack your things, Luna," he orders. "I'm taking you to a safe place, but you have to promise you won't involve Hazel."

He grabs his phone, looking at my brother. "You owe me, big guy."

I walk toward my bedroom. Any other day I'd fight their safety concerns. Not today. He's taking me right where I want to be. Now I have to convince that bitch that she can trust me. Should I beat the shit out of her before or after my mission? The former will get me some respect, the latter might get me more information.

"If you touch her, I'll kill you. My little sister is off limits." I hear Tiago threaten Harrison.

"Dude, you offend me with your mistrust."

"I decide if I'm off limits," I warn my brother as I begin packing my clothing. "If I want to have sex with him, it is none of your damn business. I'm thirty-one, not thirteen."

"Jesus, Luna," my brother complains cursing in Spanish.

It doesn't take me long to pack. I have a system to ensure that I can leave within minutes without leaving a trace. When I step outside, I glare at my brother.

"Watch your language," I warn him as I serve him with a glare.

The words might not mean much to many, but I understand what he's saying. "And just a reminder, I'm not a virgin and if I want to have sex. That is s-e-x with him, it's none of your business."

"I mean it, Luna. Do not sleep with him."

"Thirty-one, not thirteen," I repeat, looking at his friend who is grinning at me. "He seems good enough to keep me entertained while I work."

Harrison laughs, flashing a cocky smirk. "I could entertain you in so many ways."

"Harrison, is it?" I ask again, batting my eyelashes. "Please, lead the way."

He walks toward me and grabs my bags. His eyes focus on me, his smile is gone. "Just so you know, I don't have s-e-x before or during the first date." He winks, turns around, and leaves me with an open mouth.

Who does he think he is?

7

HARRISON

When did I step into the twilight zone? Tiago has a sister. A beautiful, smoking hot, sexy sister who is anything but normal. And she's an FBI agent too. Bradley and I have to have a chat about recruiting her. With that innocent face and killer instincts, she'd be a great undercover asset for us.

Why isn't she working for us? If she's half as good as Tiago, I want her on our payroll. *I want her . . .* my core tightens when my big brain begins to work again. She might be fucking gorgeous and a wet dream, but I can't act on it. She's my friend's little sister. Plus, I've never mixed business with sex before.

Thank fuck I decided to send her to Hazel's house. I can't imagine her staying with Scott and me. One of us would be having flower girl for dinner . . . and lunch. It wouldn't be my brother because I'd kill him if he tried. Just like I'm not allowed to sleep around with my sibling's employees, they aren't allowed to sleep with anyone who is linked to my business. Not that Fitzhenry follows those rules.

My phone buzzes on my way downstairs. I ignore it until I arrive at the lobby.

Hazel: *I have a bedroom available. The question is, why do you need a room for the next couple of months?*

Harrison: *If I tell you . . .*

Hazel: *Cut the crap, Everhart. If you tell me, I might say yes.*

I huff, what happened to my happy girl?

Harrison: *Anyone know why our little ray of sunshine is angry at the world?*

Hunter: *Scott, I thought you were going to tell him.*

Scott: *At dinner, I said that it'd be during tonight's dinner.*

Harrison: *What happened to our girl?*

Scott: *Her mother committed suicide, and her father is in jail.*

Harrison: *Why is he in jail?*

Hunter: *He claimed to have pushed his wife.*

Scott: *He meant metaphorically since he wanted her to go to therapy.*

My heart stops. I read his texts three times. Hazel's mother was mentally ill, undiagnosed, and estranged from her daughters. They practically abandoned them at a young age. Hazel has been trying to help them with the hope that someday they will decide to move closer to her.

Harrison: *Are we leaving him in jail?*

Hunter: *Fitz and I are working on his release. But neither one of us is in a hurry. It can take another month or a year. I don't give a shit.*

Harrison: *How's Willow doing with that?*

Willow is Hunter's live-in girlfriend and Hazel's sister. She has borderline personality disorder, and she handles her emotions differently.

Hunter: *She had a few rough days. At her request, we went to a retreat last weekend.*

Scott: *FYI, it's business as usual with Hazel. However, she's not in a playful mood. I advise you to approach with caution.*

I want to ask more questions, but I focus on my plans and how they'll affect Hazel.

Harrison: *I have a low-key undercover operation. The asset needs a place to stay, and I considered Hazel. Thoughts?*

My phone rings and Scott's name flashes.

"What?"

"Are you fucking kidding me?" His voice is loud enough to leave me deaf. "I won't allow you to put Hazel in danger."

I sigh, looking out for the service car I just called. This day can't get any shittier.

"I wouldn't do anything stupid, Scott. It's a white-collar crime . . ." *I lie.*

He wouldn't allow me to continue if I told him it's about human trafficking. Actually, he'd either kick me out of the state or take Hazel somewhere safe until this is over. I can look after her, but Scott can be overprotective of her.

"You know what?" He sighs. I can just imagine him closing his eyes and pinching the bridge of his nose. "Hazel might get a kick out of this if you pretend to include her."

"Actually, I might need the two of you to join us at some events."

"That's what we're here for, managing your investments and undercover events." He chuckles, but the tension in his voice remains. "Be careful, if something happens to Hazel—"

"Yeah, yeah." I pause, as the service car parks right in front of me. "A piece of advice, little brother—you should make a move before you lose her."

I hang up, hand over the bags to the driver, and text Hazel what I know she wants to hear. Her response comes fast, *I'm in.* I reply telling her that I'm on my way to her. The building is located on Park Avenue. The area is one of the safest in the city, and that apartment is secured with a state of the art security system. But after seeing how Luna can use a sharp pointed object, I have no doubt she'll be fine.

I caress my neck, swallowing at the memory of that needle-like instrument she threatened me with. My heart continues beating fast. That woman has surprised the fuck out of me for the past hour. Tomorrow I have to go back into training. A girl almost kicked my ass. I sigh as I recall her long legs and how I'm going to slide . . . don't think about her legs or her beautiful pussy. Fuck, if there's an image I won't ever forget it's her . . . "eyes," I sigh as she comes into view.

"Ready to go?" I ask, grabbing her tote bag and yoga mats.

She turns to look at her brother giving him a kiss. "I trust you." Then she turns to look at me. "You not so much."

"Where are you taking her?"

"Hazel's place," I answer. "The penthouse on Park Avenue where we set the latest security system a couple of months ago."

He nods, looking at the car.

I tap his shoulder a couple of times. "She'll be safe with me."

"If it's okay with you, I want to be around for the next couple of days. Not to be in the middle of the operation, but to hang out with her."

"Yeah sure, we have plenty of room at my house. You're welcome to stay."

I text him the lock and security codes to access my place and wave at him.

"I'm good at what I do," Luna says when I climb into the car. "You don't have to babysit me."

"Can we talk about the operation?"

She turns toward the window, her hands curled into fists. "Our sources claim Gia is dating the leader of a human trafficking cell."

"Let me guess, your job is to become her best friend."

Luna pulls on the hem of her sexy, short dress, smoothing the skirt. "Something like that." She sighs.

"You have to tell me everything. From this point forward, we're partners."

She sighs, shaking her head, her long, slender fingers drumming against her leg. "You don't want to be my partner. The last one died because he pissed me off."

"What?"

She laughs. "Lighten up. You don't have to do anything but introduce me to her. I'll do the rest."

"How often do you go undercover?"

"Not as often as I'd like. Most of the times I'm left behind profiling and doing desk work."

"With your kickass skills?"

She huffs at me in response.

"Have you considered doing something else?"

"Like what?" Her head snaps, and her eyes ignite. "Homemaker? You think I should be behind a desk filing the cases that the male agents work?"

"I—"

"Because let me tell you." Her voice gets louder, and her hands begin to gesture. I flinch, afraid that she's going to slap me just because I didn't phrase my question right. "I'm capable of doing more than getting married and having children. There's nothing wrong with that, I respect it. But since I was a kid that's all my grandmother has wanted me to be. My father thinks I should be a teacher. My gender is a major hang-up in the bureau. My former boss undermined my skills and knowledge but pretended to come up with brilliant ideas—*my* ideas. Now, he's trying to push me to Quantico because I should work on profiling. I didn't work my ass off for years to be sent to a place that won't fulfill my dreams."

"All valid points. Though, I meant like working for us. HIB would love to have someone like you."

Her eye twitches. "I don't work above the law."

"That's the beauty of working for our company. We go on top, the bottom, and any position necessary to get the work done." I use a low voice as I lean closer to her.

She's beautiful. We're going to be around each other long enough to show her she can use her skills somewhere she'll be appreciated. I can appreciate all of her for that matter. It hits me—I can take advantage of the situation and make these next days, weeks, or months not only bearable but exciting.

"To get close, you have to be close to me." I reach for her hand, and a powerful surge of electricity zaps my entire body. She turns to look at me, her eyes wide, and her mouth slightly open. Did she feel that too? I kiss her hand lightly and enjoy a second electrical rush. "With our chemistry, this cover will be perfect."

"Cover?"

"We are here," the driver interrupts.

"This will be our test, darling," I say, grabbing her hand and kissing it gently. "To convince her we're together."

"Who is *her*?"

"Hazel," I say as my eyes land on her. She's waiting right outside the building where she lives.

Hazel knows me well enough to catch me if I'm fake-dating someone. If we pass her test, we're gold. We have that kind of connection. Plenty of people confuse it for something more. There's a depth to our relationship that no one will understand. But there's no physical attraction. Fitz says it's because she's a male version of me. Whatever it is, neither one can fool the other.

Hazel turns slightly to her left. Her somber face changes when she spots my brother. Scott walks toward her wearing an unusual smile. I watch them from the tinted windows. Somehow they seem different. My brother reaches out to her, caressing her cheek, and bending to whisper something in her ear. She nods slowly, kissing his cheek, and closing her eyes briefly. I wouldn't make too much of it if it weren't for the length of that lingering kiss.

"They're a cute couple," Luna says.

I narrow my gaze watching them interact. Are they together? "No. They aren't a couple."

"Is that jealousy I hear?"

It's not jealousy, but curiosity and anger. Something happened to her, and she didn't reach out to me. I'm her person. When I glance at them a second time, I feel like an outsider, but I don't think about it more as the driver opens my door. I climb out not moving my eyes from my brother and my best friend. They are looking at each other, no words are exchanged, and yet I feel like I'm missing an entire conversation.

Hazel jolts, taking a step back and turning to look at me. "Hey, Everhart."

"Beesley," I greet her. I turn around to help Luna and lean closer. "Show me how good you are at this undercover shit."

"What are you doing here?" Hazel points at Luna, charging toward us.

"Scott," I call my brother, tilting my head toward Hazel.

We don't need to witness a catfight. Hazel only knows the basic self-defense training I gave her. Luna will send her to the hospital. Scott picks her up from the waist and mumbles something in her ear. Hazel's nostrils flare as she watches us, but she stays with my brother.

"How do you know Hazel?" I ask Luna while retrieving her bags.

"It's a long story."

I release her hand, running it through my hair. We need another plan. Hazel is about to kick Luna out of her apartment, and that will ruin my plan. Unless . . . "In a few words, tell me, what happened?"

Luna gives me the short version while I take my time getting her things together. She tried to get a job, but the background check was too precise. I pride myself on knowing everything that happens at Everhart Enterprises. Scott runs the show, I am the guy who provides the security. All of our clients have been screened. Mostly the ones who have enough funds to buy a third world country. Knowing that we stopped an FBI agent from being hired is good, but now being told about the entire incident, it doesn't sit right with me. I could've had a different plan if that had been the case.

"Follow my lead," I order her.

"I'm sorry about your mom, Hazel," I begin the conversation, giving her a tight hug. "How are you?"

"Better, thank you." Her voice is guarded.

"I'm here if you want to talk about it." I'm trying to feel her mood, but she's guarding herself from me.

"Thank you." Hazel glares at Luna. "I rescind my invitation."

"Are we watching *Vampire Diaries* again?"

"It's *True Blood*," Hazel corrects me. "She's not welcome in my house."

"Luna recognizes the error in her approach. She should've been straightforward with you and Scott."

"Sorry for that. It was my first time going solo." Luna gives her that warm smile I'm starting to dig.

"As much as I'd like to continue this conversation, we have to do it privately," I remind them. Looking around us. "Give me five minutes before you kick us out, Hazel."

Hazel turns around and waves at Carter, the doorman. Scott greets him, and I salute him. We follow behind them, but I detour toward the elevator. Hazel taking the stairs is the equivalent of her blowing off some steam. Scott is the one who pokes the elevator. Turning around, he crosses his arms, studying Luna and then me. His gaze doesn't hold anger, but he's waiting for more than what I had said. I appreciate his silence.

"Hazel loved Luna's application," Scott says as the elevator doors open. "We were ready to hire her until the background check arrived. If Ms. Galvez had come to us requesting our help, Hazel would have been open to it."

He looks at me, crossing his arms. "Did you know about it?"

"Bro, I'd have told you and worked it out differently."

"Since her mother's death, Hazel's mind is in a strange place," Scott offers. "What is it that you need from her?"

I take Luna's hand, squeezing it slightly. "She's a yoga instructor and my girlfriend. My plus one during the social events. Hazel has to help us get the right clothes and introduce her to the right people."

Luna snatches her hand away from me. "I'm not Julia Roberts, and you're not Richard Gere. There's no fake dating."

"That's the only way this will work," I inform her.

"True, being Hazel's friend won't get you as far as being Harrison's girlfriend," Scott backs me up not knowing what I'm talking about.

When my parents died, we became Hunter and Fitz's, guardians. In some twisted way, we became their parental figures—dealing with teachers, grades, and all the growing pains being in charge of teenagers implies. We perfected the good cop/bad cop shit and not only do we support each other, but we never contradict the other.

Luna stares at her feet. She remains quiet until the doors open. "Fine," she sighs. "Tiago said I should trust you."

"The elusive Santiago?" Hazel asks, arching an eyebrow.

"Yeah, Luna is his sister."

"Hmm." Hazel crosses her arms analyzing Luna. "What's my role? House mother for the innocent girl?"

"I'm not a girl, and you don't need to use your sorority knowledge on me."

Hazel presses her lips together, exhaling loud. "If you think you have me figured out, you're wrong. Why should I help you, Harrison?"

She's losing her last strand of patience, and if she kicks us out, I'm fucked. "Are you being a bitch?"

"Probably," she snarls. "What's the goal? Is it catching an inside trader or saving the world from terrorists?"

"Human trafficking," Luna responds, her voice is calm. "My department handles missing children. The best part of what I do is reuniting families. In this case, I'm searching for a trafficking cell. According to our intel, the head is dating someone in your social circle."

Hazel bites her lip. Her chin quivers. Luna has demolished the wall of concrete. She points at the luggage and then looks at me.

"The room next to the library is available. Everything she needs is there. Clean sheets, towels, and toiletries for the bathroom." She glances at Scott. "We have to go back to work, but please give her a tour of the apartment and explain to her how everything works."

"Thank you." Luna bows her head slightly. "I wish I was sorry for the way I tried to become friends with you, but it seemed like the only way to do it. Can we start again?"

Hazel looks at her, then she looks at me and her light brown eyes have this funny look. The smirk appears and then she speaks. "I understand. Harrison does that often. I like how this worked out though."

"What did she mean, 'I like how this worked'?" Luna asks after Scott and Hazel go back to work.

"Nothing," I say, shrugging the nagging feeling in the pit of my gut.

Hazel has some ulterior motive. I'll have to keep an eye open, or she's going to fuck this mission.

8

HARRISON

Luna didn't want to become my pretty woman, but Hazel used her like a doll. Friday morning, they went for a run. Later, she joined the yoga studio where Luna teaches, and by the end of the day, they were at my house with a professional buyer who helped them pick a brand-new wardrobe for her cover-up—which I had to buy. The service was two thousand dollars too expensive. Plus, the cost of all the clothing. I wanted to protest, but Scott reminded me of Hazel's state of mind. One of the ways she copes with her depression is by organizing. Luna hasn't complained about Hazel's micromanaging personality, yet.

"What's the event?"

"An engagement party," Scott checks his phone. "Demetri something. His uncle's account is one of the biggest we handle."

"And he is . . ."

"He is dating Gia's cousin." Hazel finally walks out of the bedroom where Luna is staying. "That reminds me, the story has changed."

"What story?"

"How we met." Luna comes out of the room wearing a short, lace burgundy dress. Her dark hair covers her bare shoulders.

"Hazel and I are old college friends. I quit my high-paying job in LA. She's letting me stay with her while I figure out what I want to do in New York."

"Why did you quit?" I fire up.

She lowers her face, slumping her shoulders. "I caught my fiancé cheating with his assistant." She pauses biting her lip. "We worked for the same company."

I feel sucker punched, reaching for her hand I kiss it. "I'm sorry."

Luna and Hazel start laughing and high five each other.

"You are brilliant," Luna says, hugging Hazel. "We should hire you at the bureau."

"I can't take credit for your acting skills." She pretends to pat dry under her eyes. "You almost made me cry."

"Why are we switching the story?"

"The elusive Harrison Everhart suddenly has a girlfriend because . . ." Hazel pauses, crossing her arms as she waits for my response.

"Because . . ." I frown, lower my gaze, and rub the back of my neck. *Think fast, think fast.* "I like her."

"That's a stupid reason to have a serious relationship," Scott points out, arching his eyebrow.

"We met during one of my trips, it was love at first sight."

"Where was the trip?" Hazel throws out the questions. "If it's so serious, why is she living with me and not you? How long have you known her?"

"I have to think about it."

"Your story has to be simple and credible," Hazel explains. "The less you have to explain, the better. Tonight, you flirt with her, get to know her, and the chase begins. You two become inseparable, and no one will question why you have a girlfriend."

As I'm about to ask about the cover they came up with, Grant Beesley makes an appearance. Hazel smiles at her grandfather, giving him a big hug. His eyes go from Scott to me and then back to Hazel.

"If you plan on staying out all night, send me a message, sweetheart." He kisses her cheek.

Then, his gaze goes to Scott. "I trust you'll keep her safe, Scott."

"Yes, sir."

"Harrison, please be a gentleman with our guest. She's a close friend of my girl and has had a rough couple of months."

I tilt my head, arching an eyebrow. He believes the story?

He believes it, I repeat inside my head, smiling.

Reaching out for Luna, I touch her hand lightly and smile at her. Another surge of energy hits me, and I'm starting to enjoy the jolt. In fact, I want more.

"Don't worry, sir," I respond. "She's in good hands. If you'll excuse us, we have reservations at eight, and then we're going to the party."

☆ ☆ ☆

"I'm starving, and the food is . . . too small?" Luna stares at her entrée. A piece of salmon the size of a credit card. The side of mashed potatoes isn't much bigger either.

The waitress sets my filet mignon, which is also a small portion, in front of me. This place is known as a boutique restaurant. They serve sophisticated, unique plates. The menu changes daily and the portions are enough to satisfy the patron's palette, not their appetite. At least, that's what Hazel explained during the drive.

"Next time, I'll choose the place," Scott, who is a pretty patient man and never complains, offers. "This is a joke. I'm going to starve all night. You'll starve."

"Why here?" Luna looks around, leaning closer and lowering her voice. "If neither one of you like it."

There's not much to see. The restaurant is inside an abandoned bodega. The high ceiling holds multiple mason jar pendant lights. The tables are metal and wood. It has an industrial-modern atmosphere. However, there's a crowd outside waiting for a table. They're booked until the end of the year, and their takeout-delivery service is an hour and thirty minutes behind. We heard a customer complain when he came to pick up his food.

"Visibility," Hazel responds. "Part of the story."

"Yeah, what's the cover?" I try to keep my voice down too.

"That's all. You get to know her, sweep her off her feet in front of your audience." She shrugs. "It can't get simpler than showing them what's happening in real time."

"But it's not real," Luna remarks.

"They don't have to know that," Hazel chides with a sweet smile. "It's about perception."

She kisses Scott really close to his lips. Then she turns to look around. Everyone is watching her next move. "See, they're waiting to find out if we are a couple, or if that's just a friendly kiss. I'll keep them guessing until they see either one of us dating."

"I feel like I'm a box of chocolates and you're selling me to these people." Luna sets her forearms on the table, looking at Hazel intrigued. "How does that work in this case?"

"I'm displaying you two at the trendiest places. People notice." Hazel scans the area.

"You'd think that in a city with millions of people, no one would notice who you are, but some people aren't invisible," Hazel says as she tastes her salmon. "Everyone knows the Everhart brothers. They are on some kind of watch. Hunter not so much since he's taken, but these two are a hot commodity."

She grins, touching my hand and Scott's. "My hot commodities," she cackles. "If I wanted, I could auction them and get a lot of money for them."

"You're a hot commodity too, sweetheart," I remind her.

"I bet there're a few pictures circulating on social media of the four of us." Hazel ignores me. "Harmless comments regarding the mystery woman sitting next to Harrison, across from Scott. Is Scott finally with that Beesley girl? They have married, engaged me, knocked me up, and divorced me from them a million times. And I enjoy playing with that."

"You need a hobby, Hazel." Scott stares at the plate. "Is there going to be a real dinner afterward?"

Hazel smiles at him and steals a cherry tomato from his plate. "We can go to your place and order pizza after. Unless you want to cook something. I promise to bake cookies in exchange." She takes a bite of his food and pushes her plate. "In fact, let's go now. I'm starving."

"Let me ask for the check." I stop them.

She turns to look at me with that wicked smile I hate. "You two are staying. We'll see you at the party in about an hour. Start working the Everhart charm on Miss Luna, Harrison."

"Hazel is an evil genius," Luna implies, eating her food.

"Evil. Take the genius away from the title."

"You two remind me of Lucas and myself. She's like your sister, isn't she?" Luna deducts and laughs.

I frown, not understanding her statement. "Who is Lucas?"

"My brother. He's the middle child. Santiago is the oldest." I nod a couple of times. "Tiago's our half-brother."

Her smile disappears. I take her hand, squeezing it lightly. "Everything all right?"

"Of course, my sugar levels are down."

"Eat your food, and I promise to buy you a sandwich on our way to the party. Now tell me, is this ex-fiancé real?"

"Nah, I've never dated anyone for too long. You?"

"I lived with someone, but it didn't work out," I respond with the short, light version. "It happened fifteen, sixteen years ago."

While we eat, and I eat Hazel's and Scott's too, I ask her more questions. She doesn't have a favorite color but likes pastel tones.

"I'm not kidding, *Harry Potter*. The entire series is my favorite book. I'm not saying it just because your name is Harrison," she claims. "How about yours?"

"It's a tie."

"*Lord of The Rings* and . . . hmm, what else could it be?" She taps her chin, smiling at me.

"You'll never guess," I invite her to surrender.

But she doesn't, she continues with a long list of books, then mentions authors like Orwell, Asimov, Twain, King, Poe, and Hawkins and I finally stop her.

"You're never going to guess."

"Well then, tell me."

"Instead, why don't you tell me what your favorite food is?" I brush a strand of hair from her face and kiss her lightly on the cheek.

Luna isn't a picky eater. In fact, she loves all kinds of food, liver included. Is liver edible? She lives in Alexandria, but she was born here in Manhattan. And we discovered that her father hates me.

"Special Agent Cristobal Santillan," I repeat his name and massage my forehead.

I'm sitting next to the hottest woman I've ever met, and she happens to be the daughter of Cristobal Santillan. This is a cruel irony. If I make an attempt to even kiss her, her brother and her father are going to eliminate me. When this is over, Tiago is going to pay for this. Why hasn't he mentioned that he's related to him before . . . to them? The last name Cordero is way different than Santillan. "Wait, your brother is Luc Santillan?"

"It's safe to assume that you know them, but you had no idea about our relations to Tiago." She frowns.

"Tiago only talks about his mom," I explain to her. "Your father hates me."

"What do you mean he hates you?"

"We've worked with him a couple of times. He thinks I'm a useless piece of shit, his words."

"That sounds like my father." She beams. "He's a teacher now at Quantico."

"Telling the new recruits they're pieces of shit?"

She laughs, and the sound is melodic, contagious, and addictive. Maybe this mission isn't as bad as I thought. I'll spend several weeks with my brothers, and the company isn't as bad as it could be. Not my type, but she's easy on the eyes and decent to talk to.

9

LUNA

Stretched T-shirt, dried blood, and a badass attitude looked good on him. But that's nothing compared to Harrison Everhart wearing a suit. His tall, broad, body wrapped in dark gray is a sight I want to photograph, frame, and stare at forever. He's the type of man who behaves differently depending on the place and time. For the past five hours, we've chatted pleasantly about our families. Nothing too superficial but nothing terribly intimate, either. If I had time to date, he'd be the kind of man I'd choose. Easy to talk to, funny, and a gentleman.

A refreshing change from the guys who I hook up with when I have time to go out with my friends. Which lately has been never. Maybe I have time, but I don't want to waste it by doing the same thing over and over again. Meeting a guy who has few social skills, only talks about himself, and by the end of the date is the only one who is satisfied, isn't great. I have little friendly toys that do a better job, and I don't have to listen to nonsense.

This would be a great subject for a sociology class; the interactions between humans, and how that they're so out of touch with one another that dating has become a joke. What happened to love letters? The chase is so much different now than it was back when my parents dated. I should quit the Bureau and go back to school—finish my psychology degree, go into anthropology or sociology. I would enjoy doing that more than having to jump through hoops to show that I'm capable of more things than my superiors like to acknowledge. If anything, I can write a book with Mom's letters and notes.

A manual on how it's done.

"Everything okay?" Harrison asks when the service car stops and the driver opens my door. "You've been quiet since we left the party."

Define okay? My skin tingles every time you touch me, your deep voice makes me shiver, and dancing in your arms was a bit torturous because everything inside me wanted you to touch more than my bare shoulders and my waist. But yeah, I'm cool.

"Your brother and Hazel never arrived at the party," I comment, not disclosing that I'd like to find out how my fake future boyfriend kisses. "Gia wasn't there either."

"I'm sorry about that. If you want, I can try to find out her whereabouts. My people can hack her phone and track her daily activities." He smirks and winks. "We can start stalking her."

"Stalking?" I boom, laughing and covering my mouth when a couple walking close to us turns to glare at me.

"Yeah, that's the word, and you know what they say, 'couples that stalk together stay together.'" He grins, his blue-crystal eyes shining with the street light.

That grin is addictive. I shouldn't mind pretending to be with him while I'm working. A little fun on the side, some sexy times. Sex. I haven't had that in a long time. So long that I can only remember what my toys can do for me. But I care. He's a distraction. Each time he smirks touches me, or talks with the low-bedroom voice, I want to jump him. That's not only unprofessional but also illogical.

"Anything for the sake of the case, right?" My voice comes out a little throaty, needy.

He clears his throat, looking around and poking the elevator. "We should do this again," he says, leaning closer to me.

"Technically, we *have* to do it again."

"Have I mentioned this is the best case I've ever worked on in my entire life?" He leans forward, kissing my cheek. His lips lingering close to my ear for one too many seconds, his musk-wood scent makes my stomach flutter.

"Thank you." I swallow hard, turning around and stepping into the elevator. "We can discuss our next move tomorrow."

I poke the elevator button. Looking through the doors that start closing, his gaze locks with mine. His eyes darken, the intensity of that gaze makes me feel vulnerable, bare. I imagine my skin searing with the touch of his big hands. As the doors close, my phone rings. An incoming message. Unknown numbers read across the screen.

Unknown: *This was the best first date I've had in a long time. Thank you.*

The corners of my lips stretch toward the sky when I read his words. Relief washes over me. I had no idea that his opinion mattered to me. I have to agree with him. This might be the best undercover operation I've had in my entire career.

Luna: *It was great, wasn't it?*

Unknown: *I propose that we take full advantage of the situation and spend the next few weeks doing what normal couples do.*

Luna: *Is that what you do during your undercover missions?*

Harrison: *This is a different kind of mission. You have your orders, I don't have any. We can mix it up, and find a middle ground where we can enjoy each other while we work. What do you think?*

I stare at the phone. This is new territory for me. The undercover operations I've taken part of usually include finding female informants. In most cases, I meet the family members of the missing people, run their profiles, and work some insider investigation. This is different from any other case I've worked before because I'm away from home and the operation could take more than only a couple of weeks. Would it be possible to entertain the idea of being with Harrison while I work? It could work. As long as feelings aren't involved.

Luna: *It might work, we'll have to talk about ground rules.*

Harrison: *We can make a few of those as we go.*

Luna: *Then it's a deal.*

Harrison: *Good night, Moon.*
Luna: *Good night, Harry.*

☆ ☆ ☆

I put my iPod on the speaker, turn on the music, and soft jazz fills the air. I want to set a light atmosphere. Dad has been trying to get in touch with me, and I've ignored him. However, he threatened to come visit if I don't call him tonight.

"Luna bear, I'm glad you decided to call your old man."

"Hello, Papá," I greet Dad.

"How are you doing?"

"Great, this city is interesting. I can't believe you moved back to Alexandria after . . ." I pause, we don't speak much about her, but I wish he could tell me more about her. He doesn't talk about his years living with her in New York. That life disappeared once she died. "Do you still miss her?"

There's a sigh on the other side. The pause is long. I wish he would talk about Mom a lot more than the usual, *she loved you. She was the love of my life.* Or my favorite when he's drunk, *I wished I could've saved her.*

"Is that why you accepted the assignment?" His voice is severe.

"They wanted to move me to Quantico, Dad," I answer with a different reason.

"Quantico isn't bad, you'd be working next to your father." The tone is lighter, the worry still tangled with his words.

I slip down my dress, walk to the dresser, and search for a T-shirt to sleep in. Mom's blue journal is under my 1986 Journey World Tour shirt. That was one of her favorite bands. I like them but not as much as the ones she has on her tapes under Spanish rock.

"Papá, do I look like her at all?"

"Her?"

"Mom," I whisper. Unlike me, my mother had porcelain skin and blond hair. She was Caucasian. Her family came from old money, and for her birthday she traveled to other countries. I've never gone out of the country, or on vacations. "I look nothing like her."

"You have her eyes, her smile, and her fearless, compassionate, and sweet personality." Dad's voice sounds lost. "I miss her every day."

"I wish I had spent more time with her," I tell him, searching for some comfort through her words. "Can you tell me about Mom?"

"Luna, why are you in New York?"

And we are done discussing Mom.

"I'm working, Dad," I remind him. "Children shouldn't be taken away from their families. But when they are, someone has to find a way to bring them back home—alive."

"That won't bring your mother or your sister back, Luna. It puts you in danger."

"One life exchanged for another is not a fair price to pay," I repeat some of the words he's said throughout the years.

During the eighties, he led several missions as a Navy SEAL. He has worked cases of national security while in the bureau that have saved millions of lives and put him in danger.

Dad's a hero, but he couldn't save his own family.

"Luna, don't talk that way," he pleads. My heart hurts as the pain in his voice squeezes it tight. "I wish I could send you to your room for the next hundred years. Do you have any idea what'd happen to me if I lost you or your brothers? I wish you had been doctors, teachers, cooks or another professional career that wouldn't put you in harm's way."

Mom was a teacher, she still died young, I don't say that out loud because the words will hurt us both.

"I'm safe, Papá," I say the words he wants to hear even when neither one of us believe them.

No one is safe from death. That's the only thing in this world that doesn't discriminate.

"New York isn't a safe place, I'll make a few calls. Have a good night, *mi Chiquita linda.*"

I can't believe he still calls me his little beauty. I'm thirty-one, not three. The men in my family have a hard time remembering my age, but their sweetness makes me feel loved. But what kind of calls is he going to make? Is he going to ask my superiors to pull me out of my post?

"Night, Papá."

I open the journal to a random page, I have to hear her words.

☆ ☆ ☆

He's here. I saw Cristobal walking along Central Park with a woman holding a little boy. He has a family. My heart beat fast when I recognized him, but slowed down when I heard the kid call him Papa. His mother was right, I wasn't meant to be with him. We're different. My parents warned me, he's not in love with you.

If only I could stop loving him. I surrendered my heart to him. My body and soul belong to him. Even when I've let other men touch me. I'm his.

I console myself looking at Sammie. Having her is the best thing that's happened to me. I can't regret breaking up with him. That'd mean not having my little girl. She's the only one who matters to me.

10

LUNA

Sleeping after my conversation with Dad is impossible. He's miles away from me. We don't discuss my cases. He doesn't know that I've read all of Mom's journals several times. But for some reason, he's aware that I'm here for more than one reason. I'm here because Mom deserves justice. Sammie ought to have gone back home after she died, with her family. They never came home. I hate to imagine the life we could've had if they had never been taken away from us.

My stomach tightens as the memory of the last time I saw Sammie before she passed strikes me. Lucas found her. She lived in DC. My sister was part of a gang. She was linked to one of the biggest dealers in the city. His boss found out and transferred him to another case. I, on the other hand, tried to help her get out of that life.

I failed.

I parked my car at the subway station and made my way to the city. Sammie hadn't contacted me or responded to my emails. She had agreed to leave and go to rehab. Dad would help her if she was willing to get clean. I walked downstream through the mass of people rushing toward the street, swiped my card, and boarded the car just in time. With food and enough money to buy her a ticket to wherever

she wanted to go, I was ready to fight her. Once I arrived at my desti-
nation, I walked outside the subway station at the corner of the street.
I stopped waiting for the light to turn green so she could cross.
Looking around, I worried about her safety. The road was polluted,
litter everywhere. A man sat next to the building across the street,
begging for money.

As I crossed the street, I watched the people surrounding us. Men
eyeing me, licking their lips and whistling. They could stare all they
wanted, but if any of them got close, I would make them regret it.
My brothers and father had taught me to fight. I have practiced judo
and karate since I was four. I continued past a fruit stand, a nail salon,
and a chicken rotisserie store, and stopped at the front door of the
third building. It was a complete mess, to put it nicely. A few boarded
windows, the peeling door, the trash around it. Everything looked
threatening. I rang the bell five times.

"Who died?" A guy wearing a pair of boxers opened the door.
Glassy eyes, bruises on his arms.

"Who are you?" I glared at him, releasing my hand and pushing
him so I could get through.

There was only one rickety staircase leading to the first floor with
a worn, beaten banister.

The first floor wasn't any better than the ground floor with the
paint clinging to the walls and doors. A thick layer of dirt settled on
everything in sight, I bet untouched by any cleaning supplies.

"You're high," I whisper, walking toward my sister.

Her brassy blond hair was matted, she only wore a T-shirt, and
her legs were bruised.

I set the food I brought on the table next to the piles of trash.
"You have to be at work in an hour."

Lying on the couch, she releases a loud laugh. She's skeletal.
Barely any meat on her bones. "I made enough money to pay the
rent. Get the hell out of my house."

"You made enough money? I loaned you money yesterday for the
rent." My voice comes out as a raging scream. "What happened to 'I
want to get better'? You asked me for help."

"I. Don't. Need. You."

I shook my head, ignoring her hurtful words. Opening my purse, I search for the paper bag with the herbs. "Here's some tea. Mom would've wanted you to drink it."

"You still think she talks to you, poor little girl." She cackles, her angry words puncture my heart. "She was my mother. Not yours. You look nothing like her. I wished they had killed you when they killed her. I will never understand why they let you live."

Sammie was so high she spit nonsense just to be hurtful. Lucas told me to ignore her. That when I was born, she adored me. It was the drugs, but I hated how she treated me. Yet, I tried my best to save her.

"Stop," I ordered her. "You're doing it again. I might not have met her, but she was mine, too. She loved me, I know it. I want to help you because you're my sister."

"Get the fuck out of my house and my life. You're nothing to me. If I see you again, I'll kill you. This is your only warning."

Sammie's dad was granted full custody when Mom died. As her stepfather, Dad didn't have any rights over her. I don't think anyone helped her work through Mom's loss. She lost herself in drugs when she couldn't deal with reality. She once told me that meth allowed her to achieve some of the happiness she lost when Mom left us. She liked to reach for that magic potion that helped her forget whatever it is she wanted to ignore.

It wasn't long after that last meeting when I received the call that my sister overdosed. I wish I had saved her, but maybe her addiction was like terminal cancer. I could only prolong her life for so long, but it was best for her to leave. A part of me hopes she's happy with Mom by her side, that she finally got to be in peace. According to the few articles I've found, Mom's body was discovered by her daughter. She saw what happened to Mom, lived her last minutes. That can scar any child.

She was thirty-one when she died. She was sick, very sick.

Mom's killer is free. He might not have pulled the trigger, but he's the one who did it nonetheless. Like in all my cases, if I can't bring them home, I have to bring peace to their families. In this case, my father, my brothers, and maybe me. They took a piece of my heart when they took them away from me. It's not about vengeance, but opening a case that was mistakenly closed.

Will Harrison help me bring the killer down if I ask him?

11

HARRISON

"**H**ow was last night?" Hazel is handling the espresso machine while Scott is in front of the stove.

"Good morning?" I stare at her. How does she know I'm here?

"Morning, Harrison. Do you want some coffee?"

"I wasn't expecting to see you this early, and dressed." I stare at her mini dress and sandals. I saw her sleeping in the media room, wearing pajamas, only a few hours ago. "Where are you going, the beach?"

Her shoulders slump. "That sounds better than Vermont." She smacks her lips as she pours the frothed milk in the two mugs she has in front of her. "We are going antique shopping. I want to redecorate your Scott's office."

She sets one on the breakfast table, then hands me the other one. "It doesn't have any sugar or flavored syrup," Hazel warns me and goes back to the cupboard for another mug.

"We haven't discussed your parents." I bring up the tricky subject.

"There's nothing much to say, Harry." Her voice is steady, but her body tenses. "Mom decided to call it off, Dad is brokenhearted."

Scott shakes his head, giving me a death glare.

She sets the gallon of milk back on the counter, taking a few deep breaths. "There's more, but I have to process it, slowly."

Hazel turns around. Her eyes are slightly red. "Dad blames me for Mom's behavior. He said that if I hadn't been so insistent on trying to change her, she wouldn't have jumped."

"It wasn't you." Scott's voice is gentle.

"I know, but that doesn't make it hurt less." She drinks some of her coffee and stares at the pancakes on the table. "We should buy maple syrup. Vermont's is as good as Canadian syrup. I should get my passport in case we decide to cross the border."

"Can we plan Canada for October?" Scott redirects her attention. "You already have the month of September booked."

"Sorry," she whispers to him.

"You don't have to apologize. I've wanted to travel like this for a long time, actually I welcome the opportunity."

"You do like to travel," I agree with him. "That was part of the plan until . . ."

"I have a list for you." Hazel snaps her fingers, chasing away the thick, gloomy atmosphere we were creating.

She grabs her phone and starts firing messages. "I gathered some likes and dislikes from Luna. Things I know you won't find out soon but are imperative. Study it. It'll help you."

She finally takes a seat and grabs a couple of pancakes. "Now tell me, how was last night?"

"You abandoned me." I fake hurt, but I'm glad they left me alone with Luna.

"We didn't want to be your third wheel, plus we were starving. Scotty treated me to fish and chips since it was Friday," she informs me. "We went to O'Leary's."

"And came back to watch a Harry Potter marathon," I finish her adventure.

Hazel frowns.

"Scott was still watching it when I came back, but you were already asleep."

"Yeah, poor guy, he slept all night on the couch because of me.

For your information, I think he's starting to sneak into the top spot of who is my favorite Everhart." She shrugs. "Just in case you want to up your game."

"Nah, I think I'm good for now. Having that position for the past ten years has been hard, I'm glad he started working his ass to win the number one spot."

"Speaking of which, you should head to my house and check on Luna," she suddenly says before taking a bite of pancake. "Do something fun with her."

"I don't understand why I'm actually dating her." I bring it up casually, it doesn't bother me, but Hazel is pushing the envelope a little too far.

"Visibility and transparency are key during this operation," she corrects me. "Follow my lead, I know what I'm doing. In exchange, you can have so much fun with her."

She finishes her coffee, holds her mug and smiles at me. "The woman is amazing, enjoy your time with her."

"You like her?" I narrow my gaze, studying Hazel.

She has never liked any woman I've gone out with. Not even when she knows they'll be gone the next morning. I wonder if she likes Luna genuinely or . . .

"Are you sure?" I cross my arms. "You've never liked any of the women that my brothers dated. Why this one?"

"I do like her," she says, honestly. "As for the other women, they were less than average . . . no one has ever brought home a Luna. Everyone else was . . . unappealing."

"We need a Luna for Scott?"

She turns to Scott. "He's content right now. I don't think he needs a woman. Do you, Scott?"

"No," he groans. "I'm happy with my life. Leave me alone."

"Hunter has Willow. My best match so far."

"But you like Luna." And fuck, why am I so relieved to know that they are getting along?

"If I were into women, I'd be snatching her away from you. She's witty, fun, smart. And have you seen her practice yoga? She's very . . .

bendy." She smirks. "I want to be like her. Actually, I'm going to prac- tice yoga every day. My next man is going to love my . . . elasticity."

"Time for me to go," I declare, then turn to Scott. "Good luck. You have your hands full this weekend. She's going to tell you all about her . . . yoga poses."

I leave, laughing at the fact that my brother will be fighting a hard-on while he's next to who I think is the love of his life. He should man up and just tell her how he feels.

☆ ☆ ☆

I could get used to seeing her beautiful face every day. And that smile she uses to greet everyone around her is contagious. Luna waves at Carl as she exits the building, shooting happiness and sunshine around her. Until she halts. Her precious face becomes an ugly scowl the moment she spots me.

"What, I don't get to see that beautiful smile?" I hand her a cold matcha green latte, her favorite drink for the summer according to Hazel. Hot cocoa during the fall, peppermint chocolate during the winter, and hot tea after New Year's Day. The little micromanager emailed me a list of helpful tips. Favorite flowers, drinks, food, music, and hobbies. Based on Luna's preferred sports, she suggested the shooting range or a boxing ring for one of our dates. She loves her family and spends time with them every Saturday.

Since Hazel is a professional matchmaker, I trust her judgment. Though, there's also the possibility that she'd enjoy watching me die slowly in the hands of her new best friend.

"What do you want, Everhart?" Luna narrows her gaze at the large cup of iced tea in her hand.

"Did I do something to you that I don't remember?"

"No, I just don't trust you." She takes a few sips of the drink; her eyes never leave mine. "Thank you for the drink though. You shouldn't have."

"You're welcome?" I stare at her, feeling like we are on a chess board and the other one is waiting for the next move. "But you have to stop telling me what I should or shouldn't do. I enjoy spoiling you."

"Why are you here?"

"You have trust issues," I observe, not understanding what exactly is going on between us. The plan was simple. I bring her a drink, we take a walk around Central Park, and maybe if things work out, we can go to the shooting range. I was going to let her borrow Clarisse.

Does she have plans?

"Where were you going so early?"

"Why are you here so early?" she counters, then shows me the large bag she's carrying with her. "I am heading to work."

"Work?" I repeat with confusion.

"That physical or mental activity that one does in exchange for monetary remuneration," she sasses me.

"But it's Saturday," I highlight. "At seven f—" I stop when a couple of children holding their mother's hands stare at me. "F-reaking in the morning."

"Why are you here on Saturday? At. Seven. Freaking. In. The. Morning, Harrison Everhart."

"Everyone woke up early at home," I say, shrugging. "Hazel and Scott are going to Vermont. Fitz left for the gym . . . I hoped you'd want to hang out with me."

"Another time." She lifts the cup, biting the straw. "See you around."

Luna waves, giving me a cautious smile and walks away from me. I stare at her sweet, round ass. Those yoga pants make my mouth water. But I snap out of the trance as she turns to the right and I lose sight of her. If she thinks we are done for the day, she's wrong. I can wait for her outside of work. I can't remember what she does for a living?

Oh, right, she's a yoga instructor. A very bendy yoga instructor.

I jog to catch up with her. Though, I stop when I see her pull out a bag and hand it to a homeless man sitting with his back to the building wall. When she continues her walk, I stop in front of him and stare at the bag. It has water, a protein bar, and money. I pull out my wallet and hand him a twenty-dollar bill. For the next seven blocks, she hands a total of ten bags out.

Harrison: *Do you know about the Ziploc bags?*

Hazel: *Yeah. Wouldn't you want to date her for real?*

I hate to agree with her. When I agreed with Tiago, I had zero expectations about meeting his sister. After I met her, I liked her a lot, but still had a chance to keep myself away from her. Now . . . I'm not sure if keeping myself away will be easy.

Harrison: *I'm watching you, Beesley.*

Hazel: *Can't read more texts. We're losing connection. There's a tunnel ahead.*

Then she sends a gif with white noise. She's ridiculous, but I think I'm starting to understand her game. And I hate to admit that I kind of like it. Because I kind of like her—Luna.

12

LUNA

"You did great for your first time," I praise Harrison who not only stayed for the first class but the second yoga class too.

Both classes were for beginners, and a man as fit as him could take it. But the fact that he bought yoga shorts, joined the studio, and paid for an entire month was sweet—and heart melting. Just like dropping in at seven in the morning to bring me tea. I was in bitchy mode because I had zero sleep. Thinking about Dad and my sister, and reading Mom's journals trying to find some words of wisdom, took a toll on my mood. Seeing him too early made me suspicious about him. Or maybe it was the fact that no one has ever shown up at my doorstep with my favorite drink and said "Hey, I couldn't wait to see you" with just a smile. He didn't need to say a word.

"It was different. You made it . . . interesting." He smiles down at me.

His arm is right next to mine. The car of the subway is full. There's no place to sit and not much room to move. He puts my body in front of his when we step inside. His broad frame covers my figure. And surprisingly, it doesn't bother me that he's protecting me. I only trust my safety to myself, but right now, I'm letting my guard down and letting him be the one to look after me.

There's something about him that fascinates me. Or I should say that everything about him mesmerizes me. I could stare at his sculpted body, his bright blue eyes and get lost in them. However, Harrison isn't just that. He's the guy who makes sure that everyone in his family is taken care of, who worries about his friends. And I could listen to his husky voice for an entire day and never get tired of it. Among the best qualities, I've found so far is that sense of humor he uses to deflect an uncomfortable moment or to make the other person feel at ease. He surprises me every second we spend together.

He's not the person I thought he was during our initial encounter —a bitter guy who couldn't smile by himself. I keep wondering what was bothering him that he wanted to shut the doors the first time we met. Now that I've spent more time with him, I know he didn't shut the doors to be an asshole. He's actually attentive with most people.

"Do you work tomorrow too?"

His voice snaps me out of my trance. I move my gaze toward the floor feeling silly for staring at his forearm and fixating on him so much.

"No, Sundays and Wednesdays are my days off," I tell him, holding tighter onto the railing.

"What should we do tomorrow?" he asks, putting his arm around me when the car moves abruptly.

"I got you," he says, his lips almost touching my neck.

"Not sure," I stutter, as I try to move away from his hold.

He's too close, and I want him to step back because if not, I'm going to turn around and hug him, expecting him to hug me back . . . tightly . . . for a long time.

"Why are we back to small talk?"

Because I'm starting to enjoy your company too much and I'm not sure how to react to it.

I stay quiet, flustered since I have no idea how to respond to this question. Harry, I think you have it all wrong. I had an entire conversation with myself about my fixation with your powerful legs, your rough hands and how I'd love for you to run them over my body.

"Is it something I did?" His voice is a little off, I would've never guessed in a million years that Harrison would be a little insecure. "You didn't enjoy the shooting range?"

The shooting range was the weirdest, best date I've ever had. Wait, was it a date? I shouldn't consider it a date. Maybe an activity with my new partner.

"Thank you for letting me use Clarisse," I say, hiding the laugh.

Who names his guns Clarisse and Hannibal? Harrison Everhart.

"But did you like it? Was it okay?" He presses the subject. "I haven't gone out on a day-date, and . . . maybe this was way off for you."

So, it was a date. Interesting, and now my stomach has millions of butterflies fluttering inside.

"It was unexpected," I confess. "Thoughtful. I enjoyed shooting and learning a little from you. I had no idea you're a sniper."

The man zeros in on a target and doesn't fail. And those hands . . . ah, his calloused hands, positioning my body, so it was in just the right place before I took a shot was a religious experience since I kept praying I wouldn't drop the gun and just push the man against the wall.

This fake dating isn't as easy as I believed it'd be. I'm beginning to see the challenges ahead of me. How am I supposed to say no to him when all I want is for him to kiss me?

"This is our stop," he says, releasing my waist, but grabbing my hand. "You have to have an idea of the places you'd like to visit. Like a wish list."

"I thought you said that you hated to do the touristy thing." I bring up the most absurd part of yesterday's conversation.

"But you're new in town, I want to show the sights," he says, looking around when we come out of the station. "I have to confess . . ."

"It's confession time," I say excitedly, waiting for some torrid secret from his past. "What is it?"

"I don't like crowds," he whispers so close to me that his breath tickles my ear and makes me shiver.

His face is serious, and he continues walking without looking at me.

"I couldn't tell." I stay by his side, but every few steps I turn to him.

He's mumbling something and bouncing his head. As I think about all the times we've been together, he's done that just when we're in the streets, walking. He glances around, his head bounces, and he mumbles.

"AFTER I LEFT THE RANGERS, it took me a few months to adjust to them." He halts, opening the door of a small restaurant.

The music isn't loud, and surprisingly it's not some mariachi band, but just pop Latin music. Like the one my parents used to listen to, according to Mom's ultimate playlists.

"You seem pretty well-adjusted," I say when we sit at the table right next to the exit.

He exhales. "Now I can tolerate them. That doesn't mean I'm a fan."

"What is it that you do while you're walking?"

"Count people, remember where the CCTV is located, check plates . . . Watch out for the enemy." His head tips back at the ceiling briefly. "There are things from the war that stay with a soldier even after he's left the battlefield."

"Thank you," I say.

"Are we drinking a whole bottle of tequila?" He changes the subject.

I want to thank him for his service, for trusting me, for watching out for me while we're in the crowd, because even when he didn't say it, I know he wasn't just looking out for himself. But he closed the conversation, and I have to respect him.

"You and Dad have a lot in common. He was a SEAL. He doesn't like crowds either. Which is hard when our family is big and loud."

Harrison turns his gaze to the emergency exit, drumming his fingers on the table. As he's about to jump out of his seat and leave me—or at least that's what he wants to do—the waitress approaches our table.

"Harrison," she greets him. "Where is the family?"

"*Hola*, Clarita," he greets her. "*La familia me abandono*," he complains that the family abandoned him, "*pero mejor, porque asi puedo disfrutar a esta mujer hermosa.*"

I gawk as I hear him call me beautiful and that he prefers that they left him so he can enjoy me. He speaks Spanish with almost no accent. And suddenly, I want to bring him home to show him off to my family.

"This is your girlfriend?"

"Not yet, she's playing hard to get." He gives me that charming smirk that melts me and makes my entire body jitter. "I'm working on it, that's why I brought her here."

He winks at her as if they're sharing some kind of secret. "Luna, meet Clarita."

"*Mucho gusto*," I answer, nodding at her.

"What would you like to drink?" She hands me over a menu.

"Water, please," I say in Spanish.

"Bring a bottle of Don Julio, all your salsas, and guacamole, please," Harrison requests.

"Your Spanish is impressive," I praise him after Clarita leaves the table. "How did you learn?"

"Mom believed in immersion, so she dropped us in each country and didn't pick us up until we knew the language."

My eyes open wide, not understanding how that worked. What does he mean? And the idiot begins to laugh.

"Your face was priceless." He can't stop cackling. "It's Fitz's joke, but I use it sometimes. The reaction of most people is priceless."

"Everyone in your house talks like you?"

"No, you know how some people are great at math, others at

learning how to play instruments . . . well, I could learn how to speak a new language fast. That's my party trick."

"That's cool."

He nods. "And you, I assume your family speaks Spanish at home all the time."

"Yeah, we have to speak both languages as if they are both our first languages. It's a pain."

I sigh, shaking my head. It's almost two in the afternoon. On a regular Saturday, I'd be complaining about the noise, most likely holding a baby or talking to one of my cousins. Watching a soccer game, or perhaps, hiding from one of my aunts who brought a new guy for me to meet. I never thought I'd say this, but I miss them.

"You miss home." It's not a question, it's a statement. "You want to visit them?"

"Though I'd love to, my job doesn't pay that much." I am about to explain further when Clarita sets the chips and a bazillion salsas in front of us.

I'm glad she did because explaining further now feels silly. Why would he care about my life or my family? I doubt he wants to know that most of my salary goes to my family. We help each other, and since I don't need that much, I just give it to Abue who knows where and how to distribute it. Suddenly, the difference between his world and mine somehow makes me feel uncomfortable.

"It's my turn to pay for our food," I offer, but my voice sounds off.

"As I was saying, I could drive us to Alexandria," he suggests, ignoring my change of mood. "We can spend next weekend there."

"Drive?"

"Yes, Hazel told me you spend time with them every Saturday."

"Ah, Hazel. She has a Rolodex filled with useless facts from everyone she meets. What's the catch?"

"She does?" His eyes widen. "I knew she was crazy, but that's borderline insane."

"Nah, it just sounded like it when she began to ask me too many questions at the same time."

"She only does that with people she likes." He pours two shots of tequila and pushes one of them close to me. "To new and long-lasting friendships."

I sigh, getting lost in his blue eyes, repeating what he said. "To new and long-lasting friendships."

13

LUNA

I never thought I'd say that I miss Harrison Everhart. I only met him a couple of weeks ago, but last weekend we spent almost every minute together. Saturday, we drank a little too much tequila and ended up walking around the Museum of Natural History, making up stories for each exhibition until they kicked us out for being too disruptive. We weren't, but Harrison couldn't control his f-bombs in front of little children.

"When you have children, your wife is going to put a shock collar on you," I told him.

He gave me a weird look and shook his head. "You're going to be my predator mantis, aren't you?"

"Praying mantis, it's called praying mantis," I corrected him, *shaking my head. "Let's get you a coffee. The tequila is still swimming in that head of yours."*

"It's you, I'm drunk on you."

Sunday, we went for a run in Central Park, ate hot dogs for lunch, and spent the rest of the day flying kites. It was different. I have the feeling that he's as lost as I am about the dating world. I wonder when the last time he dated was. Maybe I'll tell him the next time I see him. Which might be tonight, or in a month. I have no idea. He had a special job that only the "A team" could assist. I'm curious to know what makes the team so unique.

There is one benefit to being alone, though. I have plenty of time to work out the logistics of my current case and study Mom's file. I believe someone tampered with the evidence. This week, I plan on going to the archives where they have the original paperwork. Hopefully, I can find out more about what happened to Mom. That'll be another step closer to catching the killer. The noise of the elevator doors opening draws my attention back to the present.

"You're here!" I jump when I hear Hazel's voice.

"Are you going somewhere?" I ask, stepping out of the elevator to find Hazel in the foyer waiting for it.

She glances at me, narrows her eyes and smiles. "Yes, you might want to change if you want to join us."

I look at my yoga pants and tank top, comparing it with her solid-white T-shirt and jeans. There's nothing special about it. Even her flat shoes are bland in comparison to what she usually wears— high heels, business attire, or fashionable dresses. Her hair is tied into a ponytail, and she only wears lip gloss.

Where is she going? I check the time, nine in the morning.

"Why would I want to join you?" And where have you been?

"Because we are doing our Sunday run."

"I already ran," I respond. "You might want to change for that though."

"Errands, we run errands," she clarifies. "I don't know if you want to come with us. However, I hope you do."

She opens the flap of the small purse she's holding and pulls her phone out, tapping it a few times.

"We are going to St. Catherine's soup line," she explains further. "And we're short four people."

"As in volunteering?" I raise an eyebrow looking at her outfit one more time. "What's the catch?"

She looks at the time. "That you'll be working your butt off for the next five hours without stopping," she responds. "And we have to leave in about five minutes . . ." She eyes me again. "Which means you'll have to hurry up."

"Four people bailed on you?" I frown.

"As you know, Harrison is on a 'secret mission.'" She uses her index finger to draw quotation marks up in the air. "The other two Everhart boys and my sister are out of town."

"Will there be press, something to cover the news?"

She rolls her eyes. "I'm not sure what you think about us, but we're anti-media." She pauses, scrunching her nose. "We don't help to attract attention, but to help . . . unless you delivered those supply bags to the homeless just to get media time."

I stare down at the floor, remembering last Sunday morning when Harrison helped me make them and deliver them. He mentioned something about St. Catherine's too. My heart skips a few times as I realize how much I want to see him. Why do I miss him?

"I'd be happy to help you."

I head to my room, searching for a pair of pants and a shirt. I put on a pair of flat shoes and adjust two of my bracelets on my ankle. Running a brush through my hair, I tie it into a bun, grab my small crossbody purse, and join Hazel in the foyer.

"Are we ready?" I ask when I find her whispering something to Scott, or were they kissing?

"Of course, we were just waiting for you." They step away from each other. She lowers her gaze, dusting off her jeans.

"Luna," Scott greets me. "It's good to see you."

"Hello, Scott. It's good to see you too."

Hazel lifts her chin, straightening her shoulders and turning to Scott. "Lead the way, sir."

✮✮✮

The loneliness I felt during my morning run dissipated. I had a busy, fulfilling day. According to my horoscope, the entire week is going to be productive. I should have read the rest, but Hazel has trouble saying no. She insisted that we watch movies, she promised to cook, but Scott didn't allow her. Scott explained to me that Hazel isn't allowed to cook, only to bake. She's terrible at the former.

"I can cook whenever you want me to," I offered.

"No, you're my guest," she responded, glaring at Scott. "How am I supposed to get better at it if I don't practice?"

"Take-out, we can cook, just stay away from the stove," he insisted.

"I planned a three cheese, Mexican lasagna for tomorrow."

"There's no such thing as Mexican lasagna, Hazel." His voice sounded a little frightened. "We can buy tacos for Mexican Monday." Scott cut her off.

"I can cook Mexican food," I intercede. "And I can teach you, Hazel. I promise you won't mess it up."

Today's big lesson is never judge a person without knowing her. Which I always follow, except today. The polluted air in this city tampers with my judgment. Or is it rich people? I admit that I'm intolerant of rich people. Mostly, against Mom's family and any others that seem to be like them. After Hazel and Scott rejected my application, I believed they were just like them. My entire perception of those two changed within a day.

When Hazel rejected my application, I hated her. The night we went to dinner with Harrison and Scott. I liked them, but I think I have a serious crush on both of them. In fact, it's kind of sad to learn that they aren't a couple. Scazel or Hazott would be a hit in my world. There's so much more to them than what they give away. Hazel spends her Sundays serving at a soup kitchen, except when she's out of town. She drags the Everhart boys and her sister if she's available. Hazel and Scott have a non-profit company that helps people start their own business. She doesn't just serve food. She asks every person that is in front of her how they are doing. Or if some family member is doing better. She knows them all by name.

I thought taking an SUV was over the top until I realized that they brought clothing, toys, and toiletries for the people who came to eat. Scott isn't bad either. While serving, I heard a few people talking about the boys and those girls who visited often. But my heart stopped when Scott said, "She's like Harrison."

"Who?"

"Hazel," he commented. "They come up a little dry, but underneath their cynical posture they are the most caring people I know."

That's exactly how I saw Harrison at the beginning, but he's so much more. My heart stops when I piece out his words.

"Why aren't they together?"

"They're like twins. Two positives don't attract." He grinned at me. "But I think that you and Harrison could be a hit."

"No, I shouldn't mix work with . . ." I repeated the words I've been saying for the past few days. "Maybe you should be with her," I fired back at him.

He sighed, looking at Hazel who was playing with some of the children. "It's a lot more complicated than anyone would think."

I felt the same about Harrison. If he were as amazing as Scott, I wouldn't hesitate to try something. Except, I can't open myself to a serious relationship. It's pointless.

As I'm about to turn off the light, my phone buzzes. I can't help but smile when I read the text on my screen.

Harrison: *Hey, I'll be there soon. Have you missed me yet?*

I missed human contact, does that count as missing you? Instead of responding that, I feign ignorance.

Luna: *Who is this?*

Harrison: *Silly woman. I heard that you covered for me in the soup line today.*

I laugh at his response, yet, I'm intrigued that he knows where I was today.

Luna: *It was interesting. How do you know I was there?*

Harrison: *I usually contact Scott when I'm back on the grid.*

Grid, hmm. I wonder who Tiago contacts when he's in and out. There's so little I know about my brother.

Harrison: *Maybe we can go together next week.*

Luna: *I'd love to do it again. Today turned out to be much different than I imagined.*

Harrison: *Wait until I'm there, we're going to have fun ;)*

Harrison: *I'll miss you for another day, but I'll see you soon.*

14

LUNA

Yoga is my outlet. It's not a hobby, but a way of life. Even though I've practiced yoga since I was in college, teaching it is new to me. Doing it with a few hours of sleep and the distraction of Mr. Crystal-Blue Eyes was almost impossible during the first class of the day. I blame him, stupid Harrison Everhart. That Everhart boy isn't going to see the light of a new day if he continues surprising me at work tomorrow. Today, he came holding a matcha green tea and wearing that dazzling smile that makes my heart stop . . . and then thunder so hard I'm afraid it's going to break my ribs.

He has to stop being all wonderful, caring, and attentive. The mission comes first, and his flirting advances should be banned.

We need rules.

First rule, he isn't allowed to drop in at my place of work and say, "I woke up thinking of you," and give me a deep, soulful kiss in front of everyone who was going to take my beginners-Vinyasa class.

Rule number two, he isn't allowed to take my classes and wink at me while everyone is watching us. That panty-melting-heart-stopping smirk is forbidden. That should be rule number three. Rule number four, keep that eight-pack hidden behind a thick layer of clothing and his thick, long appendage should be covered at all times when I'm around. Who goes commando while wearing jeans? Doesn't that hurt?

I'm just thankful that he didn't book a Reiki session with me after I got a good glimpse of his perfectly shaped, naked body when he was changing in the locker room. Otherwise, I'd have quit on the spot. I couldn't stand the torture of touching him for thirty minutes. Harrison Everhart has to stay away from me. He might not realize it, but I need his help blending. Not the animosity of the women who want him.

After my second class of the day, I went to the Reiki room. I'm better at practicing it, except, it's six o'clock and I've been having back-to-back appointments. Everyone wants to take my classes or enjoy the healing power of my hands. According to Jess, the owner, people are starting to use the studio's app and RSVPing to all the classes I'm teaching for the next two weeks. She wanted me to add one more at five in the morning. As much as I'd love to get paid seventy-five dollars for that hour, I prefer to sleep.

"You're incredible. I feel so much better," the lady whose name I can't remember says as she sits straight up, rotating her neck. "I'm going to recommend you to my friends."

Please don't. I can't take another round of interrogations while trying to heal you. If this continues, I am going to quit.

Just quit, Luna. These women might push you too far and you'll end up snapping their neck.

"Thank you." I plaster the friendliest smile I can fake on my lips.

"I hope you don't mind all my questions, but when I heard that you're dating Harrison Everhart, I couldn't contain myself. I knew his mother. She was a sweetheart."

Here we go again. Wait, what? She was? As in no longer existent or they are no longer friends? Now, I'm intrigued.

Do not engage, Luna.

I press stop to the music and wash my hands.

"How serious are you two?"

"It's new. We just started dating recently," I respond the same way I did the last seven times or was it a million?

I lost count after the second person that interrogated me about this phenomenon called Harrison Everhart.

"He's a catch, isn't he?"

I'm the catch, lady. Not him. He wishes he could date me in real life. Would he? I wouldn't know. He's not my type. My type is . . . do I have a type? I'm sure his type is more like Hazel. Dressed in the latest fashion, high heels and picture-ready face and hair.

"I wouldn't know. This is brand new for the two of us." I hand over her purse.

"We thought he was going to marry that Beesley girl."

That Beesley girl will laugh when I tell her that at least ten people mentioned he was her man.

"Beesley girl?" I yawn, feigning ignorance.

Opening the door, I tilt my head toward the reception area. I turn off the lights and grab my tote bag. She's my last appointment of the day, thank God. "If you don't mind paying Jess on your way out, here is my card in case you want to schedule another appointment. My schedule doesn't allow me to take walk-ins."

"Oh look, your young man is waiting for you." She stops right in front of me, looking around, then giving me a coy smile. As if we're accomplices or best friends. "And he brought you flowers."

Why is he here?

"Hey," I say, walking toward him.

"Babe, these are for you," Harrison greets me, handing me the small, beautiful bouquet of wildflowers. "Ready to go home?"

I reach for the back of his neck with one hand. Stand on my tiptoes and press my lips close to his ear so only he can hear me. "Call me babe again, and you'll die, *baby*."

Harrison grabs me by the waist, pulling me closer to him. "Ever since I met you, you have nothing but loving words and affection for me."

He grins, looking around and then looking down at me. "This girl is a keeper."

Leaning closer to me, he grabs my mouth with his, kissing me deeply and soulfully. My toes curl, my heart hammers against my ribcage and my tongue dances along with his. I rise above the earth, dancing through the clouds. The world spins as the magic of the kiss sinks in. His heartbeats are so strong, so loud that I can hear it inside myself. Or is that me?

I push him away; my stomach tightens as I try to rationalize what just happened between us.

We kissed. But it's not just that; it's so much more. Suddenly, his beat matched mine, and I was somewhere far away with him. It was only the two of us sharing more than just a kiss. This is beginning to be too much for me. I might be open to everything, but not to someone like him. I feel like he's sucking me into his life and I'm losing perspective of what matters . . . and I just met him.

"We have dinner with the family, Luna." His voice is calm, soft. It caresses my insides and my entire body tenses. Why am I reacting this way?

He nods at everyone and says, "Have a good evening, ladies."

Harrison grabs my hand. I hate, and I love that when he intertwines his fingers with mine, they fit perfectly together. Something about him just feels right. We haven't known each other for long, and yet, I react to his charm. These fluttering stomach, weak knees, fast heart-beating symptoms shouldn't exist. Since when do I care for the sexy, playboy kind of guy? Never. I've never liked those guys who catch the stares of every female in the room. I used to date quiet, smart, and sensitive men. But that was a long time ago. My last "relationship" was . . . when was it? Was it Tony, before I joined the FBI? I think so. And since then, men aren't part of my permanent agenda. They occupy too much time that I can't give them.

So, why am I reacting like a woman full of lust when he's around? I must have hit my head hard and didn't realize it until my hormones began to react to his presence. That's the only explanation I come up with.

"We need rules, Harrison Everhart," I speak as we step outside the studio.

"Rules?" Harrison glances, shrugs and pulls me toward the left through the sea of people walking toward Madison Square Garden.

"You don't seem like the kind of woman who likes rules. I swore you'd be more like a 'go with the flow and let go of what is useless.'"

"You don't know me," I rebuke his stupid observation.

I follow that philosophy, letting things go. In fact, "go with the flow, be the flow, and create the flow" is my mantra. Outside of work I prefer to live a little less organized and a lot more . . . soulful? Is that even a word? I just like to breathe, trust, and live with an open heart. It's a balancing act I enjoy performing often. He doesn't have to know it. In fact, he shouldn't be analyzing the kind of person that I am.

"We are working together, not . . . getting to know each other." I huff.

My words make me sound out of character. Knowing people is my favorite part about life. I hate superficial relationships but . . . this man is a heartache waiting to happen. Wait, why am I going from getting to know him to crushing my heart? I stare at our linked hands. Is it the electricity we produce every time we touch that's making me act like a teenager with a crush?

As we arrive at a crosswalk, he stops and turns to look at me. "It's one in the same. We are partners in crime. Partner 101, you have to trust your companion, blindly. For that to happen, I have to get to know you."

"Rules," I insist. "We need rules."

He frowns, exhales, and we resume our walk. Is he against rules? He was a Ranger. Aren't they programmed to follow procedure? My mind races as I focus on what to do with Harrison Everhart. Ditch the man and do this alone. I can't. I need him for a few more days, maybe weeks. People responded well to our bogus relationship. They want to know me, be friendly with me. My heart will burst out of my chest if he kisses me the way he did at the studio.

The ongoing fight I have in my head is part confusion and part frustration.

15

HARRISON

I hate to admit it, this get-to-know each other phase isn't as bad as I recall. Actually, I like it. Scratching my head, I attempt to remember the last time I tried to get to know someone who I was attracted to. The only three women I talk to include Hazel because she's my best friend. My brothers like to add that she's a female version of myself. We know each other pretty well. Then, there's Willow, Hunter's live-in girlfriend. And Sarah, our house-keeper. She has known me since I was a teenager.

"Why do we need rules?"

"You fluster me," she responds.

I like her reaction toward me. The cheek biting, eye squeezing, squeaky voice combination she has every time I frustrate her. It's insane to say that I fucking missed her while I was away. Now that I'm back, I want a lot more from this temporary relationship. Sex is part of the agenda. I just have to approach her from the right angle. No strings attached can be so easy.

It doesn't make sense as to why we have to set rules. What kind of rules is she talking about? The kind of rules people set before having non-commitment sex is simple. No feelings should be involved. The moment one of the parties starts having feelings for the other, it should be terminated. That calls for an irrevocable termination. Though, I admit that I'm looking forward to having monogamous sex. It's been a long drought for me. One-night stands at my age don't excite me. I blame it all on my friend and partner, Anderson Hawkins, and my brother Hunter. They are happy with their women.

Then there's Hazel who wears her rosy love goggles. She's always talking about families, and how life changes once you find the one. That one creates some kind of magic that makes you never want to be alone, ever.

I have no idea if there's such a thing as my one. I might be too old to find a girl to spend the rest of my life with. My parents married in their early twenties. But Hawk found Aspen at my age. Maybe my match is out there. Do I want to find her? I glance at Luna. If finding the one means losing her, then I don't want to find anyone. At least not for now. I want to spend as much time as I can with her. I'm not sure. For now, I want a woman who I can enjoy having sex with more than once. We can be in my bed, her bed, in a hotel, on a private island, or wherever we please. Without romantic expectations, of course.

I am ready to have steady, monogamous sex with Luna. We can fake the whole happily ever after in front of whoever she wants. While in bed, we can send each other to a state of eternal bliss. I just have to show her that we can work things out, my way.

"Define flustered. Do I excite you?" I wiggle my eyebrows. "Or do I frustrate you?"

Either scenario works for me, I like how her eyes brighten, and her nostrils flare simultaneously. I like to think that I get to her and that excites me. There's nothing frustrating about this woman. Except, her father. We have to discuss that man and her brothers. It's the big guy who scares the fuck out of me. Tiago has more muscles than me, and he knows my weak points. He can break me like a twig if I don't tread carefully.

"Frustrating." She rolls her eyes. "There's nothing exciting about you."

Her gaze moves toward the floor. She chews her cheek. And I

believe I just found out the way to tell when she's lying. She's not as hard to read as I thought.

"That's because you forgot how good we are together." I wink at her. "In a couple of days, you'd choose me over Disney World. And remember what they say, that's the happiest place on Earth."

My groin tightens when her tanned skin flushes every time I get too close or when I say something that embarrasses her.

I pull out my phone to ask my family about dinner. Since I have nothing to do but be with Luna, I was assigned to bring them food.

Harrison: *Sushi?*

Hazel: *It's not Sunday. You're ruining Sushi Sunday.*

Hunter: *Yes to sushi.*

Fitz: *I can go for sushi, stop designating food for every day of the week. I hate French Friday.*

Hazel: *You hated the escargot. I promised not to cook them.*

Fitz: *You shouldn't cook, period.*

Scott: *Sushi is fine.*

Harrison: *Perfect, just text the order. I'm almost there.*

The group chat continues buzzing, but I ignore it. The majority agrees on eating that for dinner. Unless Luna doesn't like it, that's what we're having tonight.

"Do you like sushi?" I ask as we get closer to Kurosawa, the Asian bistro close to Hazel's place. She nods. "Then we can have some Sake and a long chat about *your* plans during your time in New York City."

"*My* plans?" She shoots me a glare and shakes her head. "Rules, we need ground rules. For starters, you aren't allowed to drop by the yoga studio."

"I never got a thank you for the flowers. After you, my lady." I open the door of the restaurant and bow to her.

She smells the flowers I gave her earlier, angles her face toward me, and smiles. "Thank you, they're pretty."

"You're welcome. I'd like to point out that you're more beautiful." I kiss the tip of her nose and walk to the counter.

"Did you memorize every page of Cheesy Pick-up Lines for

Dummies?" she fires back. "Or was it How to Impress Your Girl for Sixth Graders."

"I take it you're not amused by my approach." *Or that my approach is making you uncomfortable because it's working.* I take her hand and kiss it lightly.

"Umm." She claims her hand, dropping her chin for a few moments.

"What kind of men have you been dating, *dear?*" I shoot her an inquisitive gaze before paying attention to the guy behind the counter. "Hello, John."

John's eyebrows furrow. I point at his name tag, and he smiles while nodding. "Welcome to Kurosawa, will this be for here or to go?"

"To go, please." I turn to Luna who is staring at the menu board. "Are you ready to order?"

"Can I have a SoHo sushi plate and two amazing rolls, please," she requests, turning back to me when she's done.

"Two more SoHo plates. Three orders of lobster rolls, two poke bowls with tuna, one with salmon, and one with shrimp; and five orders of tuna sashimi to go." I read the order from my phone and then read the last text.

Hunter: *Can you bring teriyaki chicken for Willow? She can't eat raw fish. And hurry, Hazel is going insane.*

Harrison: *Why?*

Hunter: *We can't give the news until everyone is here, including you.*

News? What kind of news?

"Can you add an order of teriyaki chicken?"

"Name on the order?"

I scribble it on a paper while handing Luna a cup to distract her. "Do you want water?"

When the total comes up on the screen, I swipe my phone on the scanner.

But she's busy going through her purse. I stretch my neck trying to see what she has in there other than those sharp chopsticks that almost killed me the day we met. She might have an entire arsenal to kill a gang without breaking a sweat. Fuck. Why do I find that hot?

My new addiction is petite girls who look harmless and can kick my ass.

Or just this one.

"Water?" She finally pays attention to me.

"No. Thank you. I . . . just . . ."

"Next," John calls the person behind us, he's done with us.

Luna exhales, dropping her weight on one of her legs. "You don't have to buy me dinner," Luna says, holding a rose-pale pink tooled leather wallet. "I can pay for myself."

All her things are original, handmade, and as cute as her. Plus, disorganized too. That wallet is full of folded receipts and papers. Does she need to save all that?

"Is that for your daily expenses?" I lightly touch her wallet. "Because there's an app you can use to scan your receipts and email them as you go."

"App?" She crooks an eyebrow staring at her wallet. "You're a strange person, Harrison Everhart. Can you stick to one subject?"

"Probably," I answer, smiling at her frustrated face.

The subject would be, *I pay when you're with me. It's not because I'm the man, but because that's what my mother taught me. But your answer will probably be in the form of physical injury or threatening my man parts.*

Yet, I find it adorable when she's irritated. Why do I find her adorable?

"As I said, I could've paid for my own dinner," she repeats, taking out a twenty-dollar bill and handing it to me.

"You're welcome," I say, pushing her hand lightly back to her wallet.

"Huh?"

"That's what one says when someone buys you dinner," I explain to her.

"One is talking in third person." The corner of her lips pull slightly. The smile brightens her face. My heartbeat accelerates as the scowl disappears. "Honestly, I should be the one paying for your dinner."

"Why?"

She looks at my crotch, her eyes shining. Those eyes remind me of one of Mom's stained-glass windows. The one she donated to a church in Belize. This woman has angel eyes. "Well, that little incident while you were changing in the Reiki room after yoga class."

Luna bites her lip, her face flushes.

"Dinner wouldn't make things even—maybe you should show me yours." I wink at her. "Just a glimpse, like the one you saw today."

Her angelical laugh makes my heart beat fast.

"We need rules before things between us become blurry. Blurry isn't healthy," she pauses, "or so I've heard."

"Twenty-twenty vision." I point at my eyes lowering my voice and getting closer to her. "There's no way things can become blurry, for me. I'm a sniper. I'm trained to detect things that many can't. I see better than the average guy."

Caressing her hand, I continue. "Like the way your skin flushes. Or the way you bite your lip when I say something that . . . excites you. You call it frustration, but I call it sexual tension."

Mumbling in her ear, I say, "Your condition is pretty obvious."

She chuckles, closing her eyes briefly as she shakes her head. "I have a condition. Is there a cure to what I have, Dr. Everhart?"

"Order ready. Luna Everhart, your order is ready," they call when the order is up. "Luna Everhart."

Luna gasps, looking around the restaurant. "You have a death wish, Everhart. That's not my last name." She scowls at me, again.

"Yes, you have sexual frustration. And I know how to treat it. We can make rules around . . . your problem." I smirk before going back to the counter to pick up our food but not before murmuring close to her ear. "Since you seem to like roleplay, we can play doctor while I take care of that itch."

She gapes at me. If we were keeping score, I'd say Harrison one Luna zero. Unless we count the time, she almost kicked my ass. That takes at least five points away, easily.

16

LUNA

Doctor, roleplay. Itch.

What itch is he talking about?

This entire conversation doesn't just blur the lines, it erases them. There're no lines. With so many people around us, I can't stop and talk some sense into him. Maybe he's the one who hit his head. It was my fault. Did he hit the floor too hard last week? Or maybe during the mission, something happened and he has a concussion.

"Did you hit your head while you were working?" I walk close to him, making sure that he can hear me. "Should we take you to the doctor?"

He chuckles but ignores me.

Will another hit on the head fix whatever is wrong with him?

Violence shouldn't be the answer, but I'm ready to experiment with it. I try to reclaim my hand, but Harrison holds it tighter. His steps are longer, faster. I have to almost jog to keep up with him. I wish he would slow down so we can talk. But we continue walking in silence. My question remains up in the air. I'll repeat it later when we are alone. This situation has to be resolved soon. We can't take things too far.

You're fearless, Luna. Why can't you let yourself do something different with him? I glance at him. His eyes are focused forward, but the times I glance at him he smiles at me. Pulling my hand, he kisses the back.

"Don't overthink. This has to be simple, easy," he explains. "Once you begin to use your heart and your mind to solve what's between us the moment is gone."

We are close to the building where I'm currently staying. He pulls us to the side and exhales. "Have you ever had one-night stands?"

"Yes, but the day after I'm gone." I lift one shoulder, slumping it right away. "We never see each other again."

"Okay, we apply the same concept. The difference is that you'll see me."

He angles his head to the entrance, and I follow him. "Carter, how are you tonight?" he greets the doorman when we arrive home.

"Miss Santillan, Mr. Everhart, good evening."

"Hey, Carter." I wave at him.

When we step into the elevator, I speak. "There's no itch, frustration, or roleplay. We have to set ground rules. I can't sleep with my partner."

He pulls his cell phone out.

"I propose that we take full advantage of the situation and spend the next weeks doing what couples do," he reads last night's text.

"We're not a couple," I remind him.

"Yet," he adds.

"We are partners."

"Partners?" He wiggles his eyebrows. "I like that. Live-in partners have more fun than your average couple."

"You're insufferable."

"But you already accepted that." He stares at his phone. "Luna accepted by saying, '*It might work, we'll have to talk about ground rules,*'" he mocks my voice.

"It's right here, in writing. You want ground rules. We only need one." He pushes me against the metal wall, caging me with his strong body.

Harrison nuzzles my neck, murmuring. "We don't tangle our actions with emotions. I offer you steady, monogamous sex while we work together."

His lips brush against mine. The fire they evoke leaves me weak, a low, throaty moan escapes. The wait for more is almost too much for my heart to take. Reaching for his lips, I kiss him. My skin catches fire as his hands slide down my bare back and land just above my ass. He presses me closer to him as he strips me bare from the walls I try to build around myself and exposes my soul to his.

"You can't fight this," he says, breaking our kiss.

My breathing hitches. Shivers travel from the nape of my neck all the way to my toes. Yet, my skin burns as it remembers his touch. The low voice weakens my knees, tightening my core. "That's unprofessional," I whisper.

"There's no professional link between us, Luna," he reminds me, straightening his back, and stepping away from me.

His face is somber, his gaze holds mine. "There's chemistry between us. We're both consenting adults. Why not take full advantage of our situation?"

"Situation?" I sigh, gasping for air. "There's no situation. We shouldn't be . . ."

Wait, Luna. Why are you saying no to steady sex? He's sexy, and the ache between your legs could use his assistance. The little voice of unreason speaks. That one I never allow to speak when I'm having second thoughts about guys.

The elevator doors open and I run toward my room without looking back. There's such a cluttering mess inside my head that I have to search for a second opinion. Mom's journal doesn't have any advice on no-strings-attached-sex. My second choice is my phone. I tap on my password and access my daily horoscope.

Dear Cancer,

With the Moon so close to Jupiter, you are searching for more comfort than usual. But with a Mercury-Jupiter play, there's a part of you that wants to do things differently. Get out of your shell and try something new. Combine the old comfort with the new aspects happening in your life. Nevertheless, try on that new feeling you're trying to avoid. Work doesn't have to be boring, you can experiment with a new method.

Your personal life is about to receive its own makeover, be open to change. Let the ordinary become extraordinary. That might lead to pleasant surprises if you know what I mean, my dear crab. Have more courage and welcome a new associate into your professional life. That might be the key to success. Don't forget that this is a great month to make some new connections that might lead you to love.

Good luck my lucky crab.

My comfort is not sharing feelings. Should I assume that the new is Harrison Everhart's bed, he said emotion free. Didn't he? The tightness in my chest mirrors every muscle of my body. Can I be emotionless while my body is responding so strongly to his attention? Love, I can't make any new connections that will lead me to love. There's no such thing as love for me. No future. But wait, Harrison said no feelings. That's hard for me. I like to make real connections. How do I handle him?

"Luna, we're waiting for you," Harrison says, knocking the door.

"Give me a second, I'm taking a quick shower."

17

HARRISON

Family comes first, always.

My father repeated those words to us since we were little. They've stayed with me since the day I heard them. I applied them often and made them my number one rule the day that he died. Scott and I are the parental figures of this household. And even though our youngest brother is thirty, we still look after him. Tonight, it isn't the exception. Hunter has some big news for us, and my duty as his big brother is to be with him.

I wanted to go out with Luna; spend some time with her while we discussed our new arrangement. One she's trying to avoid. Last week we had a great time together. Our chemistry is undeniable. Her body responds to mine with the slightest touch. Our conversations over the phone were simple but enjoyable. Her irritated texts had me laughing while I was out of town.

She denies there's a connection. Yet when we touch, and when we kiss, there's a fiery energy that burns us and makes us feel alive. I want more of her, more of us. I have to convince her that what I propose is safe. We can keep the wick ignited until the candle burns and our time ends. Tonight, I have to convince her that I'm safe, but is she safe for me?

I will start our talk with her plans during her stay in the city. According to the conversation I had earlier with Tiago and her father, she has some hidden business that includes her mother.

"I can't stress how important it is that you keep her away from anything that doesn't pertain to her current case, Everhart," Cristobal Santillan said with a voice that was firm, yet worried.

As soon as I'm done with this family affair, we have to talk about everything—her plans, my plans, and the possibility of more.

The room goes silent as Hunter claps.

"Now that everyone is here." Hunter takes me away from my inner thoughts.

"Where is Luna?" Hazel looks around.

"Who is Luna?" Willow raises an eyebrow, pressing her lips together.

"Hi," Luna steps into the room, coming into view.

She changed her yoga pants and backless tank top for a short, flouncy mini dress. The bracelets are back, and she tied her hair up into a messy bun. She's barefoot, and I eye her ankle where she has a tattoo of a small elephant holding a heart with his trunk as if it was a balloon. Fuck, even her ink is cute.

"Luna, let me introduce you to my family," I say, taking her hand, pulling her body toward me.

I place her right in front of me, kissing the top of her head. "Everyone, this is Luna. I'm sure Hazel will bring you up to date later. Luna, meet my family. From left to right we begin with Scott and Hazel."

"We've met before," she reminds me, lifting her chin and looking up to me. I lower my head and kiss her lips lightly.

She doesn't kick me in the nuts, progress.

"To Hazel's right is Fitzhenry, the middle child," I introduce him. "He's our special little brother."

Fitz shows me his middle finger. "That's because I'm the best of the four, sweetheart. Don't let him fool you."

"Next to him are Hunter and Willow. He's my youngest brother, and she's his girlfriend, who happens to be Hazel's sister." I eye the solitaire diamond she wears, arch my eyebrow and gaze at Hunter. "Or should I call her your fiancée, Hunt?"

"As usual your observational skills don't fail you, big brother," he responds, taking Willow's hand and kissing it.

"That's not the big news," Hazel announces clapping her hands.

Willow rolls her eyes, smiling at her little sister. "We're pregnant," she reveals. Her voice is calm, sweet and joyful.

Grant Beesley stands up to hug his granddaughter. She cries while he murmurs things to her. "Love you too, Gramps," she says, kissing his cheek.

"I'm going to be an aunt." Hazel stands up giving her a tight hug too. She is over the moon. But she's not surprised.

"You told her first?" I feign resentment as I walk closer to them and hug them both. "Congratulations, little brother."

Willow shakes her head. "She guessed, I can't hide much from her."

"Congratulations to both," Luna utters, walking closer to Willow and Hunter. "Nice to meet you by the way."

Scott hugs them both and smiles at Hunter. He then looks at me and we both nod, knowing that our job with him is over. He's happy and has his own family. We couldn't ask for more.

"Mom and Dad are as happy as we are for you two," I tell Hunter, patting his shoulder.

"Their first grandchild," Scott seconds my words. "Mom would be over the moon, Hunt."

"You think so?" He looks at both of us.

The news couldn't have arrived at a better time. It's almost the anniversary of their death. Scott and I smile and nod at him. My parents were happy when we were happy. I bet they are watching from heaven and celebrating too.

"We aren't sticking to Mom's desires, are we?" Fitz eyes widen. "Five children per son, so she can have twenty grandkids, is difficult when I can't have children."

Hazel glances at him, blinking twice. "There're options. Surrogates, adoption, and fostering. You can have as many as you want."

"I'm not having five children," Willow protests, then she turns to Luna. "Are you planning on having five mini-Everharts?"

Luna raises her hands, shaking her head. "Ummm."

"We just started dating, Willow." I stop her before she begins to ask more questions.

"She's not there, yet, don't scare her, please," Hazel warns her.

I frown at her, but she ignores me. What is going on with little Hazel? I will find out later. It's time for me to go. They are going to scare Luna, and we are in the middle of some very important negotiations. Walking toward the bags of takeout I grab her food, my food, and some chopsticks.

"Do we have any special plans for . . ." Hunter looks around the room.

"Our parents' anniversary?" Scott finishes for him. "I have a conference. Hazel and I are leaving tomorrow."

"I booked another week in Arizona," Fitz says, casually. "I'm hoping that one of the monks will break their vow of silence."

Scott slaps him on the back of the head. "Hey, it's a joke. You need to get laid."

"Hunt?"

"We might go to LA." He shrugs.

"I'm staying in town, with Luna. But call if you need me."

"Same goes," Scott adds.

"Dinner is here, I'm leaving with Luna." Then I turn to Scott. "I'm going home, do you have any plans for tonight?"

Hint, I need the apartment for myself.

"I do," Fitz responds. "Don't wait up for me."

He sighs, checking his phone. "We're traveling tomorrow. We'll be gone until Saturday. I can call the charter company and change the time of our flight." He turns to look at Hazel. "Would you mind leaving tonight, Haze?"

"Whatever." Her response is short and dry. The fake indifference might work for everyone, but that light smile on her lips is a dead giveaway. She can't wait to leave.

"Please don't do it on my account, Beesley." I poke around. "In fact, if you wait, I can join you two."

"If you think it's necessary." She doesn't snap. She focuses on the food on top of the table, avoiding everyone.

I stare at her, hoping she'll look at me but she doesn't. She seems to be ignoring everyone, but it just hit me. Hazel is avoiding *me*. What is going on with her? I glance from her to Scott who happens to be touching her hand. They have been casually touching since I came back from my other mission. It's not obvious for everyone, but too obvious to me.

"Be careful," I warn him, angling my head toward Hazel.

He nods once, and I leave the room.

"Hey, get a bag ready, you're not coming back," I tell Luna, pulling out my phone.

Luna laughs. "No. I don't plan on going to your place."

"Do you want to talk about our plans and the rules you want here while we eat with my family?"

Luna huffs, and storms toward her room. I go back to the dining room and ask Hazel to join me in the library. She closes her eyes briefly but joins me.

"I'm giving you space, but I know something is up with you," I say it as it goes. We don't lie to each other and try to be a hundred percent honest.

"Thank you for that." She smiles and walks toward me to give me a hug. "I love you."

"Love you too, just be careful," I warn her because I know that my brother can be an asshole and I don't know what'll happen if my hunch is right and he hurts her.

"You too. I'm here for you." She squeezes my forearm. "Don't fuck it up, Harry!"

"It?"

"Luna." She looks toward the door. "You like her, a lot. Be smart about it."

"It's just casual."

"You keep saying that to yourself." She lifts her nose and smells the air. "You two smell like Happily Ever After."

"Be safe, Beesley," I repeat, making my way back to the foyer.

"I'm ready," Luna announces, holding her tote bag. "Just don't expect any s-e-x tonight. And tone down your commanding persona."

"As you wish, my lady," I vow to her, calling the elevator.

This is going to be an interesting night. I glance at her curvy, petite body and my core clenches. Rationality be damned. There's something about Luna that bypassed all my walls. Only days after meeting her, I have the deep urge to have her under my skin. The next few weeks might be the best ones of my life.

18

LUNA

Harrison lives in what can only be described as the ultimate bachelor pad. The foyer, living room, and dining room are almost an exact replica of a swanky sports bar. Pool table, air hockey table, big screen televisions—three of them—a poker table and a recliner sectional leather couch. The walls are decorated with three neon signs that read, *open, exit, and bar.* But there are also a few pieces of art hanging and a couple of tall, glass sculptures on the floor. There's a faint scent of cookies and vanilla that has nothing to do with the décor of the place.

"We like to party, don't we," I say with a smirk as I picture all the parties these guys must have every weekend.

"You're judging." Harrison clears his throat.

"It's different," I confess, feeling my face heat as I realize that he's not amused by my comment. "I don't mean to criticize. I'm just wondering . . . Why did you guys decide to convert this into the ultimate man cave?"

He sighs, scanning the room. "This was my parents' apartment. The family home," he says, walking toward the terrace.

Harrison opens the door, and I decide to go after him, expectant of a longer explanation. He marches to the fire pit, turning it on. He then saunters to the brown, plastic chest in the corner of the patio and gathers two long cushions. He sets them on top of the iron chairs.

"Would you like something to drink?" He tilts his head toward one of the chairs, patting it.

"Water is fine, thank you."

"Okay. I'll go get some napkins and a beer for me, then." He sets the takeout food on top of the coffee table and leaves me for a few seconds.

The terrace is gorgeous, peaceful, serene and yet it is in the middle of one of the busiest cities in the world. I rise from my seat and walk to the railing to admire the view. I'm taken aback as the beauty in front of my eyes isn't what I had expected. Central Park is like a stunning photograph of woodland with green tones and small lakes spread throughout. I can just picture the brown-orange tones during the fall, or the white layer after a snowstorm.

The sound of the wind chimes that hangs on one of the walls is hypnotic. I close my eyes and imagine myself in the middle of a forest. My emotions sink back, and my brain reboots. I could stay here forever enjoying myself.

"This was Mom's favorite place." Harrison's voice pulls me out of my happy place. "She would come out after dinner with a book and read while we played."

"I'm sorry about your parents." I spin my head slightly to face him.

He leans his forearms on top of the railing, looking around the city. "They died on nine-eleven." He breathes out hard as he says those words. "Fitz and Hunter were kids when it happened. Scott was a freshman in college. He was barely eighteen when everything happened."

I reach for his arm, squeezing it lightly as he closes his eyes for a few seconds. When he opens them, he stares at me showing me his pain. The anguish reflected in his face pinches my heart. For some unknown reason, I want to take away that pain. Moving closer to him, I kiss his cheek wishing it was enough to make everything better.

Looking over his shoulder, he speaks. "Well, Fitz wasn't exactly a kid. He was a teenager already dealing with his sexuality. Losing them fucked him because no one would understand him or love him the way they did. He was lost." He shakes his head and puts his arms around me, hugging me tight to him.

He sighs. "We were lost. Hunter wouldn't come out of his room and would hide under the bed during his bad days. Scott became a heartless son of a bitch, and I decided to enlist and avenge my parents."

"How about Fitz?"

"He partied, a lot. Scott had it rough. He was the one who stayed with the younger ones while I fought for my country. During those years, Fitz destroyed the living room furniture. Scott and Fitz's therapist decided to make it a place where Fitz would want to hang out with his friends. That's when he began to calm, and by some miracle, the kid graduated high school and settled his anger."

He chuckles. "It wasn't just the makeover. Therapy helped too."

We remain in silence for several minutes. I rest the back of my head on his chest while listening to his heartbeat, and the rhythm matched my beat. The thought of them being synchronized didn't sit well in the pit of my stomach, but I preferred that emotion to the thought of losing the moment. We were silent, but it felt as if we were sharing our deepest, darkest secrets.

"I'm sorry for your loss." I touch his jaw, stretching my neck and kissing it. "Why did you decide to enlist?"

He snorts. "You can judge me, but I was only twenty-one, and my brothers were losing their shit after Mom and Dad died. Scott had a better hold of them than I could so . . . I went to unload bullets." He scratches the back of my head.

"Why did you retire?"

"Well, what I stood against after training was the real world. A war. I was thrown in the middle of a country where children, women, and men were being tortured by the same people that attacked us."

He looks around and takes a few deep breaths. "The reason I enlisted changed. It wasn't about vengeance. It was about justice. I had to recognize and defend the innocent. My trust fund meant shit while I was fighting. My perspective on life and the world changed. I learned that not everything is black or white. There's a gray area. And that there's evil in this world. But after many years doing the same thing without seeing any real change, I decided that I had to find something different. Something I could stand behind while helping others. And that maybe it was time to go back home with my brothers.

"For an entire year, I tried to take over Dad's company. It turns out that I'm not cut out for that. Scott, who never planned on working for him, aced that shit. After a long year searching for my thing, I found the place where I could make a difference and be happy. My brothers and Hazel were there for me while I worked through it. And once I had it, Hawk and your brother called with a new job." He tosses his head back, laughing. "I have two jobs that fulfill me as a person and the need I have to give to others. That is fate working its magic."

HE RUBS HIS CHEST. "I miss them, but I hope they're proud of us. I'm sorry about your loss too," he says, resting his chin on top of my shoulder. His arms tighten around my waist. "Cristobal called me earlier."

"Dad?" My body tenses. "What did dear papá want?"

"He's concerned about you, Luna." His voice doesn't change, it's steady, relaxed. "Mr. Santillan told me a few things."

I hold my breath, waiting for more. Is Harrison going to send me back home? Does he have that kind of power? No one understands that I have to bring justice to Mom and my sister.

"It's my understanding that this city wasn't kind to him nor his family," he continues. "He has this crazy idea that you have a hidden agenda."

"Agenda?" My heart beats harder, and it's so loud that I can't think clearly.

Harrison nuzzles my neck, feathering kisses through my nape. I shiver and try to loosen his grip, but he doesn't budge. "If things are going to work during your stay, we have to set rules. Rule number one: you have to tell me everything. There're no secrets between us."

"But—"

"Rule number two: we plan before we make any movement. *We* are working this together, as a team." He nibbles my earlobe. "Rule number three: you use my assets, not the FBI's assets. Rule number four: any side gigs that you plan on heading have to be discussed and agreed on before *we* work them."

We? What is this we? There isn't a we when it comes to my mother. I am the one in charge of solving the case and bringing that man to justice. They are crazy if they think I'm going to follow their lead.

"I have the right to do whatever I want during my free time," I counter, fighting his hold. "You can't stop me."

"You're right. I can't stop you. However, I can help you." His voice is quiet and calm but commanding.

I stop fighting his grasp.

Did I hear him right?

Will he help me?

"What does that mean?" I want to trust him, but my father and my brother are involved. "The babysitter got paid for one service, but he's willing to do more than that."

"I'd like to point out that I'm not your babysitter. They didn't pay me," he corrects me, his lips tracing a line around my jaw. "If you recall, you can kick my ass. Why in the world would you need someone to take care of you? I need a bodyguard to protect me from you."

"And don't you forget it." I wink at him, exercising more force and stepping away from his distracting arms. "Keep talking."

"I'm willing to help with whatever it is that you came to do. I just need you to trust me."

"Trust isn't easy to give. People have to earn it. We just met."

"That sucks, doesn't it? We just met, and we have to trust each other, blindly. I think I can do it, can you?"

I shrug. "It's hard. Not even my family believes my claims."

"Why don't you start from the beginning?" he suggests, shoving his hands into his jeans pockets. "Tell me what happened, and what you're planning on doing. I want to understand you."

I bite my lip, looking at the marble floor for several seconds before answering him. "My mom died when I was a baby," I start my explanation. "The guy who pulled the trigger is in jail, but I know it wasn't him."

"How?" He crosses his arms, his brow arching and his lips pressing together.

Swallowing hard, I hug myself tightly and narrate some of our family history. "My parents dated in high school. It was a private school. My father had several scholarships. Mom's parents hated him. The entire class was nasty to him. Everyone knew him as the poor undocumented Mexican kid. He wasn't. He was born in America, but people didn't care. He wasn't rich, or white, so they called him names. But Mom didn't care. She loved him. They broke up after they graduated. He was leaving to serve in the Navy. Mom was moving to New York for college. Plus, Abue hated Mom. You have to know that my family history is full of drama."

"Let's eat while you tell me the story. It seems that it's longer than I anticipated," Harrison offers, holding my hand.

We eat as I continue telling him about my parents. "Mom went to Columbia to study education. One of her old classmates and a family friend was studying pre-law. They dated for a couple of years, and he knocked her up. My grandparents forced her to marry. The marriage didn't last. He was abusive and a cheater. The guy didn't care about his daughter or his ex-wife until she rekindled her relationship with my father."

"Dad had a little boy by then, Santiago," I explain. "He never

married his mother, but they had a good relationship. Dad married
Mom almost immediately, and when he tried to adopt Sammie, all
hell broke loose."

"What happened?"

"Sammie was four by then," I continue. "Her father hadn't given
any alimony or child support or seen his kid since the divorce. But
now that Dad was back in Mom's life, he fought her for custody.
Sammie spent half the time with us, the rest with her father."

"And Tiago?" he asks before popping a piece of sushi into his
mouth.

"He and his mother moved to Florida with her family." I shrug
because after they moved, I didn't spend as much time with him as
Lucas did. Being the baby isn't all that great, I miss so much. Mostly,
Mom time. "Mom's theory is that Estella, that's Tiago's mom, realized
nothing serious would ever happen between her and Dad. She chose
not to stay around. Tiago came to visit during summers and
holidays."

"How did your mom die?"

"She disappeared for a couple of days. They found her in the
woods in Piseco Lake. Three gunshot wounds. One in the forehead,
one in the heart, and the other in the eye. Her daughter was crying
next to her. Sammie went to live with her father after she died."

"And you say the guy who shot her is in jail. But you believe he's
not the one who planned it. Why is that?"

I set the empty container on top of the table and drink some
water before responding. "Mom's journals. She wrote every night
since she was a teenager, but I don't have all of her journals. In the last
entries, she talks about Sammie's father. She thinks he's hitting my
sister, and Mom was building a case to take her away from him. Dad
wanted to move to Brooklyn. He . . . that man threatened her. That if
she continued with her plans, she'd die."

"Have you talked to your father about it?"

I bob my head, taking a few cleansing breaths. "He told me to
stop. That I had no idea what I was doing. '*No busques tres pies al
gato,*' he repeats every time I bring that up to him. That's a Mexican

saying. It means something like 'don't go sniffing around somewhere you know it's dangerous when there might be harmful consequences.' Simply put, I shouldn't ask for trouble. Things were settled, according to my father."

"Your dad let things be, just like that?" he trails off, using the back of his hand to caress my face.

"Yep, my dad." I bob my head, sliding my gaze to him, staring at his eyes. They are so blue, I can feel myself being sucked inside those blue pools. I move my gaze away.

"He's very thorough," Harrison says. How well does he know my father?

"He is," I admit. "The guy who solved every case he's worked during his entire career let this one go. The murder of his wife."

"I'm sure he knows more," he states. "Including what will happen if you get too close, Luna. The man lost his wife, he has to protect the ones that are left behind."

"Every person deserves justice," I argue with his last statement.

Harrison narrows his eyes and rubs his stubble a couple of times. "Tiago mentioned that your sister died too. What happened to her?"

"OD, she was extremely sick." I sigh, pressing my lips together. "She was thirty-one, like Mom." *Like me.*

The women in my family don't live past their early thirties. My mother's Mom died at thirty-two of cancer. It's creepy to know that the end is near, yet, I try to be ready for the inevitable. But I don't want to go until I know the guy who took away Mom from us is behind bars.

"What if this puts you in danger?" he counters.

"If it were up to my father, I'd be inside a bubble. His ideal job for me is from home as a housewife. Dad doesn't understand that I can die crossing the street," I point out the obvious.

"I don't have children, but I have my brothers. It's natural to worry like that, don't be too harsh on him." He rises from his seat and starts picking up the trash. "If you were mine, I'd put you in a bubble too."

Then, he laughs, throwing me a glare. "But you'll get yourself out of it and punch me for holding you back."

"I'm glad we understand each other." I follow behind holding my empty glass and the empty bottle of beer he drank.

"So, are you going to help me?

19

LUNA

Harrison crosses his arms, those blue eyes are dark, his face is masked, and I want to know what he's thinking. Is he going to disregard my worries the same way my brothers and father have done each time I ask them to help me with this case?

"I have a concern." He rubs the back of his neck, clearing his throat.

Fiddling with the crystal charms on my bracelet, I ask cautiously, "What is it? You can trust me. After all, we are a team."

He clears his throat. "Are you going to protect me from the big guy?" His question surprises me. "Tiago is going to beat the shit out of me if something happens to you."

"Aw, is Hawy afraid of big old Tiago?" I can't help but laugh as I hold my stomach.

His eyes become slits. "If something happens to you, you bet your ass that I will be hiding for years from him. That motherfucker goes batshit crazy when someone he loves gets hurt." Then he releases my hands. "Not that I'd let anything happen to you."

"Someone he loves gets hurt? Is my brother in love and I don't know it?" I snap, staring at Harrison.

He stares at me cautiously. I wait for him to answer my questions.

We breathe almost at the same rhythm, one waiting for the other to answer. I am trying to get a read on him. He's learned how to read some of my reactions, but I have yet to read this man. Guarding myself against him is counterproductive. I should open myself up a lot more, but will that be counterproductive?

He raises his hands, shaking his head. "I don't know. I meant his brothers, us."

"You're lying to me," I bluff.

"Certainly not, I have no clue about your brother's love life. If he is, he hasn't told me. We don't just sit around and paint each other's nails." He smirks, winking at me and melting me. "Though, I would do it with you. We can sit down and talk about your love life."

Why do I melt when he winks?

"I don't have a love life," I protest, trying to go back to my mother's case.

He cocks his head to the side. Shooting an eyebrow up, he speaks, "Rule number five, we work on your love life." He lifts his arms, tracing a line across the air. "It'll be called, an 'affair to remember.' Your future boyfriends will have trouble measuring up to me, but I can live with the title, 'the legend.'"

I gape at him, speechless. Luna Santillan, you've met your match. Two brothers, dozens of cousins, and years of training hadn't prepared me for him. I have to restart my brain before I can think of a comeback and even then, it's weak.

"You're too cocky and definitely not going to become, 'the legend.' Or get close to me." Yeah, too stupid. I scrub my face, trying to get the reins of this conversation and wonder how he'd be in bed, or against the wall or . . . *Mom, Mom, Mom, think about your mother, Luna.*

"About Mom, would you really help me?"

"Yes, you have the right to know what happened. But . . ." His eyes open wide, he walks closer to me, and once he's right in front, he grabs my shoulders firmly. "We are doing it as a team. Send me everything you have, and I'll have my people work on your mother's case."

"I can't pay you." I frown, thinking if this is the best-case scenario for my investigation.

They charge millions. Millions. I can't afford them. I should go with Plan B. Infiltrate the family and interrogate that man and go from there.

"My services are free." He throws another smirk while wiggling his eyebrows. "But if you insist on paying, we can come up with . . . an arrangement."

"Idiot," I mumble under my breath.

"As long as your plan doesn't include kidnapping or torture, I'm all for it."

My heart beats as I picture the blood of that man on my hands. "What?" I take a step back, wheezing. "I wouldn't ask for that. I just want justice for Mom."

"We'll solve this, Luna. I have a good feeling about our partnership." Harrison's gorgeous smiling face gives me a sense of security, some hope. I reach out and take it.

"So, we're partners." I fight the hold he has on my hands, but he doesn't let them go. "Partners don't touch. They don't kiss."

He winks at me. "You know, as you talked about your mom, I was thinking. What the hell is this woman doing spending time with the FBI?"

"This woman works for them. I like what I do," I respond, ordering my heart to stop that stupid thundering noise. It's not allowed to answer to Harrison's touch like if each time our skin makes contact it's a life-altering event.

"I understand that. What I mean is that the FBI isn't for you."

A lump lodges in my throat. He's no different from my father or my brothers.

"You're passionate, strong, caring, and smart. They are wasting your talent," he continues, and my eyes sting at his praise. "I want to hire you."

Hire me?

For two seconds, I consider his words. Then I remember what he does and what he stands for. "No," I respond without thinking about the proposal.

"Keep my informal offer on the back burner. We can come back to it later," Harrison responds. "You need a little more room to spread your wings and achieve what you really want to."

"And you know what I want?" I ask dismissing his tone and offer. "We just met."

"I've been watching you since we met." He doesn't let the subject go easily. "Luna, I'm offering you more than what the FBI will ever give you. If you work for us, you can help us profiling and run our human trafficking division." He might not know me, but he's saying just the right words, meaningful words.

"You will have an entire team at your disposition," he continues enticing me. "And technology that the FBI has no idea exists. You'll lead teams. And during some of the undercover operations, you might be able to join me. Most of all, you'll have more assets to bring people home or find justice."

"Why only during some undercover operations?"

"With your experience and knowledge, I doubt that Bradley will put you to do fieldwork. You're more like 'A team' material, and we aren't sent in the field as often."

I gasp. My eyes widen, and my heart accelerates. He's offering me a dream. I stop myself immediately. He's luring me with the things I want to hear, but what if I accept and they won't deliver on any of those promises?

"I will only work for rich people?"

"You're a little prejudiced." He shakes his head, running a hand through his hair. "We work for agencies like the FBI, governments, and private parties. We also take pro bono cases."

I frown. "Who pays when you do that?"

"That's why we overcharge," he answers without remorse.

He smiles at me, and I feel like he's offering me the sun and the moon. He's waiting for me to take it, but . . .

"What do you say, Luna?"

"I'll take it into consideration."

Am I crazy for even considering working for him?

I've criticized Tiago for working with these men. The day he told us that he had bought part of the company I ranted about his lack of honor. He's a mercenary, a rent-a-cop. A cold-blooded killer.

"You have no idea what you're talking about, Luna," he would retort, not fighting me. He never released too much information.

"That's all I'm asking for. Now, can we talk about our other deal?" Harrison releases my hands, but his corded arms loop around my waist. His face is only inches away from mine. His breath caresses my lips.

"There's no deal," I say, breathless.

"Oh, but there can be if you want to," he states, his eyes finding mine.

My breath hitches and I shake my head trying to escape him.

"I want to continue that kiss we started at the yoga studio. I'll kiss you so thoroughly that we'll lose ourselves maybe for an eternity, at least for a thousand years." His eyes don't leave mine, he's too close but he doesn't kiss me.

"None of those lines are going to convince me. That kiss was a small slip," I say, trying to strengthen my weak knees. He's so close, too close, and if he comes closer I swear . . .

"Don't fight it," he whispers. "I know you feel at least some of the heat. The way you kissed me back told me that I'm not the only one wanting this."

He leans in and kisses me.

It's a simple kiss.

Nonetheless, it's his kiss.

Everything in this moment becomes him and me. We are one. He's underneath my skin. His breathing becomes mine. We share one beat and one breath. All I can taste in this moment is him. All I can feel is the warmth of his skin, the fire underneath us burning. The heat suddenly becomes unbearable, but I want more. I want to be consumed.

"Is anybody here?" I jump away from his hold as the voice of my brother vibrates around the place.

"Everhart!"

20

LUNA

"The big guy is going to kill me, but my death will be worth it." Harrison's stupid grin doesn't falter. "Have I mentioned that your kisses taste like honey and heaven?" He runs a shaky hand through his hair and asks. His eyes burn like two blue flames. Harrison is as affected as I am. Is his heart threatening to jump out of his chest too?

I gasp for breath, trying to control the fervent heat that's blazing through my body.

"Are you okay?" He has trouble controlling his breathing too.

I nod slightly. He has left me numb, speechless, and needy. I swallow, unable to respond. Am I okay? A tornado just swooped me inside of its vortex while I was catching fire. I fan my face with my hand. New rule, no kisses. Harrison Everhart isn't allowed to kiss me like he's trying to swallow my heart and own my soul in just one bite.

"Luna, what a surprise?" Tiago enters the kitchen glaring at Harrison, then looking at me. He steps right in between us and shoots a murderous look at him. "Everhart, you're too close to my little sister."

No, he's too far from me. I want him closer, his body against mine. But all I can do is stare at those blue pools filled with desire.

"Close? I didn't know we had set parameters on how many inches we need of separation between bodies," Harrison says, breaking the stare.

When he takes a step backward, my body misses his heat.

"How close do you want me, big guy?" Harrison asks, stepping too close to my brother and serving him with an unapologetic grin. "I need the ground rules, so I remember that the next time I have to carry your useless body across the battlefield."

Harrison angles his head, our eyes meet. "Do you have any restrictions I should know about, Luna?" He says my name slowly with a smile plastered on his face. "Twelve thick inches, maybe?"

My face heats up when he blurts the inches, but I grin when my brother growls. I'm between a rock and a hard place. How can I rant to Harrison? And tease my brother at the same time? This is torture.

I shake my head. My eyes lower when my brother's nostrils flare. These two are amusing together. I've never seen my brother so worked up and he's been here for only a few minutes.

"We have rules, Everhart," my brother reminds him, Harrison rolls his eyes.

"What's with your family and all these fucking rules, T?" He walks toward the refrigerator, takes out a couple of beers, and hands one to my brother. Twisting the cap off, he takes a couple of swigs, those blue eyes staying on me.

"I swear, I've never seen this tight ass side of you." He then looks at my brother.

"Rules? Are you trying to make a pass on my sister that she has to set you straight?" My brother looks at me, his voice is demanding.

Divert, Luna. Divert this conversation.

If we continue talking about Harrison, his twelve inches of separation, that hot body, those rough hands and . . . wait we weren't talking about any of that. But that's all my mind can focus on. My body is sizzling, and my core is aching. Every cell of my body is waiting for more. If I don't find release soon, I might die. Even if it's Harrison, who has to take care of it. Would I prefer if he uses his hands on me?

My cheeks heat up when I picture our mouths exploring our bodies. Those hands . . . I press my thighs hard when I picture the heel of his palm pressing hard against my clit, as his callused fingers pump inside me, hard . . .

"Mmm," I moan, closing my eyes. This can't be happening. Why am I so turned on and on the verge of having an orgasm in the middle of the kitchen?

"Are you okay, Luna?" Harrison hands me the beer he's holding. "You look a little flushed, should I adjust the air conditioner?"

I wave away the beer. "I'm fine. Water, do you have any water?"

Cold water, cold shower, I need to run away from here!

"Are you getting sick?" My brother rubs his brow, studying me.

"I didn't know you were in town. We could've done something." My eyebrows draw inward as I try to fake annoyance, but it's not working. All I can think about is Harrison and that kiss, his mouth.

My brother raises an eyebrow. He looks at Harrison who slumps his shoulder. Then, his attention is back at me. "You're shitty at taking care of her. I'm not sure if I should head back to Seattle."

"How's Kevin?" Harrison crosses his arms, smirking at my brother. "I was thinking about visiting him soon to get a tattoo."

A tattoo? I jump into that subject. "I want a tattoo too," I say, unable to hide the excitement. This is perfect, I was hoping that I could do it soon. "Are they good?"

Harrison nods.

"They are the best," Tiago confirms.

"Can I come with you? I've chosen these quotes from Mom's journals that will go great right around here." I touch under my right breast.

"Never," Tiago and Harrison answer simultaneously.

Tiago's hand raises, his finger points at me. "Are you reading that shit again?" He breathes loudly. "Dad is right, isn't he? You're here looking for trouble."

"Mom's journals aren't shit. And I'm looking for justice. Not trouble." I cross my eyes, tilting my chin. "I'm doing it the smart way. Harrison is helping me."

"What the fuck, Everhart?" my brother growls.

"Thank you, beautiful," Harrison mutters, tipping his head. "Being close to you reminds me how precious and short life can be."

Harrison touches his index finger as he begins to count. "First, you tried to kill me."

"You broke into my place," I remind him, clenching my teeth.

"That doesn't erase the near-death experience." His attention goes back to his fingers. "Then, you threaten me for calling you, babe."

"Because I hate that term." I poke his chest twice. "So, don't call me *babe*."

"Duly noted," he acknowledges scribbling something in the air. "But now you throw me under the fucking bus."

He tosses his hands up in the air. "Your family is lethal, T. I've almost died a few times because of you, and now your little sister is pushing me on the train tracks so to speak."

Then, he gives me a stern look. "What's next? Are you going to tell him I've kissed you senseless?" He jets out of the kitchen but stops for a few seconds. "I'm just glad he can never outrun me."

"I told you not to touch her. You're going to regret being born, Everhart," Tiago yells, charging after him.

I grab his shirt. "Stop, Santiago Federico Cordero, or you'll be the one who is sorry."

"Is everything okay?" Scott steps into the kitchen, Hazel right behind him.

"This isn't a good time, Hazel," Harrison protests as she pulls him with him.

"Don't be such a baby. I'm sure I can protect you against any spider you might've found in the kitchen." Hazel halts when she sees me. "Oh good, a strong woman is here to protect you. See there's nothing to fear."

"What are you doing here?" Harrison releases her hold and stares down at her.

"I'm helping you," Hazel responds. "We didn't go through your schedule for the upcoming week. I scored us an invite for a gala on Saturday night. That's a great place for Luna to meet and greet. I tried to call you, but neither one of you answered your phones. Since Scott has to pack a bag, we came hoping to catch some action." She ends the fast talk with an innocent grin.

"Ooh, no one told me that Tiago is in the house." Hazel walks into my brother's arms. "How are you?"

"I'm doing well, Little Hazel," Tiago greets her, then, turn his body to shake hands with Scott, but his eyes remain on Hazel. "I see you're taking care of my sister, thank you."

"Of course. Anything for you, T," Hazel sends a flirty smile his way.

I stare at them, surprised by their camaraderie. Feeling a pang of jealousy in my chest. My brother has kept himself too far away from us. I'm meeting his friends and learning that he's loved by so many people.

"Haze, would you mind giving me a hand so we can leave sooner?" Scott requests, his jaw tightening.

"Yeah, give me a second, Scotty."

Hazel's focus is now on Harrison and me. "I like what you two are doing." Her voice is professional.

"Hunt and Willow bought the entire thing. I didn't correct them, and that's how we're running things." She claps. "For the upcoming days, I suggest you two continue working on convincing everyone that you're a new couple and that this relationship is going strong. Walk around New York, shop, have some ice cream while strolling around Central Park. You need to share lots of PDA. Small touches and casual kisses too. I emailed you a list of suggestions for where to go during the week."

"No kissing," Tiago growls. "Or dating. They aren't a couple."

Hazel glares at him, and I swear her lips peeled and her eyes widened. "You better not ruin this, Tiago. I spent a few hours planning this, and your part is to keep that big brother attitude hidden."

"Just a few hours?" Harrison questions, grabbing my hand.

"Yes, I invested . . . fine, maybe it was several hours pulling something credible. I know what I'm doing, Tiago." Then, she smiles at him. "Say hi to everyone in Seattle." She kisses his cheek and dances out of the kitchen.

"She's vicious." Tiago frowns at her.

"Especially if she's hungry or you try to tamper with her plans. I'm just not sure what her plan is." Harrison shakes his head.

Harrison pulls out his phone and starts scrolling on it. "We have a packed week." He frowns at the screen. "Pedicures? We are not doing couple's pedicures."

"But that sounds just perfect." My brother smirks. "I'll book it for you, Everhart."

I massage my temple when I look at that email. "Dance lessons?"

"When is my next mission?" Harrison's eyes harbor anxiety. "I'll take saving Tiago's ass over opera."

"Can I join?" I would beg him to take me with him if it's necessary. "I'd rather slit someone's throat than . . ." Waving my phone, I deflate. "She's crazy."

"We're leaving!" Hazel calls from the door. "Don't worry, everything has been booked, paid, and scheduled. Don't flake on me, Harrison. This is your time to shine."

"I hate her!" Harrison and I say in unison.

21

HARRISON

My body is buzzing from all the sexual frustration accumulated last night. Tiago stayed with us. Luna teased me with those vixen eyes and smart mouth while hanging out with her brother and me. Well, she was teasing Tiago by flirting with me. She probably would've ignored me if we had been alone. Or I'd have finally broken through her walls. I need to show her how good we could be together. If I can just get rid of the big guy. He's following my every move. When I informed him that I was going to Luna's class, he decided to join me.

"Step your feet out, taking the side of your yoga mat and reach your arms wide as well," Luna instructs. "Now keep your gaze to the front of the room and bend over without arching your back."

Every muscle in my body shakes as I switch from one position to another. My forehead drips with sweat. Who practices yoga while the humidity is at seventy-five percent and the heat cranked all the way to hot as hell? I guess now I know what Hot Bikram stands for. Next time, I'll follow Luna's advice and do some research before I choose her classes.

"Be mindful of your body," Luna repeats, stepping right beside me. "Find your breath, and let everything go."

Tiago starts wheezing, masking his laughter, again. It's not like he's doing it right, but he doesn't have the hot teacher hovering over him and telling him that he's useless. Well, she hasn't said that to me, but I swear each time she adjusts my position, it feels like I can't do anything right. And then she has the fucking nerve of saying, "You're doing great."

If I'm doing great why the hell are you fixing what I'm doing?

"Inhale, and as you lower your body, exhale. Keep your hips straight, back straight and continue bending forward." I feel her hands adjusting my waist, her fingers move slowly up and down my back, tracing a line through my spine.

Stop touching me!

Think how Tiago is going to kill you if you take this further. Nope, dick doesn't care. One . . . two . . . three . . . nope, how about . . .

Her hands are like velvety rose petals, caressing my skin; awakening my body as if sunlight was bathing it as it rises in the morning. Her touch is making me aware of what I'm missing, what I've been searching for, but I shouldn't have right now. Luna. Yes, touch me. Slide those hands lower. But the sexual frustration is nothing compared to my swollen chest. I hold my breath, pushing away the emotions blossoming inside my heart.

"Concentrate on your breathing," she orders, her mouth close to my ear.

I want to reach out to her, hold her in my arms, and take her mouth with mine. I want to show her what her hands, what her voice and her scent are creating. But I fight it. Then she runs her hands back to my hips, and she pinches my ass.

I tense, my back straightens up, but I lose my equilibrium and fall. She promptly moves away, but I catch a glimpse of her mischievous eyes. Luna winks at me as she continues walking toward the center of the room biting her cheek. Those eyes harbor humor underneath them.

"Relax, and breathe." Luna's mellow voice fills the entire room. Her eyes though remain on me. "Stay in the present."

This is war. One of these days I'll have you tied up, naked, and under my command. I'll be the one ordering to relax and breathe. As I'm about to stand up, I notice my phone flashing.

Bradley: *I have a job for you or T. Call me.*

"Big guy," I announce picking up my mat, my water bottle, and my towel. "Let's hit the showers."

I tip my head toward the beautiful girl in the front of the room. She stiffens, her eyes trained on me for a couple of breaths. Tiago leaves behind me.

"Though I'm flattered, I'm not into you," Tiago jokes.

"Bradley has a job for either one of us." I pull my phone out to forward the message. "Can you take it?"

He promised to take my cases for the next couple of months, but I have to make sure he's going to do it. Mostly, because he will have to leave town. I want to spend more time with Luna, and with Tiago breathing down my neck, it's impossible.

"This will save you from all the shit that Hazel scheduled for you."

"Yeah, but your sister needs the help."

"You're a good man, Harrison." He pats my shoulder, and I feel shitty.

I want to stay because I want to break the cardinal rule. Do not fuck thy best friend's sister.

"That's crazy talk, T. This is nothing."

"I owe you, man," he says while confirming to Mason that he'll be the one taking it.

"Please, don't mention it. That's what brothers are for." I flinch as I say that, feeling like a complete asshole but . . . Luna.

☆☆☆

I took a shower and waited for Luna's class to be over. She had only a few minutes free between classes, but it was enough time to give her a kiss and make some plans to meet for lunch. She only worked a half day today and tomorrow she is off, which I'm fucking thankful about. I'm not sure how I'll be handling tomorrow. When I saw the date, it hit me why Mason had found a job for me, but he also knew that I was helping Tiago with his sister. I try to be away from the city when it's the anniversary of my parents' death. Before I used to spend it with my brothers, which was the worst fucking idea.

We started the day well, but by the afternoon we were throwing words, and before dinner one of us ended up in the ER because the fights got out of control. That, or we'd go clubbing and ended up fucking too many women in one night. At least that was before Hazel noticed the pattern and we began to travel.

Not this year, this year I have . . . *Luna*, I say to myself as she walks through the glass doors of the studio.

"Hey," Luna greets me, pushing herself on her tiptoes and combing my hair. "What's going on?"

"Hmm?" I lose my voice when I realize I can see through her dress. Fuck, she looks hot but she better change, or I'm going to kill any man who stares at her beautiful body.

"You looked a little lost and sad." She smiles wider, looking at me. "Though now, you're upset."

"Your dress is see through," I mumble, grinding my teeth.

She squeezes her eyes. "I forgot the slip that goes under this dress. But my yoga clothes are soaking wet. We have to go home." She presses a hand to her mouth to stifle the giggles. "Believe me, I'm not a fan of showing this much skin. Tell me what's wrong while we rush back. I'm sure no one will notice."

I take off my shirt and hand it to her, holding her big tote bag. "Just don't do this during winter or I might end up with frostbite."

"Thank you," she mouths as she slips on the shirt. "Now tell me, why are you sad?"

"Nah, I'm good. Just . . . thinking about tomorrow." I lean forward to kiss her lips and hand her the purse. "Regretting not going on that mission, but not too much since I would've missed our time together."

"Are you planning on going to the nine-eleven memorial, maybe take some flowers with you?" She takes my hand, entwining her fingers with mine and squeezing it. "We can go to church to light a candle. Maybe St. Patrick's Cathedral?"

"That's where they married," I mention, as I kiss her hand. "I think they'd like that."

"Why don't we do it today?" she offers. "That way, it won't be as crowded as tomorrow will be. Tomorrow we could go somewhere else, maybe get out of the city."

I release her hand, put my arm around her back, and press her tight to me as we continue walking. My chest grows as my heart swells with the way this woman is behaving toward me. I wasn't aware that my body was so tense because of tomorrow, until now. And unexpectedly, she brightened my day.

"I might kidnap you and never let you go," I whisper in her ear when we stop at the light.

She sighs, turning to look at me. "Have you counted how many men and women turn to stare at your bare chest?" Luna scrunches her nose. "Not sure I'm happy about this. Keep my mind busy and tell me what you did after class."

"Work."

"You have another job?"

"Yeah, one that you might like . . . and if you're good I might let you help me." I kiss her ear and continue walking down the street to her building.

22

LUNA

Two hours of yoga didn't settle my anxiety. It's not the type of anxiety that ties me to a chair and doesn't let me move. But the one that makes my stomach turn and my mouth vomit thousands of stupid things to the guy who is holding your hand. I think the last time I felt this jittery was when I dated Jeremy Paul in the seventh grade. I couldn't eat much for five entire days after he asked me if I wanted to go bowling with him, as his girlfriend. Needless to say, I shook off the anticipation after he kissed Trudy instead of me, asshole. That was the first man who couldn't take my competitive streak. I won the bowling game, he ditched me.

"Do you have more of those supply bags?" Harrison glanced toward my tote bag after handing over the last one I brought with me.

"Nope, I grabbed the last ones I had in the pantry after I changed."

"So, we give money away for now?" He looks around, then nods his head when he spots whatever it is that we are looking for.

"If you have, yes. I'm a little short on cash today."

"I went to the bank, just in case we needed it." He hands me an envelope, and he winks at me. "Unmarked ten dollar bills."

"Tyler's flowers?" I ask when we stop in front of a flower shop, and my eyes grow wide when I see all the flowers through their windows. "They have sunflowers, and mums, and . . ."

I walk inside, grinning when I read the sign on top of the baskets: Create Your Own Bouquet, Handle The Flowers With Care. Forgetting all about the knots in my stomach and the man who's staring at me, I begin choosing a few flowers. Fall is so close that they already have all shades of burnt reds and oranges. Suddenly, I stop. Turn around and look at him.

"What did she like?"

"Um, who?"

"Your mom." I close my eyes, enjoying the fragrance in the shop. It's the first time in a while that I don't have to pull the spritzer to bring back the sweet scent of flowers.

"She just loved them," he answers. "Dad brought home all kinds, almost daily. The bigger bouquets were for when he fucked-up."

"You should try to control your cursing," I suggest, eyeing the little girl close to the counter.

He flinches, mouthing fuck. I roll my eyes.

"I ordered a bouquet, while you were . . . dressing." He runs his eyes over my body.

"It was a small mistake," I remind him.

When I packed my clothing to stay at his house, I was too confused by the way his soon to be sister-in-law insinuated we'd be having five children and elated by how comfortable it felt being a part of them. At least I brought my underwear with me, or that dress I wore would've shown everything.

"We fixed it, didn't we?"

"Yeah, let's hope you make the same mistake when we're alone, little moon."

"Dream on, Everhart." I take one of the flowers out of the basket to put it back when he touches my hand and shakes his head. "No, don't. Finish it, and we can take both. She'll like that."

"What else did she like?" I ask after he picks up an arrangement of long-stemmed pink roses in a box.

"She was an artist," he responds. "Loved her family and liked to paint with watercolors. She did some pottery, and cut glass was her passion. She created the best stained-glass windows I've ever seen in my entire life."

As we continue walking toward the memorial, he tells me about his parents. His father liked to sail, his mother's motion sickness didn't allow them to take long family trips on their yacht. She loved the ocean but preferred to vacation in the cabin they owned in Vermont.

"We didn't have nannies. Only one person came to help her with the cleaning, Sarah. And just because Dad insisted." He smiles. "She grew up with seven brothers, and her mother did everything and taught them how to do everything."

"She followed your grandmother's teachings?"

He nods. "I know how to cook, clean, iron, and even change diapers. Though, I haven't done the latter since Hunter was potty-trained."

"You're a catch, Everhart."

"Take note of that." He winks at me.

He lifts his arm, his hand curls into a fist but he releases his thumb. "Good cook." He releases his index finger. "Twelve inches, babysitting training, and I could be a great homemaker."

The corners of his lips quirk into a slight smile.

"If I see any job openings that require those credentials, I'll make sure to send you the email." I wave dismissively as we arrive at the memorial, searching for my phone.

He looks down at me. "Thank you, for coming with me. This changed so much." Harrison kisses the tip of my nose.

"You've never been here, have you?"

Harrison shakes his head, taking several deep breaths. I take his free hand and squeeze it tight. Waiting for him to talk or take a step. My stomach quivers. The unsettled feeling isn't about having him next to me, but that I pushed him too far. I have no idea how this will affect him.

"Harrison?" I spot a tall, slender middle-aged woman only a few steps from us gawking at him.

"You've got to be fucking kidding me," he mumbles.

I'm sure I'm the only one who heard him say that, but the couple in front of us are stunned and frozen in place as they see him.

His face turns red, his breathing is harsh. I can feel the anger in his gaze. The grimace on his face. He restrains all his thoughts. His lungs are almost collapsing from all the angry words he swallows. I caress his wrist with my thumb, trying to soothe the rage inside him.

"Ileana, Damon." He nods at them, his voice neutral. "This is unexpected."

"The kids wanted to visit, and we thought about you're . . . parents," Ileana says as she stares at the bouquet of daisies she holds in her arms.

Two boys and a teenage girl stare at us, and those bored faces tell me they have no desire to be here. I bet they would rather be at Coney Island or the Statue of Liberty than here.

"I remembered your mother loved flowers," Damon adds, his voice shaky and his eyes on the floor.

Awkward. Can we move on people? Neither one of you wants to be here or talk to each other!

But everyone remains in place. Harrison's breathing is settling, but his eyes continue watching the horizon.

"Hi," I greet them, releasing Harrison and shaking their hands. "I'm Luna, his girlfriend."

At least, that's how people know me at the moment. You, of course, don't need to know who I am and . . . why am I babbling inside my head? Someone just get me out of here.

"Nice to meet you," Ileana shakes my hand, not moving her gaze from Harrison who is still frozen in place. "I'm Ileana. This is Damon, my husband. These are our kids. Josie, Cash, and Chase."

"Are you from here or just visiting?" Why am I making small talk, when all I want is to go inside the memorial, but everyone seems to be paralyzed.

Morbid curiosity. There's a big accident, and I am staring to see the damage and learn about the casualties.

"We used to live here. I moved to Texas with my family sixteen years ago," Ileana says.

"Fifteen," Harrison corrects her, staring at their daughter for one too many seconds.

She's almost as tall as her mother, the same light brown hair, but with her tips dyed purple and pink. She has her mother's green eyes, but her facial features aren't that similar. I hold the gasp, as I remember him saying that he had a live-in girlfriend fifteen or sixteen years ago.

"Harrison, I'm s—" Damon shuts his mouth when Harrison glares at him.

He waves his hands, shaking his head. The anger is gone, he's not with us, but he's definitely not upset. "It was long ago, Damon. It's all good. What you two did was f—" he stops, looks at me and smiles . . . "freaking wrong, but it worked out for you. Maybe if we had met somewhere else at another time, this encounter would've been . . . different . . ."

"Friendlier," he adds after a long pause.

He's not upset, but my heart tells me that he wants this to be over right about now. "Ready to go in?" I ask him.

He bends and kisses my cheek. "Yeah, I'm ready."

We step inside, he scans the big, crowded hall and closes his eyes briefly. "I think they'll understand if I just drop the flowers and we leave."

"They are with you in your heart, Harry," I repeat the words that Abue said when I used to tell her that I wish I could visit Mom at the cemetery. Mom's ashes were spread along a lavender field. "This isn't necessary, just an idea I had. But we can go somewhere else."

He doesn't say a word. We walk around, and my attention is on him, his face. Everything around me fades, I am trying to read him.

He's still too quiet, and my heart can't take his absence. But I wait for him to come back on his own. Whatever is going on inside his head is working itself out. I just wish I could do more than hold his hand and make sure that he doesn't get lost while he's away from the present.

"Thank you, for being with me. I'll be right back," he says, closing his eyes briefly before he takes the flowers from me and walks away.

I want to follow him, but I give him space. He'll come back to me soon, I feel him closer.

23

HARRISON

I place the flowers on top of my parents' names. I wanted to pile all my grief into a ball and push it away. I didn't think coming here would be this hard. All these years I've been avoiding the site like the plague. The magnitude of the despair I feel isn't as big as it was when it happened, but fuck, I am reliving every agonizing moment from that day. The hollowness in my chest increases. The stitches of the old wound break. The agonizing ache is back.

The imaginary walls are closing in on me, the people are getting louder. Don't break, Everhart, I order myself. I take small breaths of air and start replacing those painful images from that day with the happy memories we made as a family. The same way I've done it in the past years, I recall how Mom would bake chocolate chip cookies every day. We could only eat one after dinner. That's how I've lived through every day since they left me. Daily, I remember all the blessed moments of our lives, and try to bring them up as often as necessary to remind myself that life can be good. That life was good for them, and they loved us. Every time I'm about to break, I picture them watching over me, and all my troubles vanish. I can still feel my mother's love and hear my father's supportive words. Those memories accompany me always, those are the ones I need to stay with me so I can erase all traces of the bad shit that happens around.

Like right now, I'm invoking the memories I collected from this place when the towers graced the skyline of this city. On Halloween, Mom would bring my brothers to Trick or Treat. We would go through the cubicles dressed in whatever costumes she had made for us and ask for candy. Though in exchange, she would be handing a small basket of goodies for the employees. She was kind with all of them, they adored her because she was one of the kindest people in the world. Just like Dad. And they killed them. They took them away from me.

The tears burst, spilling down my face. The muscle of my chin trembles like a child who has fallen from his bike for the first time and scraped his knee. In my case, there's no mother to run to my side and kiss it to make it better. The walls that held me up since they died collapse. They crumble as the salty drops fall from my chin drenching my shirt. I'm trembling and can't stop it. Everything is back and raw. The screams over the phone while my parents said goodbye. Mom's sobs, Dad's pleas. The silence after they hung up. The darkness that fell when we lost them. That same darkness that's sucking me into the vortex of despair. I couldn't bring them back to my brothers, to me. I shiver as the shadows close up and the light begins to disappear.

"I'm with you," Luna says quietly. "You have to come back to me, Harry. Don't stay in the past. Please don't leave me, baby."

Her arms come around me. Her words make the pain bearable. Her heat warms my body. Her light pushes away the darkness. Being with her soothes me. Though, I can't stop crying.

I sob as I cling onto Luna, grasping her tight.

She doesn't say a word, she holds me in silence, rocking with me as I continue releasing all the pain I've held onto since they left. Closing my eyes, I remember the nighttime story. The routine never changed since I was little. Mom read the same books to us after reading a few chapters of our favorite book.

"*Love You Forever* and *Goodnight Moon*," I say, pressing a kiss on top of her head.

"Hmm?" Luna tilts her head. Her eyes hide behind her long lashes and all of a sudden it hits me right in the center of my chest. This woman just saw me at my worst and lent me her strength.

And I think she just stole my fucking heart.

"Those are my favorite books. Mom read them to the four of us every night. She probably never stopped. I think the last time I sat and listened to her was when I was sixteen. Her good night phrase was a combination of both books: I love you forever, I like you forever. No matter if I leave. And when I'm gone, you say good night to the moon, because that's where I'll always be watching over you."

Luna cups my face with one hand, smiling at me. "I like you forever," she whispers, pulling me toward her and pressing her lips lightly onto mine.

There's something so intimate about her words, this kiss, that I have a sudden urge to leave this place so no one can witness what's happening. Because it's happening. We are happening, and this moment is ours.

This moment is only for us.

24

HARRISON

L una doesn't say a word until I'm calm and the feeling in my limbs comes back.

"I'm ready to get the fuck out of here," I whisper in her ear, hugging her tight one more time to absorb some strength.

"Where do you want to go now?" she asks.

"Far away from everything," I mumble.

"Fucking away from this place," I repeat louder. Then I wince and glance around to make sure there aren't families around us.

"We should wash that mouth out with soup." She grins at me, looking up to the sky.

Then, she stops, her eyes widen, and she turns to me.

"Harrison." Damon marches toward me, his eyes look guarded. "Can we talk for a minute?"

I crank my neck, square my shoulders and nod. Might as well let the man release some of the shit he's holding.

Kissing Luna lightly, I mumble, "I'll be back, if you see me do something stupid, please take me away."

She chews her lip. "Just right now, or in general."

I smack my lips against hers and shake my head walking to Damon.

"Are you okay?"

"Fine," I narrow my gaze. "What do you need?"

He tilts his head toward the memorial. "Back there, I've never seen you losing your shit like that."

"We haven't seen each other in a long time. You wouldn't know."

"Yes, but you never cried for your parents. You and Scott were trying to be strong for your younger brothers. I just wanted to . . . I'm so fucking sorry for what I did."

He drops his head, his hand massaging his temples. "If I could turn back time, everything would be different."

I feel bad for my friend, the guy who I shared so much with since we were children. The asshole who cheated with my girlfriend doesn't get anything. I have no idea what to do with this man. I don't know him.

"Damon, nothing can change. You have a family, it seems like you're happy."

I glance at them and look at the girl who doesn't look much like Ileana, yet looks familiar. "Your daughter, is she . . . yours?"

He shoves his hands in his pockets and nods a couple of times. "She's mine, but not Ileana's . . . the kids are mine."

"What happened?"

"A lot of bad decisions. But I don't regret them because I have them. I love my kids."

"I wish you nothing but happiness, Damon," I tell him, taking a step toward Luna.

She's on the phone, shaking her head and moving her mouth too fast for me to read what she's saying.

"It's good to know you're doing fine, Harrison." Damon nods, not sure if he could shake my hand or hug me.

Looking at Luna, I nod. "Better than fine."

"She reminds me of your mom," he said, smiling at her. "Full of life, happy. She makes everyone feel welcome. It's like you can't believe there can be people that happy when the world is so fucking dark."

I smile, patting his shoulder. "Luna is my light, Damon."

"ARE you sure it's okay with them?"

"Hazel made the arrangements." Luna huffs, going through her purse.

"But they said they had a conference." I stare at Luna who is too busy putting on all those clingy bracelets.

"I knew going through airport security would be a shit show with you. I swear that's the first thing I thought the day we met."

She grabs one of the bracelets and threatens me with it. "Don't upset me, Everhart, or I swear I'll use this and it won't be pretty."

"Are you going to beautify me with your accessories?"

She pulls one of her chopsticks from her hair and holds it like a knife. "Shall I remind you how we met, Harry?"

"You're vicious, woman." I push the button, calling the flight attendant.

Once she finishes, she puts on the sweatshirt I just bought her at one of the stores and stares at me. "Excuse me."

"Need any help?"

"You have to move." She points at the window seat.

"Or you can try to make your way through." I crook an eyebrow. "I'd like you on top."

"Do you need something, sir?" I rise from my seat, letting Luna walk through, and control myself because spanking or pinching her butt in public might cause injuries—to me.

"The lady will have champagne," I order for Luna.

"No, the lady will have water, the gentleman too," she corrects me, smiling at the attendant, yet, giving me a nasty glare. Impressive, she did both at the same time. "We're not drinking any more alcohol."

"What's one or two more?"

"For you nothing, but I'm smaller than you."

I roll my eyes. "You win this round." She's right. I don't want her wasted when we arrive in the Keys.

"Thank you for . . . today and for this trip." I stretch my legs.

She shrugs. "The trip is all Hazel. She prepped this after I called her."

"Mind if I ask why you called her?"

"I felt like I was losing you and I needed to know who they were."

"They?" I arch an eyebrow.

"Your ex and the asshole." Her fingers brush my knuckles. "Hazel's words."

"I'm glad she wasn't there, or she would've kicked them. But they had nothing to do with . . . what happened. I had never been there, after . . . that day."

"You live in New York City. How did you manage?"

"Everything is possible if you try it. I've done it for years, almost two decades."

"What did Damon say when . . . he asked if you could give him a second."

I scratch my forehead. Today was supposed to be different. My plans included sweet talking the woman next to me into a wrestling match in my bed. The only rules would've been no clothing and lots of mutual pleasure. None of that happened. However, I feel lighter and much more different than I've felt in years.

. . . and closer to Luna. I've never been or felt so close to someone, linked.

"How much did Hazel tell you about them?"

"'The four-one-one is that she's his live-in GF, he's her BBF since pre-k, and they fucked Harrison, royally. Call if you need more.' Her words." Luna grins after she talks almost as fast as Hazel.

"He was my best friend, and he wanted absolution after what happened between us."

"Since we have a few hours to kill, can I have the longer version?"

Mom used to say that I wore my heart on my sleeve. That I loved unconditionally and that she hoped that no one would take advantage of me. She never told me how she felt about Ileana, though she always said she's lovely. I think that's Mom code for 'I can't stand her but I'll let you realize that she's not for you sooner rather than later.'

The thing was that sooner never came until it was too late and we had a fucking disaster on our hands.

Fucking disaster I repeat inside my head as I think about the teenage girl. How old is she? I don't think she's mine, but she could be and would they have hidden that away from me? To think that Damon was my best friend. We were inseparable since kindergarten and . . . he fucked me over when I needed him the most.

I met Ileana at NYU during our freshman orientation. It wasn't hard to lust after a leggy, blonde girl who kissed the same way she gave blow jobs. I had fooled around during high school but never went all the way with anyone until Ileana. I thought she was it. We spent a semester during junior year in Australia. When I came back, I had decided that she was the woman of my dreams. We made plans together. Our lives had been set right before we left Australia. We would marry after graduation, travel during the summer for our honeymoon, I'd go back to work for my father, and we'd live in an apartment right in front of Central Park.

My trust fund wouldn't become available until I turned twenty-two. I didn't have enough money to pay for the ring she wanted.

"That's expensive, Harry, are you sure you want to buy it now?"

"We want to marry, Dad," I insisted, showing him the picture of the princess or queen or whatever cut she had chosen that was about four carats and mounted with billions of diamonds. I had no clue what I was buying, only that she had asked for it and I said yes after we had mind-blowing sex.

"I'm not sure she's the right girl for you, son." He patted my shoulder. "Or that you're ready to take that step."

"She's like Mom, how can you say that?" I offered, offended by his doubts.

"Ileana is nothing like your mother, Harrison. And the fact that you think they are similar in any way only solidifies my theory. You're not ready, and she might not be the one for you."

"Then how do you know when the right woman comes into your life?"

"It's about the flaws, the heat, and the magic," he said. "You fall in love with her flaws. The heat between the two of you is palpable even when she's miles away from you. That's when you find your forever."

For a couple of weeks, I tried to think about what he said, but then he died, and Ileana was there for me. She helped me get through the funeral and Hunter's anxiety. My twelve-year-old brother had developed agoraphobia. My extended family was fighting to get custody of Fitz and Hunter to gain access to my parents' money. Scott and I fought tooth and nail against them, and Ileana lent me an ear. She was there for me at night when I was tired of battling the judges and my money thirsty relatives.

When I enlisted, she wasn't thrilled, but she suggested we buy an apartment together. A step toward our future life. She's the future wife of a soldier. I rented an apartment for us, purchased the furniture and moved a few things in with her. Ileana was the perfect girlfriend during deployments. She always sent me care packages and letters and our short conversations were sweet. She missed me, and she couldn't wait until the war was over.

Marriage became a permanent subject in every conversation we had. She added it to her letters and even sent bridal magazines a few times. I told her it had to wait. I convinced myself that once I stopped serving, I'd marry her. But that's not what happened.

Scott called me. Hunter's panic attacks were escalating, and the doctor had suggested new drugs. "We might have to institutionalize him. But I don't want to, Harrison." Scott's pleading voice broke me.

I asked for a week off, and my superiors understood the gravity of the situation. My first stop was home. Hunter hugged me as he had never done before. He thought I had died. There had been a picture of a soldier who looked like me, and he lost his shit. It was so bad he couldn't even talk. I planned on staying home for that week as Scott, Hunt's therapists, and I decided what the best way to treat him was.

Instead of telling Ileana that I was home, I decided to surprise her.

When I opened the door, she was on top of the coffee table on all fours taking it in the ass. The dick belonged to one of my best friend's.

My mouth slacked, my stomach clenched. Nausea hit the back of my throat. I already had so much shit to deal with, and now her.

"Get out of my fucking house," I barked at both of them.

I saw red as I understood why my best friend's beer was always stocked in our refrigerator. There was enough food to feed two people, and she only ate salads. I went to the second room where she had her home office and opened the closet where I found his clothes.

"You, fucking, asshole."

"Wait, Harrison," he stuttered.

"Wait for her. You fuck my woman, eat my food, and sleep in my bed," I stated, pulling everything to the floor. "How long has this been going on, Ileana?"

"I can explain." Damon ran a hand through his hair as I continued tossing everything he owned to the floor.

"Explain that you've been fucking my girlfriend?" I stopped, crossing my arms. "Good. Why don't we start with how fucking long has this been going on? I assume years. Was this before or after we moved in here, Ileana?"

I was just the fucking sucker paying for their room and board.

"It's not what you think." She used her bedroom voice, rubbing her body against me.

"I think he was fucking your asshole, maybe I'm wrong, and it was your pussy. That's what you want to rectify? Because I don't give any fucks, bitch."

"Don't be disrespectful." Damon raised his voice.

"My house, my tone of voice. Get your shit. You two have been evicted." I went to our room and began doing the same with her stuff.

"You can't just kick me out after everything I have put up with, Harrison. I've been waiting for you to marry me for a long time."

"Why would I marry you? You're a cheater, Ileana."

"I felt lonely. You're always away." She started crying. "You stole the best years of my life."

"Me?" I turn around, getting too close to her and raising my voice. "He is the one who's been fucking you all these years while I've been serving my country. Defending your fucking freedom. Guess

what, you're fucking free to do whatever the fuck you two want outside my home. The locks will be changed."

"At least let me explain," Damon pushed me. "You can't waste all these years of friendship because of her."

I turned around and connected my fist to his jaw. "You were my best friend, fucker. If you had come to me, we could've . . . but this is treason. I will make sure to have my lawyer send you a bill for all the expenses you've incurred for the past few years, with interest."

I glanced at her. "Have some decency and leave now."

After Ileana, I was an asshole with women, with myself. I had too little respect for myself, or maybe I had a death wish. I liked to have rough sex. It made me feel something while it happened. But it disappeared so fast that I'd kicked the woman or women out of my bed, treating them like trash. According to my therapist, I was emotionally numb. I had lost my parents. My little brother was mentally ill. I was fighting in a war and killed people for a living. Plus, the woman I had been faithful to since I was eighteen had been fucking my best friend. The way I chose to feel was through sex. Rough, unadulterated sex. It was my addiction for a long time until I realized that it wasn't fulfilling.

"I didn't know you then," Luna speaks after the long silence. "And though you mention a gray line, I don't think you deserve what happened."

"Seeing them was good. I'm not upset at them. Not anymore."

The plane takes off, and I exhale. "Damon wanted to make sure I was okay. He knew my parents and also knew I never cried when they died."

"You finally released the pain. You let yourself feel and maybe forgave yourself for things that you never did . . . Your aura is brighter." Luna smiles. Her chin lifts and her eyes stare at the ceiling. "Sorry, I can't help but notice those things."

"Your quirks drive me crazy, Luna."

She twists her mouth to the side and continues her interrogation. "You two were close?"

"At some point, I was closer to him than Scott." I shrug. "Age difference."

"I was afraid you'd hit him. She . . . Ileana mentioned you broke his nose and jaw."

Covering my mouth, I try to suppress the laugh. "The night I caught them. It was epic at the time. But it's over, and this situation falls into that gray area."

Being with Ileana made sense. She was the only link I had left to my past. Everything I had before my parents died was gone. I had changed, my life was so different. If I let her go, the link to my past might be gone forever.

"How did you meet her?"

"We met in college. I believed she was it. But my parents died, I went to Afghanistan . . . we should have broken up when I realized we weren't a good match."

I massage my forehead. "She tried to stay with me for the wrong reasons, money. I wanted her because she was part of my pre-nine-eleven life. My comfort. She cheated, but I was a shitty boyfriend. It took me too long to understand that it wasn't just her fault, but what she did was fucked-up. She wanted my money. I wanted my past."

Once they said that we're allowed to turn on our electronics, I set down the tray, pulled out my laptop and my headphones.

"I asked him about their daughter."

"What?" Luna's eyes land on me. "Is she yours?"

I shake my head. Damon and Ileana were fucking idiots. "She's Damon's, but Ileana isn't the mother. They had a rough start but sounds like they are doing fine now." I take Luna's hand and kiss it. "And I'm happy about it."

She rests her head on top of my shoulder. "I'm glad you're back. For a moment, it felt like darkness surrounded you. I feared that you wouldn't come back."

"Why wouldn't I when my light was right next to me?" I kiss the top of her head.

I swallow, staring at our linked hands and wonder how I'm going to gather the courage to show her that we belong together. Damon's words keep repeating inside my head like a broken record. *"She reminds me of your mom,"* he said, smiling at her. *"Full of life, happy. She made everyone feel welcome. It's like you can't believe there can be people that happy when the world is so fucking dark."*

I smiled, patting his shoulder. *"She's my light, Damon."*

25

HARRISON

"Have you ever gone to the memorial?"

"Once." Scott pours me another shot of tequila. "How come?"

He fidgets with his bottom lip while looking at the horizon. "Hazel."

Great, he is in a few words, don't bother me kind of mood today.

"That's a big word." I stare at the amber liquid in his glass, then move my gaze to the ocean where Hazel and Luna are paddle boarding. "Why did she take you?"

"It happened recently, after her mother died." He smiles, his gaze remains on Hazel. "She decided that our parents needed flowers and some attention. It was a strange experience." Scott shrugs.

That's all he says. The tin man went, saw the place, and didn't shed a tear. Can he share some wisdom on how to feel a little less? I wait for more, but Scott is closed off to the world today. His mind is lost, and his eyes only focus on one person.

"I never saw you cry when our parents died. Have you ever?"

"Not everyone reacts as expected, Harrison," he says, taking a glass filled with bourbon. He holds it to his lips, then stops and glares at me. "Spill. What's going on? Because I'm about to get shitfaced and won't be able to have a coherent conversation with you."

He drinks like a man quenching his thirst after a marathon. With each gulp, his Adam's apple bobs violently. Bourbon should be enjoyed. Sipped from a small glass. As his big brother, I should tell him. But I guess the point of this exercise is to induce himself into a temporary coma.

"Earlier today, I went to the memorial," I say, pressing my lips together.

"How bad was it?" He pours himself another glass of bourbon.

"Fuck, I wanted to run away." I tell him what happened from the moment we arrived until we left. He doesn't say a word. His eyes remain on the horizon.

"They aren't there," Scott blurts. "Mom's at home, on her terrace, making sure her plants survive my careless watering. Dad's in his office, reading a thriller or solving crosswords."

He's dead serious.

"Remember the time when you dressed up like G. I. Joe, and I was Batman?" Scott starts laughing. "I taught you how Batman would beat the shit out of your super soldier."

"We didn't have candy that year." I shake my head. Mom put us in time out without cookies for an entire month. "Sorry about your arm."

"I still won, and got to wear a cool cast for six weeks," he brags. The asshole had me pinned on the floor. Though I broke his left arm. But it seems like he believes that he won the biggest prize. "All the fourth-grade girls wanted to sit with me at lunch and help me with my food."

"You were in third grade."

He smirks. "Like I said, I won."

We laugh, I drink a shot of tequila. We tell more Halloween stories and then jump into Christmas parties.

"I hated them," we say in unison.

"Dressing in suits, only being allowed to eat two cookies and drink one can of soda," Scott complains, then grins. "Remember when we stole the bottle of whiskey?"

"My ass still hurts." Dad never believed in violence, but when he caught us drinking, he spanked the shit out of us.

"Do you have any idea what can happen to you?" Scott imitates his voice. "This isn't for children . . . I gave you one job. Take care of Fitzy and instead, you stole the liquor and ran away."

"Fitzy was with us," I defend myself. "How old were we?"

"Poor Fitz, I can't believe he survived us." Scott shakes his head.

"You were thirteen, I was ten, and Fitz only seven. Hunt stayed at home."

I'm about to say something more, but my curiosity is bigger. "What happened when you were at the memorial?"

"That place is beautiful but haunted," he says. His eyes close, his head leans on the back of the lounge chair. "No, not as though there're ghosts, but it's haunted by the memories of what one witnessed or who you lost. It's impossible not to react to it. Innocent people died leaving their loved ones behind and . . . no matter how many times I say good night to the fucking moon, I'll never see them again."

Scott covers his mouth and closes his eyes. He shakes his head while breathing through the pain, not a tear slips through his eyes.

Is he ever going to cry?

"I was sobbing like a baby when we were there."

He bobs his head. "Hazel told me," he pauses, pressing his lips together. "The day I finally broke down and let myself feel was bad, yet, the best one of my fucking life."

"Where were you?"

He smiles, opening his eyes. Sitting straight and finishing his drink. "The memorial."

"What happened afterward?"

"Do you think this is the first time Hazel has flown an Everhart out of New York because he's broken?"

"What's going on between you two?"

He pours more liquor into his glass. "I don't know. And you have to stop asking us."

"You might lose her if you do something stupid."

"What's there to win? She belongs to *him*." His words are acid, bitter and my heart hurts for him.

Hazel doesn't belong to anyone. She only wants love and someone who will love her even when she's a fucking mess. A man who sees beyond that fucking act she puts on every day. My brother sees it, he knows it. He fucking loves what's underneath the dome she built after her ex fucked her royally.

If his mind weren't floating in a pool of hard liquor, I'd beg him to get his head out of his ass. But he's not in a good place. And fuck, I'm right beside him. We should stop drinking. I want to stop the derailed train from crashing. But the waiter delivers the frozen margarita pitcher that Hazel ordered before going paddle boarding. And who the fuck can say no to a margarita? I can't.

Drinking the cold cocktail feels like the greatest luxury on earth. The numbness creeps into my brain. My fingers slide on the condensation before I regain my grip. I hate to agree that everything feels better from here.

Hazel said it when I arrived, *"You're not avoiding reality, only taking a detour to build your strength. You shut down those memories and feelings, and in one day you let everything loose. It's not healthy."*

This wouldn't be my first choice after what happened, an exclusive resort with fruity drinks and the hottest woman in the world wearing a tiny bikini while enjoying the evening with her new best friend. But I can see the appeal to it. From here, I can laugh and enjoy those memories better than I could when I was so close to where they died. It's not being shallow, it's being mindful of my heart.

"Do you think we should buy a house here?"

"Why?"

"We can bring the next generation on vacations. Hazel loves the ocean. You'd have a place to stay when she has that urgency to be bathing under the sun right next to it."

He laughs and shakes his head. "You're already planning where to vacation. Are you buying Luna a house like Hunter did with Willow?"

"Nah, I'll wait for her to choose where to live. We have the penthouse in Seattle, but . . . I sound like fucking Hunter."

When our little brother fell in love with Willow, he bought her a brownstone in Brooklyn for her birthday. We thought he had lost his marbles. A glance at Luna is all I need to know that once you fall hard for the right girl, you just do whatever it takes to convince them that you love them.

"What should I do with Luna?"

"Are you seriously asking me what to do?" Scott laughs, slurring his words. "Almost ten years ago, I fell in love with a fucking eighteen-year-old girl. Years later I'm still collecting the stupid crumbs she throws on the floor and feeding them to my heart. I have no fucking idea what you should do. Ask her. Hazel knows all about fucking love."

He picks up his wallet and watch and tries to sit down. "I've discovered that she loves those second chance romances." He laughs. "I think that I have about a year or two to enjoy whatever this is." He points a shaky finger at me. "Don't fucking fuck it up for me, big brother, or I swear I'll kill you."

Yep, he's drunk. I watch him stumble through the lounge chairs. I let him walk back by himself. It'll be good for him to break his stupid head and learn to control his alcohol. Or the impact might reboot his brain.

"Hey." Hazel comes running back. "Where did he go?"

"Back to his room, he's wasted."

She chews her lip. "Okay. I . . . ."

"Answer fast. What do I do to convince Luna that this isn't a pretend relationship? That I'm serious."

Hazel grins, and fuck those evil eyes brighten. "Honestly, keep doing what you're doing. And keep your dick in your pants."

"What?" I look at my crotch, then at Luna's curvy, perfect body. "Are you sure?"

"I'm afraid so, Harry." She nods. "Wait until she's sure that she has feelings for you."

Her gaze goes toward the hotel building.

"He needs you, go to him."

"Harrison—"

"I know, this isn't happening, it's a figment of my imagination. If I say a word, you'll have my balls tied to a light post." I take a breath. "Did I miss something?"

She leans, kisses my cheek, and runs to my brother's side.

Luna makes her way to me. The corner of her lips is stretching far. "I didn't know she's a surfer."

"And a tomboy, and one of the guys. She hides it pretty well." I'm impressed that Hazel has been authentic with Luna. When Willow came back to her life, she was so guarded . . . and she's her sister. "Do you want a margarita?"

"Nope, I want to go dancing." She smiles. "I've never been on vacation. I'm not wasting the next few days lounging and drinking. Come on; we have to go and get ready."

Dancing? Is she crazy? How am I supposed to behave like a gentleman when she's going to be flaunting her ass? I take another shot of Patron before following her. This is going to be a long weekend.

26

HARRISON

Scott and Hazel left the Keys the next day. They had other plans, and wouldn't be back in New York until Sunday morning. I didn't ask what happened, and I swore to both that I'll never say a word. Unless I felt it was necessary. Luna and I decided to bail on the gala and arrived last night. I wanted to give her the best vacation of her life.

When I asked how come she's never gone anywhere, I was shut down. Luna trusts me, but only so much. I hate that I've shared everything with her and there're still parts of her that continue to be a puzzle. Today, I went to yoga, and we agreed to have lunch together. Dinner is at my house. We are cooking together and feeding the tribe.

Scott knew when I'd be back and he scheduled a board meeting for Tuesday morning. Thank fuck they decided to hold it at home, or I would've said fuck no. I'm not putting on "business casual clothes" after coming back from yoga.

When I enter the home office, I spot a basket with pastries, a bowl of fresh fruit, coffee, and an egg casserole.

"We're having breakfast too, how fancy," I declare, taking a seat between Hunter and Scott.

"The prodigal child is back." Hazel stares at me from her seat. "You were gone for almost a week."

"You're mad?" I arch an eyebrow.

"I worked my ass off to get you the perfect dating scenes, and you didn't go to any of them." She pushes a yellow envelope. "You owe me. They were my treat if you had used them."

I look at my brothers and look at her. "Can you explain why she is part of this board meeting?"

"Scotty promised to make me breakfast, I never say no to home-made food," she jokes, pouring herself a cup of coffee.

"She's my right hand," Scott reminds me, ignoring Hazel's response. "Neither one of you gives a fuck about this company. Hazel at least pretends to care because she likes to boss me around."

"I love to boss him." She nods, feeding him a piece of a chocolate croissant. "But that's not the reason. I handle the Everhart boys' investments. Having a say in the company is part of my job."

"We're not boys," Hunter defends himself. "But I need your help. Which one of you is going to set the baby's trust fund?"

Hazel raises her hand. "Me, pick me."

"You can have that," Scott concedes, preparing a plate of fruit for her. "Can we start the meeting?"

"After he tells me all about Luna." She bats her eyelashes at me and fakes a long sigh. "And how much he loves her."

"I appreciate the family reunion. But if that's all, I have things to do." I toss a glare at Hazel. "Don't you have a company to run?"

"This meeting is a little more pressing than my other job. But first, tell me how your weekend was."

"We are here to discuss Everhart Enterprises, not how you like to meddle in my love life." I glare at Hunter who isn't paying attention. He's just texting with Willow. "You should've stayed home if that's all you're going to do."

Hazel claps. "Ooh, our boy is in love and pissy from the drought he's going through." She winks at me.

"Fuck, what's wrong with you?" Hunter groans. "You need to get laid, at least jerk off in the shower to see if it takes the edge off."

"Shut up!"

I had a great time in the Keys, but fuck, Luna was wearing tiny bikinis, and I couldn't touch her. "Do you have any idea how torturous it was?"

I glare at Hazel. "And it was your idea."

"I suggested it, and it's working." She grins.

Then she stares at the ceiling, licking her lips. "If I were into her, I'd be all over her." She starts laughing. "She is hot, and, dude, have you seen her naked?" She whistles.

"When did you see her naked?"

Hazel grins, thumping her hand on the table. "Never, but you should've seen your face. Priceless. Now tell me what happened."

I exhale, staring at Scott. "What is it, sugar, coffee? She's wired up and already driving me insane."

"Sex," Fitz responds. "She's getting some. I just don't know who the poor bastard is."

"Poor bastard?" Scott frowns.

"Yeah, I have the feeling that this one is like that bunny in the commercials that has a long-life battery included," Fitz responds, shaking his head.

Scott's face is stern, but he can't hide the fucking smirk. Yep, the bastard got a lot of action the past few days while I just watched and salivated.

"Can we focus on the meeting?" Hunter insists. "Willow wants to remind you guys that on Thursday we have a dinner party at our house. And I'll be gone for the next couple of months, we have some traveling to do before the baby arrives."

"Dress formal," Hazel adds.

"Willow asked for Luna's number." Hunter's attention goes back to me. "I'm sure she sent a text to her, but I assume she'll be joining us regardless, won't she?"

"Do we always know everybody's business?"

"Pretty much," Hazel dares to respond. "That's what families do, at least ours do it. Why?"

"You need to move out, and that will give you some room to

breathe." Hunter's two cents are spot on what I've been thinking for the past few days.

"I'm moving out of the penthouse," I declare, letting the weight of what I'm saying settle for a few moments. "There's no date set, but I'm starting to search for a place."

Hazel hands me a business card. "Our realtors have years of experience in the tristate area. We mostly do commercial. But for you, I'd do residential too. If you want, we can also set an appointment to discuss your prenuptial and future investments."

Then she glares at me. "You make her sign a prenup, and I swear I'm castrating you before you say I do."

"Aw, aren't you adorable. I might give your people a call . . . and no prenuptial will be signed."

She smiles and goes back to her breakfast. Yep, she's a little off today.

"The brownstone next to ours is for sale," Hunter announces, then looks up to me and smirks. "You're in fucking love, aren't you?"

All eyes are on me. This meeting wasn't about Luna, or how I feel for her, but I have the sudden urge to share with them. My brothers and my sister.

"I'm falling," I pause, "hard."

"She's not your type," Fitz intercedes. "Yet, I can see you with her. She's the Ying to your Yang."

"You're right," I agree with him. "She's not the type of woman I'd have chosen to date or consider . . . marrying."

"Marry?" Hazel's eyes open wide. She stares at me like she's heard that Santa Clause does exist. "Miracles do happen."

"They do, babe." Fitz pats her hand. "You just need to get me a man, and find a drone for Scotty."

Hazel presses her lips together, faking a smile while nodding. "Yeah, I'll find them. An excellent guy for you, and . . ." she clears her throat "a woman for Scott." Her tone is flat, and I hope she knows what the hell she's doing.

Luna and I have to figure out what's going on between us. More like I have to convince her that we are possible. Maybe she's not what

I had in mind for my life partner. The woman is noisy, and fuck, I like that about her. I like when she turns on her music, and she's singing off tune to some Latin song that I have no idea what it means but sounds hot because she's moving those hips. Or she decides to play an old ballad by Christopher Cross, and she grabs whatever is at her disposal, pretending it's a microphone.

She's quirky. Those fucking horoscopes she reads religiously drive me crazy. She believes that her hand holds her future. Just as she believes in justice and she fights for those who can't fight for themselves. She's ruthless, fearless, and stronger than any person I've ever met. But God, she can be sweet and passionate. So yes, I'm falling hard even when I'm fucking scared of what's happening between us. Convincing her that she can fall, and that I'll catch her is going to be hard.

So fucking hard.

But I want her to be part of my life—to be part of me. I want her forever.

"Being with her reminds me of what Mom and Dad had when they were with us," I say out loud.

Hunter smiles, looking at his phone. And Scott moves his gaze toward Hazel. Is Hazel the woman who could make him happy?

"I imagine they had the perfect marriage," Hazel says with a dreamy tone.

"Actually, it was imperfect and messy," I respond.

"But it was magical when they were together," Scott adds to what I say.

I nod in agreement. "Dad loved to bring her presents on a daily basis. He tried to hang the moon and promised her the stars."

"He always delivered," Scott continued. "Mom said that when they met, she just knew they belonged together. They fell in love slowly though, but it was inevitable."

"That," Hazel sighs. "I want that."

"One day you'll have it," Fitz assures her. "You always say it, love is real, it happens. You just have to wait for the right guy."

"What if I had the right guy? But we were too young and careless with what we had? I might die alone." She shakes her head, slamming her forehead against the table. Ouch.

Then, she lifts her head and smiles. "Tell me more about your parents. I need to hear about those blissful moments they shared. Were they happy?"

Scott and I witnessed the entire relationship. It was heaven when they were happy. Sometimes joy became apathy. There were fights. Words were said.

"It's over, Christopher." Mom's angry voice would come from the office, her craft room, or maybe their room.

She'd be packing. My stomach would sink each time that happened. It felt like hours when I had to wait for the news that they were getting a divorce. Scott and I would be camping in the media room with the little kids hoping that the nightmare would be over soon. Dad would come home with a big ass bouquet of Mom's favorite flowers and would tell her that he was sorry. That he couldn't live without her by his side. It didn't matter who had started it. He always came back apologizing.

"It was hard to think how one would survive without the other when you saw them kissing," I say, staring at the wall where the picture of the six of us hung.

"And . . . they did, they left together," Scott finishes. "It was hard when they left, but you can still feel their love."

"That's the kind of love Luna makes me want to have," I tell them. "I want to wake up next to her for the rest of my life, and go to heaven, and wait for her so we can be together forever."

"But?" Hazel glares at me. "What's wrong?"

"I have to work hard to convince her that we can be together."

"You're an excellent negotiator, Harrison, just show her how amazing you can be." She gives me her vote of confidence.

27

LUNA

"This is a mistake."

I stare at the file that Harrison just handed me. I read it, study every word and every picture. Nothing makes sense. This isn't what I asked him to give me.

I wanted the truth about Mom's death.

"You're wrong."

There's a picture of a baby sitting down next to her mother. I can't see the body of my mother but . . . why did they leave me on the floor next to her? Who picked me up from there? That can't be me. It was Sammie who was taken along with her. Not me. I was safe . . . where was I? At childcare maybe, or . . . I never asked for my where-abouts and the file I have. Standing up from the bed, I walk to the small desk where I have my files. I go through the pile searching for the folder with the original documents.

I open it and go through the highlighted notes. I check the few pictures I have. In the pictures, it's only Mom's head, her eyes are closed, and a white sheet covers her body. In the files, there's no description of the daughter, nothing particular about her appearance, age or . . .

The file is thin, too thin. I've known it for a long time. I expected that the other one would be larger, but not completely different. I compare it with the new file that Harrison gave me and laugh. This binder has interviews, testimonies, and pictures. So many pictures of where they found her, how they found her . . .

The woman on the ground in the pictures is lifeless. The naked, bruised, bloody corpse is next to some bushes. Her blond hair is matted in multiple places, stained with blood. Her eyes are wide open. Her glance is directed to the spot where the baby had been. They found her car abandoned on highway 95. Their little boy was close by, asking for help to the drivers who passed along the site. According to her husband, she was going to visit her mother. That night, they found her body and his baby daughter.

"Lucas." I cover my mouth. "He was there too, but they only took her and . . . me." My voice disappears as I continue reading page after page of the same.

A lump continues forming inside my throat. My stomach turns with each word, every new revelation. All the suffering and torturing she went through before they finally killed her. A hiker found her because the baby was crying.

And the note they left.

She's next. You can't hide them from us.

"That was an act of brutality. Why do you think he hired that man?" I'm still hoping to blame her ex-husband for taking away my mother and destroying our family.

"Who?"

"Sammie's dad."

"It wasn't Sammie's father." Harrison takes the file away from me.

"There's no other option," I insist, shaking my head. "Then why did he keep Sammie away from us?"

"He filed a restraining order against your father after this happened. He claimed that Cristobal was a danger to his child. Though your dad fought it, he never got to see her again."

"Where was Sammie?"

"According to my investigators, she was with her father," Harrison responds. "Your mom wasn't allowed to take her out of the city without his consent."

Then what happened to my sister? I thought seeing her mother die had broken her but . . . I will never know. It could've been missing her family or was it abuse. Mom said that he was hitting Sammie.

"I feel like my entire life is a lie." I plop on top of my bed, resting my elbows on my thighs and cradling my head.

"I wouldn't call it a lie," he says, quietly.

"He lied to me."

"There's always another side to the story, Luna."

"What would you do?" I lift my head, looking at him.

"If you died?" He exhales harshly, taking me into his embrace. He brushes sweet kisses up the side of my neck. "I'd die with you."

The tone of his voice and the words rock my entire system. I couldn't survive if he died. I know that's what happened to my father. He's not the same man. I doubt that he'll ever be the guy he was when Mom was around. But why hide it from me?

"Harry, help me understand, please." I push him away, walking around my room.

I can't think about Harrison and what'll happen to him when I die. Because this isn't the time to tell him, *by the way, I don't have too much time left,* but I am falling so hard for him that I can't breathe when I remember that this can't happen. Not between us.

"There has to be a better answer than that didn't happen, this is what happened and live with it." I come up with the first thing I can, pushing us away from the subject of my own mortality.

"What would you do?" I repeat.

"I probably would bury everything so deep that no one would ever know what happened. I wouldn't want my kid to know that. You have to talk to him."

"Harry," I say, as I see his face breaking.

Harrison pulls me back into his comfortable arms, and the weight of the world vanishes from my body. He cups my face, catching my lips with his. The kiss is soft first but becomes deeper, rougher, passionate. It's so much different from all the other kisses we've shared since we came back from the Keys. Meaningful, lustful, but healing too. It's like he's trying to absorb my pain with every thrust of his tongue.

"Sorry, I can't think about losing you. Not when we are finding each other and . . ."

He shakes his head. "Stop torturing yourself and talk to him."

"You think I have to?"

"That's the only way you'll find your answers, little moon."

Is he right? Will Dad finally tell me what happened? I can't think. This is too much. The past two days have been bad. My yoga classes had only a couple of students yesterday and today. I didn't have any Reiki clients. Jess wasn't happy because I missed almost a week of work. Even when I said it was a family emergency.

"I don't care that your boyfriend is rich." Jess used Harrison as an excuse to try to hook me for more classes, now she seems to hate him. "If you miss one more day of work, don't come back."

Then there's my real job. The case I'm working on is going to be handled by my ex-boss. The same man who hates my guts and the guy who emailed me to say that next week he was coming to New York to look into what's been done so far. That he has his team assembled and didn't think he'd be needing me.

Lucas hasn't responded to my email, but I have to find out what he's planning on doing with me. Is he going to fire me?

"Luna, how can I help you?" Harrison's concerned voice warms my heart. "We can fix everything . . . one thing at a time. You have my support. I can listen, suggest, or do whatever you feel necessary."

I know I could get through this by myself, but having him here makes everything so much easier. His heartbeats remind me that there's hope. His strength shows me that pain can only break you for so long. Learning the truth about the past isn't the end of the world, this might be the beginning of something different. But what?

"He's been lying to me," I complain, resting my head on his chest. "Dad, Lucas . . . I bet Tiago knows too. Why would they hide that?"

"Say the word, and I can have you in Alexandria tomorrow morning."

"Jess will fire me," I retort, but I might not need to have a cover in New York. For all I know, I have to pack and go back home.

"But I want to talk to him."

"I'll set it up for tomorrow morning. Do you want to stay here or go out for dinner?"

"Hazel is cooking." I flinch because that woman should only be allowed to assist.

"Scott is doing it. He's pretending to help her."

"Then here, and . . ." I close my eyes, blurt the words and hope he says yes. "Stay with me tonight."

"Luna, I can't. Not yet."

"Just hold me, nothing else." I smile, pretending to be fine with the arrangement. Telling him that I want to be with him might grant me a no, and my emotions are too crumbly to handle the rejection, even when his reasons are sweet.

We are not ready.

What happened to his cheesy or crass innuendos?

I'll be setting you on fire.

There hasn't been any fire. The heat between us increases, and I'm about to combust. By myself.

"Fuck, give me strength." He closes his eyes. "Let's have dinner, and we'll play it by ear."

28

LUNA

Harrison Everhart is a dead man walking. I stare at his back while he's talking with the hostess. She keeps smiling at him, batting her eyelashes, and sighing every two freaking seconds.

"I'll be with you in a moment." She flashes me a smile, then turns to Harrison. "Follow me, Mr. Everhart. I'll bring your guests to your table as they arrive."

"We have guests, dear?" I arch an eyebrow and refrain from showing her my claws.

Harrison kisses my temple, taking my hand. Then, he turns his attention to Ms. Flirty. "Mr. Santillan should arrive soon. Thank you for taking care of our table."

"Where's my sunshine?" Harrison holds the laugh. "You're in a bad mood today. Not a morning person, are you?"

"Shut up!" I say, walking behind him and Ms. Perky.

I don't consider myself a morning person, nor a night owl. I'm a mix. If I go to bed early, I can wake up early and vice versa. Last night we went to sleep at . . . we never did. Harrison found millions of ways to avoid my bed. Baking, cleaning, board games, movies. I fell asleep watching a marathon of *Transformers*, the cartoon.

"What did I do?" He moves to the side and bows slightly pointing at the inside of a private room. "After you, my lady."

Moving my head side to side and up and down I glare at him.

"I owe you my stiff neck," I declare, gently massaging the sore muscles. Falling asleep on his shoulder for the entire flight has me crying in pain.

He inspects the table, which is set only for two people, then nods at Miss Perky-Flirt. She leaves without saying a word.

"We're even." He clears his throat, walking toward the door and closing it. "I owe you my stiff dick. It's been like that since we met."

"Now you want sex." I glare at him. "My father is about to arrive, that's not something I'd like to discuss." I cross my arms, biting my lip and swallowing the next sentence.

But we can run to the restroom and take care of each other's itch. Man, there's the itch he mentioned before.

"I already apologized about your neck." He walks toward me. "But in my defense, you didn't let me buy you a neck pillow for the flight."

He reaches over to me, pulling me against his body and pressing my back against his torso. I close my eyes, leaning against him and letting him support my tired body. Two more hours of sleep will fix me, for now. He pushes my hair to one side, kisses my neck, and puts his hands on top of my shoulders beginning to work my knots with the tip of his fingers.

"Harrison!" I cry in pain after he squeezes me hard. "What are you doing?"

"Sir."

Opening my eyes, I see my father in front of us. His eyes are shooting a furious glance toward Harrison.

"*Hola, Papá,*" I say, moving farther from Harrison and closer to him.

"Luna," he exhales a groan.

"Mr. Everhart, I see that as always, you didn't care to follow my instructions."

"Sir, as always, it's a pleasure to see you." Harrison nods. And I close my eyes when I catch the humor in his eyes. Ah, this man is going to pull my father's triggers.

I stare at my father and shake my head. "You're going to be nice to him." Then, I turn to Harrison. "And you too. Do not . . . I just need you to behave." I roll my eyes, crossing my arms.

"It won't be hard because I'm leaving." Harrison looks at me. "The room is reserved for five hours. You can use it for as long as you want though. I'll be outside if you need me."

"But—"

"If you want, I can stay. But I think this is something you two have to discuss without a third party." He takes my hands and kisses them both, then brushes my mouth lightly with his.

He turns to look at Dad. "I apologize if what I did was against your wishes, but you told me to put her first. And that's what I did. My plan is to always put her first, even if you don't approve."

"You put her in danger." Dad grinds his teeth.

"I didn't, it was done cautiously." Harrison doesn't change his tone. He remains calm.

"Yet, I learned about it almost immediately."

Harrison smirks. "You heard about it yesterday. It wasn't a coincidence, sir." He bows and steps out of the room.

Dad grips the back of the chair as he watches Harrison leave. His knuckles are turning white, and his lips are pressed together so tight they are barely visible. "I don't like him, Luna. You have to stay away from him."

"Why didn't you tell me, Papá?"

He pulls on his tie, trying to loosen it. I can't believe he came dressed in a suit.

"I don't know what you want me to say." His voice is dry.

"I want you to tell me everything, or at least explain to me why you hid the truth. The way she died . . . what happened?" I close my eyes, trying to erase the jarring images from my mind. They broke her before they killed her. "It was brutal, and she didn't deserve it. No one deserves to die that way and in front of her daughter."

The little baby who lost her mother so soon in such a cruel and horrid way.

"What kind of monster does that?"

"A heartless man."

"What happened with Lucas?"

"He hid under the seats, between the blankets that she carried in the trunk." Dad's shoulders remain slumped, his eyes never leave the white tablecloth. "My brave little boy. He stopped cars asking for help. We were searching desperately. Found you a few hours later but it was too late for her."

"Why did it happen?"

"It was an undercover job. My partner sold me out and I didn't get to her on time." He supports his weight onto the chair, his gaze focused on the table.

"Who is the man behind bars?"

"My ex-partner," he answers. "I had everything to incarcerate them. I didn't have enough information to bring down the entire Russian mafia down. They are the ones who killed your mom after they discovered my identity. I could've tried to take them down. But that implied entering the witness protection program and leave everyone and everything behind. I would only be allowed to take my children with me. If Tiago joined me, he wouldn't be able to see his mother. I couldn't leave him behind, I couldn't take him away from her. You and Lucas had lost your mom. You needed my family . . . I needed them too."

"What did you do?"

"Instead, I sold my soul to them."

"How?"

"They'd leave my family alone if I blamed their crimes on my partner, William, and left New York." His gaze lowers.

"You let them go."

"I failed your mother once. I couldn't fail her twice by losing our kids." Dad moves his head, slowly. When his eyes find mine, I feel the punch of his pain. His dark brown eyes are blotchy and his lips quiver.

"My only goal is to keep you safe," he says.

"They are dangerous, and they are connected with the man you're investigating. Luna this…" He lowers his gaze. "I still work for them."

A pang hits me hard. How is this happening? My father who has always pride himself for being the best soldier, the best cop…

I feel sad for the man that lost so much, but angry at the man who hid so much from me.

I try to swallow my words, but they come out. "Keeping the truth from me wasn't keeping me safe. You could've told me the basics years ago. I kept blaming Sammie's dad, and you wouldn't correct me. I'm not a kid. I had the right to hear this from you." The last sentence sounds cruel, or at least hurtful. And I regret it for only a few seconds.

"I was protecting you." He shakes his head. "No one will care or protect you the way I do, Luna."

"Harrison does, and he didn't hide this from me, even when he knew this would break my heart."

"Everhart only cares about himself." He slams his fist on the table.

I jolt, taking a step back. My eyes widen, as my father's angry side appears with a vengeance.

"He only helped you to sleep with you." Darkness crosses his eyes. "In a couple of weeks, he'll turn to the next woman."

"Why are you trying to hurt me?" Anger burns my chest. "You just told me that the only reason he would help me is in exchange for sex, Father. That he doesn't care for me. Why wouldn't he care?"

"No, no," he huffs. "That came out wrong. You don't understand. What he did might alert them about you, about us and I can't lose you. You're almost thirty-one, Luna. It's time to change careers and do something different before—"

"Before I die?"

"Yes . . . No, I'm not saying that . . ."

"You've been saying that for years," I bark. "You keep telling me stuff like, 'the females in our family don't live long, Luna.' Or 'be careful, Luna, things happen to women.' I hate when you say, 'it happened to your mom, Sammie, and your grandmother.'" I close my eyes for a second. "And 'you're next if you're not careful.'"

I know he's right. That there's not much time left for me but does he have to remind me about it all the time. I've made peace with myself, but when that happened Harrison wasn't part of my life. Now . . . I'm afraid to die.

"Hey," Harrison enters. "This room is private, but not soundproof."

He extends his hand, curling his fingers as he angles his head calling me to him. Taking me in his arms, he whispers, "I got you."

"With all due respect, sir, you're wrong. I helped Luna because she asked me." He swallows. "I'm not a saint, but with her I'm different. I like her. I care about Luna. This isn't just a fling."

"She's not safe with you," Dad barks.

"But she is, sir. My company is taking charge of the case you couldn't solve thirty years ago." Harrison kisses my forehead. "Our people will contact you soon."

"What did you do?" my father growls.

"That's for me to know, sir. You only have to know that Luna and your family are safe."

Harrison looks at the table, then at me. "Do you want breakfast?"

I shake my head. Then, I look at my father. "I love you Dad, but at the moment, I don't like you."

"Luna . . . I . . . am sorry." He wipes his forehead with the back of his hand. "Can we talk about this?"

"Not today, I'll come back another day. Your actions. Your words. She died years ago, and you did along with her. Or maybe you've always been dry, but instead of saying the right words, you like to scare us into doing what you want." I shrug. "Or insult us. Harrison and I haven't slept together, and you just assumed things and judged the two of us. That's wrong in many ways. I want you to think about it. Consider the way you've behaved toward your sons too."

"Luna," he exhales, his gaze dropping.

"Dad, we are the only thing you have left. You sold yourself to keep us alive, but you keep yourself away from us."

"When are you coming back, *mijita*?"

"I don't know. Soon?"

"We have to talk, I'd hate to leave things this way."

"I want to enjoy whatever time I have left." I squeeze Harrison's hand. "With him. Maybe you'll have to come and visit me."

Walking to him, I give him a kiss and a hug. I pray that this isn't the last time I see him. But also that he changes his attitude, with Lucas, Tiago . . . and with me too.

"I not only care about you, Luna. I'm falling for you," Harrison says when we are out of the restaurant, pulling my heartstrings.

I gasp the moment I see some clarity. His words are like thunder echoing in the distance. My heart pounds, matching the strength of the meaning of what he just said, and my thoughts. Every muscle, every bone, and every cell in my body want it.

We are both falling. This man has stripped me of my armor, exposing my heart to his. Making me vulnerable to him. He doesn't understand that he's setting us up and risking facing the biggest heartache. I couldn't leave this world in peace knowing I'm leaving him behind.

What will happen when I leave?

Am I going to die like my father predicts?

We have to talk, set boundaries and limits. I can't let this continue any further. Harrison is a good guy, and he deserves everything. He doesn't deserve the fate of being lonely and losing someone he loves. I will never forgive myself if I inflict any pain on him. He's pushing the inevitable. I wanted to do it after I had memorized the rhythm of his heart, learned every mark on his skin and every secret inside his adventurous mind. I wanted to trap it all into my heart so I could take it with me and live forever with him. Share that invisible link with him.

I shake my head. "No, you can't. You shouldn't, Harry. I don't want you to end up like him. You . . . no. This is casual, remember? We said only casual," I repeat for his sake, for my safety. Because I care too much, I love him too much. "You said it. You said there wouldn't be emotions. You can't fall for me."

"What are you talking about?" He pulls the valet parking ticket. "Let's go home, we . . . you. We need to cool down."

29

HARRISON

I hate messy shit. Chaos, noise. I like everything to be straightforward and nothing complicated. But the woman in my apartment is the opposite of what I want in my life. She's the antithesis of my ideal woman. Yet, my heart is bonded to hers. How the fuck she managed to do it is beyond me. I did everything I could to keep it casual. I am the master of casual. Instead, I gave into the chaotic pandemonium inside my head.

But how could I ignore what I'm feeling for her when she's everything I thought I didn't want, yet everything my heart needs to continue beating? She's my next breath. She's all I can think of since she waltzed into my life. I don't know how long I can survive without her touch, her light, and that sweet voice that soothes me.

"Good afternoon, Mr. Everhart," Mark, the concierge, greets me as I step back into the building.

Her disdain hurt me, enraged me. It cracked my heart. How can she propose something casual? You can't go to Europe, eat at the best French restaurant, and then request McDonald's for the remainder of the trip. You hope that the journey never ends and that you're treated to the finest, most exclusive dates, orgasms, and lifetime adventures for the rest of your fucking life. And she can bet her sweet little ass that I'll be working hard to make her happy for as long as I live.

Thank fuck the doors are open, and I don't have to wait while making small talk. My nerves are holding on by a thin thread. Anything might push me over the edge, and I might explode. This is the first time in twenty some years that I want to grab Hannibal and start shooting. I should go to the range. But the fucking shooting range won't be as fun if she's not with me. She has to be with me.

We need to be together.

Pushing the button, I step back as the doors of the elevator slide closed. I don't have the time, nor the patience, to deal with people. The only focus on my mind is Luna. I stare at the bag of food. I'm hoping her blood sugar is so low she's talking nonsense. Instead of flying back home, I chose driving six long hours. I took the scenic route, and we hit traffic. The atmosphere inside the car was cold, sad and quiet. Too fucking quiet.

She didn't say a word.

I couldn't speak. The fear that she'd tell me to get the fuck out of her life was eating all the words.

"Don't have sex," Hazel advised. "You're doing great. She's falling. I've never seen two people falling so hard. You two are so sweet."

Fucking Hazel, I swear she's going to pay for this and her stupid ideas. If it hadn't been for her, I'd be a happy man. And that woman in my apartment would be happy and so high on pleasure she wouldn't care if I'm in love with her. Instead, she's sending me to the fuck buddy zone—without having sex. That's worse than the fucking friend zone.

There's no logical explanation for what and how I feel for her. In fact, I should be going to my shrink to check my head. I can't make any sense about what's been happening to me for the past few weeks. I smile when the elevator chimes, and it reminds me of her. I've never been so attracted to someone. We are synced to each other. At least we were until today.

My heart drops to my stomach when I find Luna in the foyer.

Her hair is damp. She wears a pair of dark leggings and the shirt I gave her earlier when she asked if she could take a shower.

"You're leaving." I take a step back as her nod feels like a blow and my legs tremble with the force of what she's doing.

"How much do I owe you for the trip?" She reaches for her purse.

"Nothing, Luna. What the fuck is going on?" I toss my hands up in the air. "I said that I'm falling for you and handed you my heart." I sigh, linking my hands together behind my neck. "You took my heart and started kicking it like a soccer ball."

How did this happen? I let a harmless woman cross every protection I've set to keep anyone at bay. This just shows that she's great at infiltrating and conquering.

Also, at destroying.

She touches her crystal, rubbing it. "No. Actually, I didn't touch it. I handed it back to protect it, Harry. This is what's best for us—for you."

Dropping her gaze, she almost hits her chest with her chin. "I can't fall for you. We can never happen."

My heart shatters.

Her words can't be clearer than that. We're done, but it never began.

Stepping aside, I mask the pain with rage. "I've no idea what your game was, but you won. Congratulations."

"There's a pattern in my family," she blurts, her voice wavers. "Have you ever heard that history always repeats itself?"

I lift my chin and look at her. She's staring at her palm. The pain in her face is unbearable. My lungs stop functioning as I witness the fear and agony dimming her light.

She walks closer to me. "This is called the line of life." She traces the squiggle mark that goes from her index finger to the middle of her palm. "Do you see how short it is?

She takes my hand and does the same, though mine goes all the way to my wrist. "Mine is too short in comparison to yours or anyone I know. It tells you how long you're going to live."

Luna chews her cheek. Her eyes don't move from my hand. "I'm going to die soon."

Luna's shoulders slump. She turns my hand to the side and traces the three faint lines next to my pinky finger. She sighs, pressing her fingers tight. I think I hear a sob, but maybe it's just my imagination. "You're going to have three children. I bet they're going to be beautiful. Blue-eyed, blond, and smart like you. If you have boys, they're going to be dynamite. But with the biggest heart. The Everhart heart."

A tear runs down her cheek.

"Luna." I dry it.

"I'm okay." She forces a smile, finally looking at me. She's not fine. I want to hold her against me and convince her that everything is going to be all right. Instead, I listen patiently. "Death doesn't scare me. I made my peace with it a long time ago. Like my grandmother, my mother, and my sister, I won't live long. Though, I hope I can say that I live long enough to make a mark in this world."

"You're sick?" I take each hand, looking at them closely. Then her eyes and I can't find anything wrong with her. But I'm not a doctor.

Once she tells me everything we're leaving for Seattle, and I'm calling Anderson. His fiancée has to know every doctor in the area, if not, she can help us find a specialist.

"There's a cure for everything." I think . . . maybe not but . . . what now? I kiss the back of her hands, cup her chin and brush her lips. "If not we will find it, together. I can quit my job, and we can travel the world as we search for the best doctors. Or we can just travel, take you to your favorite places as you enjoy your last days." I swallow hard. "Together."

Don't leave me! That's what I want to say. Please don't fucking leave me. Not when I just found you. This can't be fucking happening. First, my parents and now . . . not her.

"Don't leave me just yet, little moon," I beg her, taking her into my arms. "I just found you. What is it?"

"I'm not sick." She shakes her head, but now I'm lost. "I don't know when or how it'll happen. I just can't be with you." She's quiet for a few minutes, and I start processing what she just said.

"For many, it sounds off, but that's what my father and my abuela have told me ever since I can remember. That I'll die young."

It takes time to piece each word she has said together. This woman bases her life on horoscopes. She doesn't cross the street without verifying that Zodiacs Dot Com, Your Daily Horoscope Dot Com, and Astro Signs Are Us have something good to say about the day she's going to have. Or that she has a contingency plan for the rest of her day to counteract the bad luck. Like the stamp of the Virgin Mary in her wallet. The rosary blessed by the pope. That rabbit foot she carries around like a security blanket; the one her grandmother bought in some obscure town close to Mexico City thirty years ago. And as a contrast to that irrational behavior, Luna doesn't think twice about fighting a dangerous, armed man twice her weight and a foot taller than her.

Her father's words make sense. *You're thirty-one, you don't have much time left.* He believes that just as she does. That's some messed up shit that he's been telling his daughter, and how do I convince her that they are wrong? She can't quit on us because of some stupid superstition. As I consider it. It's not superstition, it's something that the one person she trusts the most has been telling her since she was little.

I snap from the sadness that overtook me as she delivered some fucked-up news. I regain control of my heart, the situation and fuck if she's going to mess up what's happening to us because of her fears.

"I get it, things have been crappy for you. Your mother died, your sister died . . . sorry about your grandmother. What happened to them?" I know about her mother and her sister, but I want her to repeat it out loud and realize that she's not making any sense. She can't compare herself to them.

"My grandmother had lung cancer. She died at thirty-three," she answers, frowning. She's wondering if she had told me this before. She did, but I want her to repeat the circumstances. "Mom was killed, well, you uncovered the story. Sammie overdosed."

"Your lungs are healthy, you have a dangerous job but you know how to defend yourself, and you don't use drugs." I scratch my head.

"But something can happen," she assures me.

Her conviction enrages me. But I keep myself calm because she doesn't need me to be an asshole. She needs someone who understands her—and loves her.

I nod. "Anything can happen to you, or me, or both of us right now."

"If I stay and soon after I die . . . you already lost your parents."

"You lost your mother," I counter. "Life happens, just like death. We aren't meant to live forever. Life is full of unknowns. You can't predict what's going to happen, but you can predict how you live it. Only how much you love while you're here, and how you'll be remembered when you leave."

"I know that, and I'm ready for this unknown, except . . . I don't want to hurt you."

"Then don't hurt me. Let me love you, let yourself fall in love with me." I push my fingers through my hair, walking around the foyer. "I have trouble understanding your quirks, but surprisingly, I've learned to live with them in such a short time. This one though, I can't accept it, Luna."

"No one believes me." She huffs. "I don't expect you to validate me."

"It's not about validation, Luna," I explain to her.

"I've seen the jarring reality of war. I lived in rivers of blood. Innocent people have died for the past two decades. It hurts, and I accept it. I'm not affected by death. I'm in tune with my mortality after everything I have lived through." I huff. "Nonetheless, your news fucked me up, and I won't lie, I almost cried as I thought I'd lose you."

Rubbing the heel of my palm against my chest, I continue. "But I'm aware that one day you're going to leave me, or that I'll leave you."

I tap my foot, choosing my words. "Just don't give up on what we can have because of your superstitious beliefs."

"You think it's that easy, don't you?" The bravado is back in place, the fire ignited. "Some things can't be ignored."

"How about you live your life hoping to beat the odds?" I ignore her feisty tone. "I wonder if my parents would've changed anything if they had known that they would die the way they did."

I smile thinking of Mom and what she'd tell Luna. Maybe what she'd say. "Tomorrow is never guaranteed. So, live the best you can today, don't wait," I repeat Mom's words. "Charlotte Everhart always had some lesson to teach us or a quote that would help us through any problem we told her. I miss her."

Swallowing the rock inside my throat, I look at Luna. "She loved everyone with all she had. She was messy, wild, and put her heart into everything she did. She helped everyone, and she touched the hearts of everyone she met."

"She sounds amazing."

"Mom would've loved you. She never stopped living. Over the phone she reminded me to keep going, to remember everything she'd taught me and teach it to my brothers." I twist my mouth. "She lives in this place, in my brothers' hearts. You can't just close yourself up because your father thinks it's better if you stay under his roof."

She gasps, closing her eyes briefly. There, it's out, and I said it. I hate her fucking father. He brainwashed her, and the worst part is that her grandmother agreed with him. And Luna believes them.

"He fed you fear. And you've fought it so hard that you're a warrior, but you keep pushing everyone out around you." I sigh. "I bet that if he hadn't done that, you would have fallen in love a few times. You pretend to have an open heart, but, woman, you keep that thing under lock and key."

She taps her temple several times. "My father and grandmother have repeated to me that I have to be careful. That I've been given a gift, this life isn't mine. That I have to care for it because it's going to end soon. I'll end up like Mom."

She shakes her head, stroking her arms with her hands. "And I was okay with everything until you barged into it and now I don't want to leave. Not without you."

"Come with me." I head to the terrace, open the door and walk to the wind chimes.

"Mom was a lot like you." I change the subject, letting her think about what I just said. "She drove me crazy, but I adored her. There are two things I miss the most, her chocolate chip cookies and her wise lessons. They seemed useless at the time. They've helped my brothers and me for years. However, I am more like Dad."

"I didn't have the chance to know my mom." Luna hugs herself. "I only have her words, her letters."

"What's that?" I angle my head perking my ear as if listening to something. "Mom says that your mother is proud of you. That your father is wrong, and she thinks you have to delete those useless horoscope apps from your phone. That you'll live many years and you'll have five children because that's what Charlotte wants. Unless, you only want to have one, or none. It's your choice."

She chuckles, pressing her lips together.

"Hey, I'm just telling you what my mother is saying. We have that kind of relationship." I give her a lopsided smile. "She doesn't care that she's in heaven, or that I'm almost forty. She meddles and looks after us, just like your mom does from the sky."

"You think so?"

"Are you calling my mother a liar?"

She rolls her eyes. "What if we continue this and one day we have a child, and she grows up to be like me because I died?"

"What if we have a daughter who is as beautiful and smart as you?" I touch the place on my hand that she touched earlier, where she had concluded that I'd have three children. "Or three of them. And we just love them without thinking about what can happen to them, to us. What if you let yourself think beyond what you believe is possible?"

"It's scary," she says, quietly. "Mom's journal will end and what will I do without knowing what to do next?"

I'm partially confused by this turn of events. Luna seems like a woman who doesn't need anything or anyone. She's independent, appears to know where she's going and how to accomplish it. But underneath the façade she shows to everyone, there's a person who still needs her mother at night, and who hasn't found what makes her heart beat fast. And I wish that as she finds herself, she can see how good we can be together.

"You live your life the way you think it's best."

Mom, don't fail me. I need all those lessons you taught me to help this woman.

"You have to find your purpose and your place in the world." Exhaling, I confess, "The scariest part is learning how to live once you stop doing what you believed was your purpose. Sometimes, you grow out of people, places, or careers. Staying is easy. Deciding to move on is the hardest, bravest thing to do."

"Like a divorce?"

"Or a change of careers," I add. "When my parents died, I decided to enlist. I had to kill those motherfuckers because they had hurt my family."

"I remember you telling me how you quit when it wasn't fulfilling, and searched for a new purpose."

"Exactly." I walk around the terrace, hoping to find some inspiration. Mom would've had some wise words, but I have shit. "I don't know why you decided to become an FBI agent. You are good at analyzing data, at finding patterns and at fighting." I rub my neck, remembering the day we met. "But you're also good at healing and giving."

Her brows furrow.

"I've seen your face while you're handing those Ziploc bags you carry with you. You spend your money on people who need it more than you. And that bright smile while you're doing it, fuck, that's food for my soul. I imagine doing it might be the same for you."

"I love doing it."

"What if I tell you that you can do more?" I offer but don't say more. "You have a lifetime ahead of you, whether it's two years or a hundred, you have a day or about ten thousand to find what makes you happy."

"My grandmother thinks I will only be good at marrying and having children."

Oh, I love that idea. Married to me, we can fuck all day around my apartment. I make a mental note to buy a place in New York. We need privacy over here. Though, when we're not practicing making children, she can find her place in life.

"You take it lightly, Harrison, but I can't imagine leaving the man I love so soon. It would make everything so hard."

My heart stops when she says the man she loves. But I don't say anything because technically she just threw a hypothetical scenario. I throw her a curve ball expecting an answer that might clarify what she just said.

"Why haven't you fallen in love, yet?"

She flinches, shaking her head a couple of times. "I've never allowed myself to do that."

"That's impossible," I scratch my head. "You're sensitive, passionate, sweet."

"Love hurts," she says, and don't I know it.

My heart is grieving after the pounding she just gave us.

"How could I leave peacefully knowing that I'm leaving someone behind? Dad's a big example. He's a zombie." Her face falls. "I would hate myself if I did that to you."

I'm fighting the smile because her face is dead serious, but she's throwing love crumbs, and I can't help but pick them up and swallow them as I take them.

Yes, love me.

Putting my hands on her face, I bend my head and kiss her as if it was the first time. Slow, deep, searing, like there's nothing else in the world I'd rather do but have her writhing in my arms as my tongue makes passionate love to hers. This is the prelude, a promise of what is about to happen between us. The fire begins with this kiss, but once she's blazing, I'll take her to my room and finally show her the fervent love that's growing inside me, inside us.

I'm throwing away Hazel's advice about how to make her fall for me. This is how it's done.

"Hey, we've been looking for you two." Hazel's voice feels like a bucket of ice and cold water.

"Fuck, I'm going to kill her," Luna mumbles.

I start laughing because she barely uses the *f*-word and her eyes are filled with lust and rage.

"You're not ready!" Hazel accuses us, her eyes wide.

Ready? I arch a brow, not getting her.

"It better be important, Beesley," I warn her, turning to look at her. "We're busy, and her fuse is too short. You don't want to see Luna when she's pissed."

"Why are you all dressed up?" I retort, staring at her long gown. "Are we going to the opera? Because if that's the case, pass."

"Dinner at Willow and Hunter's." She taps her watch. "Did you forget?"

I slam a hand against my forehead.

Fuck.

"How important is it?" I can't go, simple.

"Very important. You should dress up, and expect a ceremony. I think it's . . ." she looks around and whispers, ". . . a wedding."

"How do you know, nosy?"

"Willow has been avoiding me all week, but kept asking about caterers, flowers, and quartets." She shows me her phone. "Either she's organizing a funeral or a wedding. I choose the latter."

"You better be right, Beesley."

"Luna?" *Please say I don't want to go.*

"I might have a dress or two for the occasion. But I have to go back home."

"The car is waiting for us, Luna." Hazel who has a knack for micromanaging everyone's life and fix last minute fuck ups is here to save us.

Checking my watch, I realize that we only have about an hour to get ready. We can't fool around. I have to be there for my brother. "I'll pick you up in an hour. We have to finish this . . . conversation."

"I'm looking forward to witnessing how you build your case, Harry." Her voice is sultry, and I'm ready to pin her against the wall and fuck her.

But I won't.

First, we make love.

30

LUNA

Hazel guessed right. Willow and Hunter organized a surprise wedding. Their patio is decorated with twinkling lights, volcano color roses, and candles. It's beautiful, simple and romantic. The atmosphere is peaceful.

Everyone is ready for Willow to make an appearance. When the string quartet starts playing "Vivaldi's Spring," she and her grandfather walk out to the patio and toward the gazebo at the end of the outdoor room. She wears a classy, strapless, white gown.

Hunter waits for her with a big smile on his face and love in his eyes. He sports a tuxedo; his shirt is unbuttoned on the top. He's not wearing a tie. Harrison and Scott are by his side as his best men. Hazel is her maid of honor, and I'm a bridesmaid. Because according to them, I'm already part of the family. And although it sounds crazy that they've opened the doors to a complete stranger, I love it. Looking at the small bouquet, I wonder if I'll ever take this step. I never contemplated it, but with Harrison . . .

When Willow reaches Hunter, she hugs her grandfather and kisses Hunter on the cheek.

"This is my first time officiating a wedding, so be patient." Fitz stares at the paper that he's holding.

"Hunter, Willow. You two are the perfect couple, and I couldn't be more thankful that you chose me to be the one performing the ceremony." He looks to the left, then to the right and smiles.

He looks at the paper he holds. "You should've given me a little more notice, like an hour, or two. First I say that we're gathered to witness the union of these two people." He turns his attention to the guests. "I should ask if anyone objects but I will skip that."

"We should've hired someone," Hunter protests. "Why can't you do this simple? You don't have to do much."

"Exchange the vows." He looks around, ignoring Hunter and smiling at the guests. "It's my first time, be patient."

"You're doing great, Fitz." Willow touches his arm.

She straightens her back and clears her throat. "Hunter, you're my everything. My air, my sun, my love. You're that happy beat I need when my heart is about to stop. You're poetry to my soul. You're the one person who discovered my flaws and loved me more because of them. Your love takes away my insecurities and leaves me with a blanket of warmth that keeps me safe when it's hard for me to breathe on my own. I hope that I'm enough to fill your heart with love and strong enough to be your rock when you're down. But most of all, I promise to love you for eternity."

He leans in, kissing her teary eyes. "I love you." He takes a breath and continues. "Willow, I never believed in love at first sight. But I feel that my soul has been in love with yours since the beginning of time. The day we met you felt familiar. As I got to know you, it felt as if I began to remember who you are. My soul mate, my companion, and the woman I hope to spend the next eternity with. I've loved you since always. I'll love you for always. I just hope that you'll share with me your darkest days and your brightest nights."

Her words are beautiful, but his words and the emotion he adds pull my heartstrings. I've never seen two people more in love. That's what I want, for someone to just love me as I am. My heart skips a beat when I find Harrison's eyes, and he blows me a kiss.

"Stop." Fitz breaks the silent conversation I was about to have with Harrison.

Fitz shows his paper. "Rings first. According to Wikipedia, the kiss isn't happening, yet."

The room bursts into laughter.

"First time, people," he reminds us. "My first times are always messy and—"

"TMI," Hazel whispers, patting dry her cheeks with the handkerchief that Scott handed her.

"We hired a minister and a clown."

Fitz glares at Harrison. "You didn't hire me and who has the rings?"

The rest of the ceremony doesn't take more than two minutes. When Hunter leans in for a kiss, everyone cheers, and claps. At that moment, waiters holding trays with champagne flutes begin to waltz around the patio.

"Thank you, everyone, for joining us tonight." Hunter raises his glass. "We wanted to do something simple, just with family and friends. My bride and I are leaving for our honeymoon, but please enjoy the small buffet and again, thank you for sharing this moment with us."

Now I understood why they suggested that pictures were done before the ceremony. I walk close to them, hugging Hunter then Willow and wishing them the best. I've yet to get to know them better, but I hope that I stick around a little longer, with Harrison.

"Dude, what happened to the embarrassing toast from the groomsmen?" Harrison complains. "I'm ready to talk about the time—"

"That's one of the million reasons why this wedding is so small and fast. You,"—Fitz pats Harrison's chest taking the second flute —"no one wants to hear you giving poor little Hunter shit."

"I love you, but you're annoying, Fitz." Hunter shakes his head. "Thank you for coming, Harrison. You can save the big toast for Scott's wedding. Or Fitz's."

The four brothers talk over one another, and they seem to understand what's happening, but I choose to walk away, toward the food.

I'm starving. That hamburger we ate in Baltimore at eleven wasn't enough to satisfy my appetite.

"Here," Willow says, handing me her bouquet.

"Umm." I stare at it. "I'll save it for later?

"No, it's yours."

"What?"

"I'm not tossing it. I'm handing it."

"Like tag, you're it?" I push it back to her. "I'm not playing, but thank you."

What happened to tradition? Those old times when the brides-maids would rush forward, struggling to find the best spot and become the chosen one. They pull each other's hair, disarray their gowns and all because they want to be the one to snatch the bouquet and find their prince charming.

"Harrison asked me to give it to you." She winks at me, tilting her head toward the Everhart men.

I turn around, finding him, walking toward us. "Congratulations, Willow. I wish you nothing but happiness, sweetheart."

"Thank you." She kisses him on the cheek.

"You and I are leaving too." He gives me a playful smile.

"We are?" I play coy, untying his tie.

His lips touch my ear, and he murmurs, "Yes, and I got us a reservation at the Four Seasons."

I press my legs together, squeezing my eyes as I savor his words. *Finally.*

"You've got to be shitting me." He sighs. "What did I do to deserve this kind of fucking torture?"

"Everhart, distance," Tiago orders.

"What are you doing here?" I protest.

31

HARRISON

"Do you have your passport?" Tiago asks.

"Always," I respond, turning to look at Luna. I don't want to leave her.

"Where are we going?" I ask resigned, and ready to die a virgin. At least it feels like it's been a hundred years since I've had sex, and at this pace, I'm never going to have it again.

Ever.

Tiago hands me over his phone. "Yeah?"

I angle my head, grab Luna's hand and we walk toward the library.

"We need you," Bradley is on the other line.

"I take it there's no choice." I sigh, putting him on speaker. "Where to?"

"Mexico City. There's been a kidnapping, and we have to rescue the kid before they kill him."

"Don't they usually ask for money?" I ask, huffing.

"They did, but the family is afraid that these guys might claim the money and still kill the child. It happened to their neighbors a couple of months ago."

I close my eyes for a few seconds. "What's the plan?"

"The plane is waiting for you. Call me when you're in the air so we can strategize."

"Who else is joining us?" Tiago asks.

"Hawk and I," Bradley responds. "See you soon."

Luna bites her lip, she looks at her brother and then at me. "I can help," she murmurs.

Scratching my chin, I try to find a way to tell her that she's not coming with us. I want to hire her, but I can't just bring her with me. Thankfully, it's her brother who breaks the news to her.

"You're staying."

"That's it, '*you're staying*'?" She mocks her brother's voice. "Should I sit by the door and wait for you while you come back, or get dinner ready by five?"

She squares her frame, lifts her chin, and gives me a defiant look. "What happened to being partners? You wanted me on your team, to work for you. How can I trust you when you say one thing but do a different one?"

She turns around, tossing her hands. "*Carajo!* Men, they are all the same."

I lower my head, pressing my lips tight. I hated that stony expression she had as she left the library. What do I do? She's right, I want her as my teammate. My partner. If I break my promises, she's never going to trust me.

"What does she mean by working for you, Everhart?" Tiago growls. "Dad told me what you did with her mother's file." He shakes his head. "What the fuck are you doing?"

"I'm being her person. She needed the truth. You could've given that to her."

He laughs. "My father doesn't like me. I don't want to give him more reasons to hate me."

"How good is Luna?"

"She's not coming with us." Tiago's warning voice is useless.

"Big guy, think what our mission involves. A family wanting their child back. Bad guys asking for money. If we don't find the kid soon, he could lose a finger, an arm, or his life." I paint the scenario I'm picturing.

We've dealt with kidnappings before. One time, the family received a finger as proof of life, and as a warning that next time it'd be his head.

"She's good, and they are wasting her talent. We can make a difference today, and give her a chance to move to a better place, meaning our company."

And I can't leave her. I have to be with her.

I text Bradley.

Harrison: *Agent Santillan is coming with.*

Bradley: *Give me one good reason why I should agree to that.*

Harrison: *Other than the file you stole from the FBI? I'd say she's capable of holding her ground, and she focuses on rescuing missing people.*

Bradley: *Fine, you babysit.*

I send a message to Jensen, Scott's assistant, requesting he pack my usual bag. He can meet us at Hazel's where we can pick up a few things for Luna before we leave.

"This is a bad idea," Tiago calls after me.

It doesn't take me long to find her. She's leaning against the door-frame on the patio, watching the few guests eating.

"Where is everyone?"

She shrugs. "Hunter and Willow left for the airport. They said that Jensen is unavailable. That you'll know what that means."

Fuck, I run a hand through my hair.

"Hazel and Scott decided to leave. Fitz left with one of the musicians."

"Do you have your passport at home?" I kiss the side of her long neck.

Her eyes brighten, but her mouth tightens.

"I need an answer, we are leaving, now."

"I'm always prepared," she responds, staring down at her phone then back at me.

"That's my girl." I brush her lips with mine. "We have to take you home so you can pack some clothing. I have a case for you that I think you're going to love."

☆ ☆ ☆

Tiago pulls me to the side while Luna is getting her bag.

"We can't just take her with us." His entire body tightens his jaw clenches. "This ain't a field trip to the zoo. She's all my father has. If something happens to either one of my siblings, I think he would die."

He doesn't say it out loud, but his world would collapse as well. They aren't as close as my siblings and me, but he loves her. I understand. If something were to happen to my brothers, it'd destroy me. They're all I have.

"You have to believe in Luna," I suggest, treading my case with him. Not because he can convince me, but I have to make sure that his head will be in the game once we are rescuing this kid. "She can help us find him faster. I get it, you see her as your baby sister. But man, if she wants, she could take us down just by snapping her fingers."

"That's an exaggeration, Everhart." Luna walks into the hallway dressed in a black shirt and a pair of black jeans. She stretches her arms, wrapping them around my neck and kissing me hard. "But I appreciate your confidence in my skills."

"Luna, what the fuck are you doing?" Tiago scares the fuck out of me with his screams.

"Kissing, it's called kissing, Tiago." She gives me a quick peck and releases me.

"I like the way you say my last name, Agent Santillan." I wink at her, taking her bag and her hand. "I'm looking forward to working with you during this mission."

"She has a job," Tiago insists, poking the elevator button.

"They are wasting her talent at the Bureau," I counter with the same stuff I told him before. "We need her. Wouldn't you rather know that she's doing what she loves and have her working *with* you?"

"This is the last time you talk about me as if I'm not in the room," she warns us, her eyes firing up. "I haven't said that I'm quitting the Bureau," Luna intercedes. "This is a one-time mission. Why would I want to leave all my benefits, for you? I believe in bringing justice, not . . . what is it that you do?"

"Defend the innocent and help those who can't help themselves," I inform her. "While also doing some side protection for rich people for money. We do a lot, Luna."

I stare at her arms and shake my head. "No, you have to leave all that shit behind. The last time we traveled with them, it took you hours to take them off and put them on."

"He doesn't know, does he?" Tiago and Luna share a smile while she shakes her head.

Then, he changes his side. "You should join us. Lucas should too."

"Dude, now you're adding more people?" I complain, trying to remember who the fuck Lucas is. "Luc, his name is Luc." I snap my fingers when I remember they are talking about their brother.

Tiago shakes his head in exasperation. "You offered her a job, right?" His voice is loud. "I think we should offer one to our brother too. Luna and Lucas could be a good addition to our company."

Tiago's somber face makes my back straighten and my attitude change.

"I can vouch for Luna. I've witnessed her kick-ass movements." My hand covers my neck at the memory of that sharp thing pointed to my head that is now holding Luna's hair up.

"We can use someone like her." I look at both of them before stepping into the elevator. "How about Lucas, is he as good as you two?"

"He's like Dad," Luna offers. She chews her lip looking at Tiago who shrugs. "But I doubt he'd accept the job."

"Lucas will, if you do it first," Tiago utters, then he flashes me an angry glare. "Stop kissing her hand. Do not touch my sister."

"I will only stop if she protests." I smirk at her, waiting for a comeback.

The doors open on the third floor. I pull Luna closer to my body, snaking my arm around her waist. An old couple steps into the elevator. They eye us briefly, nodding curtly and turn back around to stare at the closing doors.

"Have a good day," Luna calls after them once we arrive in the lobby and they step away without acknowledging us. "Rude."

"Not many people are as friendly as you are, Luna. Actually, only a few are friendly in this city." I bend my neck, kissing her lips lightly. "But don't let this place change you. I like the way you brighten everything around you."

"You're a sweet talker, Everhart."

"Just to you." I kiss her again, this time I don't rush it. I savor her sweet lips but stop myself before I have to push her back into the elevator and to her room.

32

LUNA

I settle back in my seat as I process the information Harrison provided me. The forensic information is easy to digest. Five-year-old male, brown eyes, blond hair, forty-three inches tall, fifty-two pounds, with a scar on the corner of his left eyebrow. He was last seen wearing his school uniform.

The last time his nanny saw him was at the playground. Witnesses say that he was in the park playing with his friends. A couple of large dogs that could've been German Shepherds or Dobermans charged toward the children. Everyone began to scramble, adults and kids. The owner appeared right behind them, and though it took him time, he was able to control them and take them with him. Once everyone settled, little Esteban wasn't around.

An hour later, the father received a call from an untraceable phone. The voice on the other end demanded a million dollars in exchange for their son. According to the father, the voice sounded like it was coming from a machine. Three hours later, a box with the shoes the little boy was wearing and a note appeared on their doorstep. The note said they shouldn't call the police, and they had seventy-two hours to respond to their demand if they wanted to see him alive.

"Unmarked bills. They didn't ask for an untraceable transfer,"

I repeat, leaning my head against the window and watching the fluffy clouds under us. "You said that something similar happened with the kid next door too. Do we have more on that case?"

"There's no such thing as an untraceable transfer," Harrison clarifies.

"There are a few similarities between one and the other," Tiago responds.

The sound of typing makes me turn in his direction. Harrison's the one at the computer. My brother's eyes are focused on his iPad, and he continues giving me what I need, but without giving me the slightest glance.

"The kid next door disappeared during a school field trip," Tiago says. "His parents blamed the teacher and the principal for their negligence. There's a lawsuit pending."

"Were they the same age?"

"No, the child next door was eight, and they requested less money. Only two hundred thousand," he says.

"The two houses share something. And it's more than the neighborhood. Nannies, housekeepers, they share an activity; like soccer. What is it? We have to interview everyone."

"We don't have much time to do that. They gave them seventy-two hours. We only have fifty left to find this kid," Harrison says evenly, still typing. "And if we start interviewing people, we might be alerting the kidnappers that we are onto them. Is there something else you can use in the meantime?"

The tightness of my chest increases as my heartbeat accelerates.

"Wait!" My voice comes out harsh. "No one should know we are on our way. Whoever is doing this might be an insider. The point of not calling the police is that they want their money without losing the kid to rescuers."

Neither one turns to look at me. I bite back a snarl at their lack of attention. They want me to help them, but they are both focused on their screens.

"Can you pull any footage of the CCTV around the park?" I ask as I contemplate other ways to find out more without interviewing witnesses.

"Mason is pulling the video as we speak. He's letting the people who hired us know that it might take us a couple of days to reach them," Harrison responds.

I take the folder on top of the table, looking at the picture of the little boy. There's a glow in those eyes and sweetness in that smile. We have to reach him soon before it's all lost.

"I love that you included me, but I'm not crazy about a child being abducted." I put the picture down and close the folder again. "If Mason can do some research on the other kid. How did they return his body?"

"The file says that the parents delivered the money four hours after the deadline. A day later they received the body inside of a black bag." Harrison glances at me, his eyebrows drawing together. He takes a deep breath. "The note read, 'You were too late.'"

My heart thunders, I clasp my hands together. "Was there an autopsy that could confirm the TOD?"

"TOD?" Harrison frowns.

"Time of death," I clarify. "They could've killed the kid right after kidnapping him. It's happened."

The autopsy was waived because the reason of death was obvious. They slit his throat. There's no further information about it. It'd be helpful to learn whose idea it was to waive it. Better yet, who thought about not having the autopsy? Was it the parents, a cop, someone in the family? I hate to think that a dirty cop could be involved, but Dad has met many during his career. In some countries, they paid them so little that they accept money from criminals to protect them.

"Are these the first kidnappings around the area?" I study the plane's cabin and sigh because there's nowhere to set a board with pictures and links to the abductee.

"Unfortunately, no. These are the first cases in the past couple of months, though."

That is good news but still awful. I open the folder again. My chest aches at seeing the picture of Esteban one more time. A rock settles into the pit of my stomach. I need more data to find the pattern. Criminals who make a living out of extortion tend to duplicate their behavior with only slight changes.

"Did someone interview the dog owner?"

"They called off the investigation right after they received the call," Harrison informs me.

I press my forehead to the table, nodding a few times. Of course, they called it off.

"If I needed the report on each of the kidnappings that have happened for the past months, how long would it take?" I throw the question up in the air but hope that maybe Harrison can give me an answer.

My other option is to map the area and go on a manhunt. Which is pulled out of a suspense novel I've been reading for the past couple of weeks. However, I am aware that it wouldn't work as well as it does in fiction.

"What else do you need?" Harrison never turns his attention to me.

"Places where they happened, footage, pictures. I have to find the pattern. There's a pattern somewhere." Inhaling, I recall their request of not calling the police. They'll know what's going on around the parents' house. Either they are insiders, or they are connected with the law-enforcement of the city. "Police involvement. As in I want to know their response to each case, if they help to investigate, took it lightly or what. Do they assume these are different criminals? And how many kids have come home too?"

He checks his watch, then the screen and finally turns to look at me. "We land in three hours. Mason and Anderson will be landing in about twenty minutes. He hopes to have most of the information you requested ready in about one, maybe two."

My shoulders relax, but my head snaps. "That's a week's worth of work and you're telling me you're going to have it in a couple of hours?"

"Most of it." He closes his laptop and sets it to the side. "We can't interview people or investigate the places because we're not there. However, if there's data in the computers, we can hack it."

"Do you think everything is connected, Luna?" Tiago puts down his tablet.

I nod, tapping the folder. "At least a few of them, if not all of them. I just don't understand why no one has done something to stop this."

Harrison reaches out for my hand as he rises from his seat. "We'll try to bring him home."

33

HARRISON

"The dog owner, huh?" Tiago points at the multiple pictures of the guy.

I look at the board that Mason and Luna created. I've seen him work millions of times. He's fast and good at what he does. But adding Luna to his process was mind-blowing. Or maybe it was adding him to Luna's process that made this case one of the best I've worked on in the past few years. Everything happened fast enough, and they were thorough about it. Once Mason landed, he sent Luna some of the information he had gathered. She took my computer, and they began chatting. A few minutes later, they connected through our company's video system. Luna suggested the board he started on the wall of our hotel suite. Since then, the two of them have been working on putting the pieces together to find the kid.

We all suggested motives and found similarities between one case or the other. Each crime had been different, but they all have a few similarities. They sent Hawk, Tiago, and me to different parts of the city to gather information to give them some live footage without them having to move from the room.

Around midnight, Tiago, Hawk, and I went out to scout the park, the kid's house, and the neighborhood. Luna insisted that the perpetrator lived around the ritzy vicinity. She was right. A couple of hours after we left, I called them letting them know what we'd seen. Each house in the neighborhood is armed with a system connected to the same security company. The company is from New Jersey, and it belongs to another company. After tracking four pseudonyms, we found Oliver Wilson.

As we put all the names, companies, and photographs together, we gathered that he was at least our number one suspect, if not the guy. Then, they matched the dog owner with his picture. Hawk and I surveyed the house. We tried to break into the house, but according to the infrared report, they have a lot of guests inside the five-bedroom home. Thank God for small miracles. The residence across the street from Mr. Wilson is empty and for sale. We were able to break in and start setting up some of our equipment.

"He isn't the dog owner. He's a financial advisor to the parents of all these children," Luna explains. "The kidnappings didn't start until a couple of months after he arrived."

With her laser pointer, she shows the northern part of the city. "He lived there for four years under the name of Dawson Malone. Eighteen children were abducted. Only five came home." She smiles. "However, only ten bodies were returned. We have a theory, but I won't bring that up until later."

"Please, don't change the current conversation. We focus on this first, then we talk about the other piece," Mason encourages.

"Why does he change the ransom?" Hawk is enthralled with the board.

She stops right in front of the files, patting them with her palm. "The guy knows their worth. That's why the amounts never match."

She points at the pictures we gathered from the CCTV during Esteban's abduction. "The guy uses a way to distract everyone around and he or—" She points at another image where a woman is walking Esteban away from the scene— "His wife snatches the target while someone else is part of the distraction."

Her head hits her chest. "Also, that's why the older children never

come home. Because they might recognize them." Her voice loses
force, her eyes have a little moisture.

"Do you think Esteban is alive?"

"That's a fifty-fifty possibility," Luna answers. "He's old enough to
recognize them. Esteban went willingly with the woman in the
picture. He could be dead, or . . ." She sighs. "Already left the country
and he's being sold to a new family."

She presses a hand to her heart. "We have to find him. Mason
already has people searching the CCTV of the airport and keeping an
eye at the gates. If they are driving him away, they'll do it themselves."

"Why hasn't anyone noticed it?" Tiago walks around. "He's
making loads of money, you can't hide that."

"He's wealthy. And he's laundering the cash." Mason is the one
who responds. "He uses the arcades, nail salons, dry cleaners, and
other businesses he owns around the city. Then, he transfers it to his
account in the Cayman Islands."

Luna's eyes land on Mason, she smiles at him. "Now that we
know each other better, can I marry your brain?"

"Just my brain?" He shakes his head. "I'm flattered, but my wife
wouldn't be too happy with that."

"Then, just your computers." She shrugs. "They're capable of
everything I need."

"Luna," Tiago protests.

She rolls her eyes. "Chill, Santiago." She points at me. "I doubt
he'll let me act on it."

"She's right," I agree with her.

I'd be jealous if I didn't see her teasing smile stamped on that
beautiful, smart mouth of hers. Where has she been hiding all my life?

"What's the plan?" Anderson checks his watch. "We don't have
much time left. The crew is already waiting at the empty house for
our instructions."

"We have a crew!" Luna claps, her bracelets chiming.

"But we're not sure where they're hiding the kid." Tiago brings up
an important point.

"If he's still alive and in town, he's either at an abandoned place or at this man's home," Luna suggests, moving toward the list of properties we found under his name, his companies name or his wife's name. "Either way, I propose that we enter his house and either locate the kid or torture Mr. and Mrs. Wilson until they tell us where they have Esteban."

"There's not going to be any torturing." Mason glares at her.

She looks at her phone, counts her fingers and then glances at the four of us. "How soon can we go in? If my profiling is correct, they have an operation almost as big as ours. Maybe even weapons and professionals to protect them. He's smart and has plenty of resources. I bet that he can give us a fight—if we let him. We won't allow him to scratch us." She places her hands on her waist and says, "Just one thing, I'm going inside with you. I want to kick his ass. At least castrate him. Plus, the kid needs someone he can trust."

"And there she is, my bloodthirsty-justice-loving-ass-kicker girl," I point out, walking to her and taking her into my arms. "I was wondering where you'd hidden her."

She smiles, wiggling her way out of my grasp. "I'm bloodthirsty, but not your girl, Everhart."

Luna salutes at everyone as she walks to the adjacent room. She stops at the door. "I'm taking a shower and getting dressed. Brief me once you have figured out a plan of attack."

☆ ☆ ☆

"This is not a good idea," I protest, looking at Luna who wears a flouncy dress, her sandals, and her chopsticks holding her hair—three of them. "You're going inside that house like that. Unarmed and willingly."

My pulse is racing, my jaw clenches. I divert my attention to Mason. "You're sending her just like that," I said disapprovingly.

Luna turns to study me. Her face is unreadable. Those full lips pressed together into a thin line.

"Are you new to the team?" Mason's chest puffs. His chin rises, and his frown deepens. "I've never sent anyone, 'just like that,' Ever-hart. There's always a purpose and a backup." His voice booms through the room.

"Also, there's you. The sniper on top of the roof, ready to pull the trigger if something is about to go wrong."

I curl my hands into fists getting closer to him. "She isn't wearing any armor." I touch my bulletproof jacket. "There's no space on her body to hide a weapon. Please, enlighten me, what is the plan?"

"She's looking to buy the house across the street. Tiago is her real estate agent, and they'll go across the street to ask them questions about the neighborhood."

Luna taps her stomach twice. "Like any other pregnant woman, I'm going to have to do a quick stop to their restroom."

"Again, she doesn't have any weapons with her."

"She does," he corrects me.

"But Luna doesn't need them. Tiago is with her, and you'll be watching her from across the street. I gave you the infrared goggles. But if you have a problem with any of that, you can stay behind."

"*She* is here. I already told you that I hate when you talk as if I'm not in the room." Luna marches toward us putting herself between us and pushing us to opposite sides.

Her eyes find mine. Her hands rest slightly on my chest. "Are you doubting yourself or me?" Her chin is up. Her eyes are burning with that fire she had when I broke into her house. She looks like a spitting cat. "Because your attitude is telling me that you either don't trust what I can do or that I shouldn't trust you."

She crosses her arms. "Which is it?"

Her nostrils flare, her skin tone darkens. "I expect this behavior from my superiors at the FBI. Not from you. I want you to treat me the same way you do the rest of the guys." She smooths her dress. "At least during the mission."

God, she's sexier than fuck when she's angry. Fuck, I'm an asshole. I want to grab her by the waist and kiss her deeply, but I don't do it. Because this is work, and we have to be professionals.

"You're right." I sigh, feeling sorry for snapping at everyone, and at her the most. "I trust you."

It's just that the fucking pandemonium of emotions that she's causing inside my chest are preventing me from thinking straight.

The lust I have for her still predominates all those feelings. But there are so many new ones blossoming inside my heart. They are spreading like wildflowers during the summer rain. I can't fathom the thought of her being hurt. How do I push them away while we are working? Do I want to drive them away or will they help me during the operation?

I should at least forget about them for the time being. She needs me to concentrate on her. Focus on what's about to come.

"As long as you're under my watch, nothing will happen to you."

Finally, a corner of her mouth quirks.

"I trust you too," she says, stretching her neck and cupping my chin. "As soon as we are out of this room, I'm one of the guys. Don't forget it."

She gives me a peck and saunters away. Her feet light as feathers, her sunshine spreading around the room.

"A hundred," Hawk pulls a bill setting it on the dresser, "he's proposing in less than a month."

"She's my sister, asshole." Tiago slams his hand on the table, his eyes filled with rage just like his sister's. "Stay away from her, Everhart. After this shit ends, I'm killing you."

"Too late, T." Bradley takes the bill. "Though, I think I won the last bet. Didn't I say he'd fall for her when they met?"

"Whatever," I say, snatching the money from his hold and walking to the door. "The rest of the team is waiting for us. Let's go and save this kid."

34

HARRISON

Luna and Tiago are walking across the street to the Wilson's home after touring the empty house. According to our scouts and the infrared equipment, there are at least ten adults inside the house. Mason has another team in Seattle running a background on the couple in hopes of finding fraud or kidnapping charges in the United States to take them home and make sure they pay for the shit they've done. In this country, they might end up paying their way out in less than a year.

"I've reached Esteban's parents." Bradley's voice comes through the communicator. "They are aware that we are here and ready to bring their boy home. I didn't mention where we are, but if anyone from the inside reports that to Oliver, he might be trying to escape soon. Keep your eyes open."

There's a long pause. "Everyone in place?"

I scan the area, nod at Hawk, and speak, "Can I just say that you look hot, babe?" I touch my earpiece. "That number makes your ass look tight. I could tap it all night."

"Kick him, Hawk," Tiago mumbles through the communicator. "How many times do I have to remind you, she's my little sister?"

"Please don't kick him," Luna pleas. "I want to be the one slitting his throat. I warned you, Everhart. Don't call me babe."

"I was talking to Tiago, Luna. That's my way of letting him know that everything is safe and I'm bored to tears. But I confess, you look hot too," I add, looking through my binoculars. "Unfortunately, I can't see your curves with the dress you're wearing today. But I'm enjoying your long, tanned legs. We should go to the beach this weekend."

"Stay quiet, Everhart," Tiago warns me. "One more word and I swear I'll have someone shoot you."

"I want to see who'll be brave enough to shoot me. They'll be dead before their finger touches the trigger." I roll my shoulders, trying to loosen the knots on my back.

"What is it now?" Hawk murmurs. "Your family is far away. Why are you behaving like a two-year-old?"

I grind my teeth, clenching my jaw. *Luna*, I mouth, tilting my head toward the other side of the street.

"Imagine she's Aspen. How would you feel?" I set the scenario in a way he'll understand.

His eyebrow arches at the mention of his fiancée. Luna isn't my fiancée, but she's the most important person in my world. He nods twice and pats my back.

From the corner of my eye, I notice movement on the right side of the house. "The garage door is opening," I announce, dropping the binoculars and grabbing my weapon. "Someone might be going grocery shopping, or escaping."

"Can I help you?" I hear a rough voice through the communicator.

Focusing on the door, I see him. Oliver Wilson. He's shorter than Tiago, about five inches taller than Luna. He's lean but doesn't look too strong. At least not from where I'm watching.

"*Buen dia*," Luna greets him.

"Sorry, my Spanish is terrible," he says, blocking the entrance. "But whatever it is, I'm not interested." He taps the small bronze plate next to the doorbell.

"Oh, nice sign." She smiles.

"I assure you, we're not here to talk to you about God, vacuums, or any charity." Luna brushes a strand of her hair behind her ear, straightens up and pushes her tits with her arms. "We are here looking for a house. Maybe, we'll be your neighbors across the street."

She turns slightly to her left, pointing at the house where I am.

"Call the realtor," the guy suggests, his eyes focused on her chest.

I move the target to his forehead. *Motherfucker! Move your eyes away from her, or I swear her tits will be the last thing you ever see.*

"Oh, that part is over. Actually, we just finished the walkthrough," she continues. "It's lovely. Cozy and it's big enough to raise a family. But I'm wondering if you could tell us more about the neighborhood? I've lived in the US for the past ten years, and the city has changed so much."

"Look, lady, this isn't a good time for me." Oliver looks around, signaling his wife. Then, looking at Tiago who hasn't uttered a word. "*No buen tiempo,*" he translates in Spanish as he stares at T.

Tiago blinks twice, crossing his arms. He's served the guy his *I'm about to kick your ass* glare.

"I need a shadow for that car in case Luna can't stop them from leaving," Mason requests. There's urgency in his voice. "Santillan, ask him more questions. Bat your eyelashes or . . . keep him engaged. We're going to try to break in through the back. I've disabled their cameras and the alarm system. Once I give you the okay, you can force your way through the main door."

"Shall I shoot him?" I question, focusing on my target.

"Not yet," he answers.

"And when you do, don't kill him. We want him alive," Bradley responds, exhaling loudly. "T, nod if you're ready. Everhart, you know what to do."

My heart beats fast as I get ready to shoot. My finger is on the trigger, my eyes set on the guy.

"Are you sure you can't give us a few minutes?" Luna touches his forearm, not moving it. Her left leg bends lightly. "We're driving back to the airport. Our flight leaves in a couple of hours. I just want to know about the area. This neighborhood seems *friendly and safe*. But we want to know more about the places where we can invest . . ." she clears her throat, "our money. Schools are important."

The man narrows his gaze at Luna, then looks to Tiago. "You'll have to excuse me, but I have to leave. I'm on a deadline."

He takes a step forward. Luna swings his arm counterclockwise, kicking the back of his knee with her right leg. He falls on his back. With a swift movement, she lifts her arm, pulling one of the chopsticks from her hair. Squatting, she points it against his throat. "I'm on a deadline too, Mr. Wilson. Where is Esteban?"

Tiago sets his industrial boot on top of his forehead. "I suggest you answer her."

"You're too late," he says, laughing.

"To kill you?" Luna says. "I don't think so."

"Big guy, there's movement in—"

A gunshot interrupts me. I fire my weapon, the first gunman drops to the ground, right by the entrance. But there's a second one. Tiago moves his entire body to the left, covering Luna's from the second round of bullets.

"Motherfucker," he groans. "This hurts like hell."

I move the target, shooting the man who is coming toward them with an AK-47. Luna throws her weapon like a knife, hitting his forehead. The two men fall almost simultaneously to the ground. With all the commotion, Wilson rolls to the side, pushing Luna away from him.

"Watch my back, Harry. There're more men inside coming after us. Someone help my brother," Luna orders.

Faster than I would've thought possible, she leaps to her feet and takes out another one of her sharp hair accessories. She throws it toward Wilson, hitting him right on his spine. His back arches. The hit makes him stop briefly, but then he continues jogging toward the car. Luna pulls one of her bracelets, straightening and using it as a blade. She tosses it as if it were a Ninja star hitting him on the side of the neck. Then a second one lands on his left arm.

She wears weapons, not jewelry. What the fuck? I went through airport security with an armed woman. And no one fucking noticed.

This woman is my fucking hero.

I move my attention toward the door, shooting two men who are opening fire as they rush toward the entrance. Tiago is no longer on the floor. Where the fuck did he go?

"T?"

"We are inside," Bradley responds. "Keep an eye on the outside details."

"Shoot the tires," Luna orders, taking her shoes off and speeding toward him. "Someone stop that car before they leave."

I fire three rounds to the back tires. "Done. Whoever is on the ground, go and help the driver," I say as she's about to leave the car. I shoot her once on the left leg and twice on her hand. "She's going to need medical attention."

My eyes go back to Luna. She is about to catch up with Wilson. When she's right next to him, she pulls the stick from his back making him jolt. Then, she kicks him in the knee, flips to the left, and kicks him with the other leg in the jaw.

Wilson groans, as his head, snaps back and he falls to the ground. He rolls on the pavement and Luna pulls one of her ribbon bracelets off her arm. Her foot goes around his neck, and she lowers her body, grabbing his hands.

"I suggest you stay put and start talking. Where's Esteban?" She ties his hands together, then repeats the same operation on his feet.

"You can kill me," Wilson says. "I won't talk."

She laughs, shaking her head. "Lovely wish, but I'd rather turn you into the authorities."

"And what do you think the authorities will do to me, bitch?"

Luna touches her sternum. "Oh no, you called me a bad name." She punches him right in the nose. I hear the crack of his bones.

"Fuck. She's insane." Hawk clears his throat.

"What's next, whore, cunt? I don't care what you say." She pulls his hair, moving his head closer to where her face is. "Right now, I *own* you. You're *my* bitch. And by authorities, I meant the FBI." She releases her hold and pats his cheeks.

Luna pulls the last stick holding her hair. She draws a line across his neck with the sharp edge. Wilson's eyes widen. "I'm losing my patience. Tell me where Esteban is?" Her voice is vicious.

"We found him," Tiago announces.

Mason has the kid in his arms. "Hawk, call Aspen. Esteban is unconscious. He's breathing, but we found some medication next to him. I texted her the picture. Tell her that I think they were drugging him. I want to know if we can do something to help as we drive him to the hospital."

"You got it, boss." Hawk takes his phone.

The boss looks around, arriving at one of the vans we drove. "Everyone pick up and let's move this party. The forensic team should arrive here soon. Please, go through the house and take all the evidence that you can gather."

"Santillan, what have I told you about littering the streets?" He shakes his head. "Untie his feet and pick him up. We're sending him and his wife on a first-class trip to FBI headquarters."

Luna does as she's told and orders him to stand up.

"I can't feel my legs," Wilson complains.

"Oops." Luna sighs, her shoulders slumping. "I might have damaged his spinal nerves." She shrugs. "Who knows what happened; I'm not a doctor."

Bradley grins at her. "You did great, kid. I think I like you more than your brother."

The tightness in my body dissipates when she climbs in the van with Bradley. We have to clean the area, and I won't see her for several hours, but I know she's safe. And fuck, she was amazing. I have to have her. We have to have her on our team.

Harrison: *You did awesome, little moon.*

Luna: *You weren't bad, Harry. Thank you for having my back.*

35

LUNA

I toss my bag under my seat. The adrenaline is finally setting in after the longest day I've had since college. Thirty-six hours of continuous rush and zero sleep. I've drunk what feels like gallons of matcha green tea and coffee during the past couple of days. Closing the case wasn't my responsibility, but after the past five strenuous hours, I'd rather have done the paperwork. After we arrived at the hospital, we spent several hours answering questions to the local authorities. I called Lucas to arrange the transfer of the Wilsons and spoke with Esteban's parents about the rescue and his condition when we found him.

Thanks to the help of Aspen, Hawk's fiancée, and who I discovered is a pediatrician, the hospital was able to treat him fast. Though the medication given to him along with sedatives was dangerous, they didn't cause too much damage. At least that's what the doctor said. When I meet Aspen, I'll make sure to ask about all the medical terms they said during their conversation. The last time we checked on Esteban, he was sleeping peacefully.

Playing the part of the calm, never shaken agent wasn't hard. But I was on edge. My nerves were on fire during those hours, as we came to learn that Tiago, Hawk, and Harrison were on a manhunt. Some of the cops in the city had aided Wilson since the beginning. The men were at large and armed with high caliber weapons. I concentrated on the job. A case isn't closed until everything is settled. But the awareness that Harrison and my brother were still in danger didn't settle well with me. Anxiety swelled up inside me, threatening to swallow me from the inside out. My lungs threatened to collapse several times. Breathing became almost impossible. I concentrated on the job, but not thinking about Harrison was a full-time job.

Relief arrived in the form of good news. They had tied all the loose ends and were on their way to Texas to meet Lucas and his FBI team, who are going to take care of Wilson and his people. Then, Harrison and the rest of the crew would fly to HQ. I had no idea what headquarters they referred to. The FBI, their company . . . are they going to New York or Seattle?

The lightness of knowing that everyone is all right balanced the weight of the stress and heavy work I experienced since we jumped on the plane. But soon, relief and tiredness invade my body. I yawn, closing my eyes briefly to suppress the need to break down into tears. It's normal to collapse after going through an extreme physical and emotional journey, but I refuse to show the rest of the team any weakness. They might claim not to be like the FBI, but they are still men who can judge me for not looking strong and manly. Though, I would trade my regular job for one of these cases any day of the week.

"How are you feeling?" Mason asks, taking off his bulletproof jacket and shoving it in the overhead compartment.

My eyes concentrate on the impressive cut muscles on his arms. Although I'm more fascinated with his beautiful brain. I'm not attracted to him, but I can appreciate a handsome man. He's tall, built, smart, and those slanted gray eyes and his mysterious pose make anyone around turn their heads to appreciate him.

I wonder how long he has been married. And what she does for a living and if they have a big family or is it just the two of them. I smile when I see him pulling his platinum ring from his wallet.

"As I said earlier, you did amazing, from beginning to end. I do wonder how you are feeling after being awake for so long?" He sighs.

"We all took a nap, except for you and Harrison, who insisted on staying up as long as you did."

"Exhausted," I respond, finally taking a seat, putting on my seat belt.

Harrison's actions were cute. That's how I decided to compartmentalize it until we were done working. But I'm dying to see him and hug him—and kiss him. If there's ever another case like this, we need our own room. But now I just have the urge to be with him. To make sure he's all right. I haven't talked to him or seen him since we left the hotel room. I touch my lips lightly, recalling our spark —missing it.

"We're about to take off, everyone be seated." The announcement comes right after they close the jet's door.

"What happened to cordiality?" I complain this might be a private flight, but hello, where are his manners? United's greetings are better than this guy's.

"Wings has too little patience for us," Mason responds quietly. "He's one of my closest friends, and the best pilot I have. He does pretty much whatever he wants, but he always keeps us alive."

"We will be taking off in a few minutes. The weather looks ideal for a late-night flight. We plan on landing in about seven hours." He pauses, clearing his throat as he comes back to the speaker. "I've been informed by the other pilot that the team is still in Texas. I will update on their whereabouts as they update me."

Everyone finds their seats and starts settling down. I pull my purse out, take out the NYU hoodie that Harrison loaned me and the wireless headphones he bought me on the way to the airport. I make myself comfortable. If I'm lucky, I might get a few hours of sleep.

"Where did you learn how to fight?" Mason asks, his face creased with a smile when his phone rings.

"Hello, my Nine, I miss you, baby," he utters the words, and they sound like a chant, a prayer, an entire love song. "It's over, yes . . . we found him. I thought of Noah and Seth too. Yeah, on my way. About seven hours, we have to refuel in California."

He frowns when he checks his watch. "Breakfast, I should be there by breakfast. I can't wait to see you either . . . love you more."

"Sorry, I had to take this call."

"Who are Noah and Seth?"

"My kids." He taps the screen and shows me a picture of him with a gorgeous woman under his arm and three little ones with them. "Ainsley is my wife, Grace is our princess, Seth is the one in the middle, and Noah is our little one."

"Wow, you have three kids."

"Four," he corrects me. "James, our oldest is in heaven."

"Sorry," I say, pressing my lips together. I can't imagine the pain of losing a child.

"You have some impressive skills, what is it that you do at the FBI?"

The abrupt change of subject doesn't surprise me. He's shown that he's a man with an agenda who is also reserved. Mason won't feel too comfortable discussing his family until we know each other well, and he has a plan. Like Harrison, he wants me on their payroll. I just don't know what I want to do with that offer.

"Profiling. My undercover work is minimal, and they're trying to transfer me to Quantico," I say simply.

This man knows more about me. He's too precise and too technical to offer me a job on the spot if he didn't have more information than what he witnessed for the past couple of days. Is he about to make me a formal offer? Should I accept? I'm not ready to analyze an offer, let alone accept it. Though, I admit that having the freedom to proceed as I feel best is liberating. Exciting and I dare say the refreshing sensation made me want to repeat it as many times as possible.

"And you have another brother, is that right?"

That's not what I expected him to say. In fact, the words I was ready to say were, "I'll think about it" after he offered me a position with him. Are we playing chess?

"Yes. Lucas," I inform him. "He's younger than Santiago but older than me."

I'm puzzled about my brother. Why hasn't he mentioned us before? I thought he loved us. We have to have a serious talk about this. Maybe he's like our father and likes to compartmentalize everything, his family included. Neither one mixes one thing with the other. They never mix things together. Each part of their life is separate, like work, family, friends, love lives, and everything else. Lucas does it sometimes, but I don't allow him to keep things away from me. I don't care if he doesn't share with anyone else.

"We might want to keep him working for the FBI. He can be a double agent. At least for the first year," he speaks, looking at his phone. "He helped immensely today. Are your fighting skills part of what they taught you at the Academy?"

I can't help but laugh. "Dad wanted me to learn martial arts, like the boys. That didn't mean that I would fight, only that I could defend myself. He was hoping I'd be a teacher, like Mom."

His eyes land on my face, they are wide. "I never thought of that. Fuck, what if Grace wants to do what I do?"

"You support her," I advise. "Without giving her any shit about it."

"I assume that your father isn't happy with your choice."

"I continued training with different martial art teachers and learned how to use weapons." I touch my bracelets. Like him, there are things I'm not planning on sharing just yet. "I joined the FBI because I thought I'd be in the field, chasing bad guys."

Lara Croft and Wonder Woman were my heroes back then. I wanted to be them. I believed that anything was possible. After years on the job, I know that anything is possible as long as it's approved by my supervisor. That's just after I had filed the necessary paperwork and as long as it follows protocol.

"The real world is different. I get to do some stuff, but not everything I wanted to do when I decided to join the FBI." Pulling my hair into a low ponytail, I use one of the ties and say, "All my weapons are mostly jewelry. I don't like guns. While working, I've used them only a couple of times, pretending that they are just jewelry and they slipped out of my hands. Tiago gave me these beauties."

"You're welcome," Mason says proudly. "It took me a couple of years to design them. My sister who is a jewelry maker helped me with them."

"They're yours?"

"Tiago volunteered to find us someone to use them. He's never given me a report on how they work." He bobs his head a couple of times. "I assume they do their job."

"I use them mostly when I'm training." I stare at my bracelets, which are gorgeous. "Tell your sister that she's amazing."

"Thea will be happy to hear that." He nods. "Send me your feedback so I can work on them. I'll be searching for a way to get you an armor that you can use when you're in the field."

I swallow, nodding. Back at the house, I thought today was going to be my last one. The bullets hit Tiago, but if he hadn't moved in front of me . . . I shiver. We almost lost him. Those seconds after he had been shot felt like hours. But thankfully, he was breathing.

"Tell me about your current case with the FBI."

"I'd rather not," I retort.

"That's the wrong question, sorry." He puts his phone away and pulls out his computer from his backpack. "Don't you think we can solve it faster if you join me?"

"Who'll pay you?" I fire back.

He doesn't know my current situation, and I don't want to discuss it with anyone until I know what's going to happen next.

"Most likely someone in the Bureau will owe us a favor." He shrugs. "That's more valuable than money, trust me."

He clears his throat. "I'm not asking you to decide now, but think about the offer that Harrison put on the table. You'll be a good addition."

36

LUNA

My heart thuds inside my ribcage, threatening to jump as Harrison stands right outside the airplane holding a bouquet of flowers and a couple of metallic balloons. A sudden storm of emotions moves up my chest, expanding it as I take one step after the other. He's here, waiting for me, safe. I break down in tears as every single event that happened since we boarded the plane finally hits me.

"Fuck, you're exhausted, my little moon," he says gently, harboring my body between his arms. "Did you sleep at all?"

I shake my head, trying to control myself but there're only two things I can do, cry and hold onto him tightly. I bare my teeth, fighting to control those tears but they come faster as the rage travel through my veins. All these people are witnessing me breaking down.

"Harrison, make sure that the two of you visit the counselor before heading back to New York," Mason orders. "Luna, this is the only time you can work on a mission without sleeping for so long. We have certain rules too. You have to take care of your emotional and physical health."

I dry my tears roughly, pushing myself away from Harrison's

grasp. "We have to go back to New York, I have work to do," I demand.

His eyes soften, he hands me the flowers. "I understand, but we can't leave. Each of us has to file a report. You have to sleep at least for a few hours, and after what happened we are required to visit the therapist."

"I didn't shoot anyone," I say with a steady voice.

"You killed one person using your weapons." He touched my bracelets. "Fuck, you're the coolest kid on the block now."

He hands me the flowers, kissing my cheek. "Can we go home, sleep for a few hours and then discuss what's next, please?"

"Home?" I look around. "This is Seattle. You live here?"

"I have a place here, and it's also my home," he comments, playing with the laces of the sweatshirt I'm wearing. "I like how you look with this, if you want, I have a T-shirt you can wear to bed."

"Bed?" I sigh.

He wraps his arms around my waist. His forehead rests on mine. His soft breath caresses my face, and every cell in my body finally settles. "I'm going to kiss you when we get home," he says, quietly. "I want to lose myself on your lips and erase the anguish I lived through while I waited to have you in my arms again. I need to feel the beat of your heart close to mine. There's no name for what's happening inside me, it's beyond love. And I swear Luna, I don't want it to stop."

Yes, I want those strong arms wrapped around me, his breath caressing the side of my neck. Don't stop it, never stop it. Let it blossom and spread through the entire universe.

☆ ☆ ☆

"I know what you're doing," Harrison says when we enter his apartment. His lips are red and swollen from all the kissing we did while his driver drove us from the airport. "You're stalling the inevitable."

"We have to talk," I sigh, touching my tingling lips.

"Does it matter to you what I say? Or how I feel?"

"I—" I bite my lip as he comes closer to me.

His blue eyes blaze. He slips a hand behind my neck, leans in, and kisses me.

It's slow.

Tender.

Delicate as the petals of the flowers I hold.

His lips fit perfectly with mine.

This kiss is different from the first one. I see as the elusive threads from his heart weave a strong bond with mine. A spark ignites the small flame as our tongues continue dancing. It grows, burning my body. My soul jolts as the blazing heat awakens my dormant soul filling it with passion. An unknown tune plays inside my head. It matches the rhythm of beats as our kiss intensifies. It's a song I never want to end, a melody I want to continue for eternity as I'm consumed by him.

And then all at once, everything stops.

He sighs, moving his gaze to blink up at the ceiling for a few beats. Then, our eyes meet. Those magnetic blues are liquid pools of desire. "I want this to happen between us." He runs a hand through his hair, closing his eyes. "I want us to be together. But once it happens, you have to know that I'll never let you go."

My brain fizzles. "I want to stay." I find my voice, even when my legs are shaking, and my mouth only wants to continue swaying with his.

I'm desperate for his touch.

I need more from him.

I want to burn slowly as he caresses every inch of my body.

And I'm willing to give him whatever he needs in exchange.

I'll give him everything.

"Please," I whisper.

"Not here," he says against my lips. "I want this to be special. To be perfect. To be ours."

He leads me through the hallway toward a bright room. The bed is against a wall of glass. He takes the remote on top of the nightstand and uses it to lower the drapes to cover all the walls of windows. In only a few seconds, the place has darkened. With just another click, a softer light illuminates the room. Tossing the remote back where it belongs, he lifts his shirt over his head and tosses it to the floor.

I stare at him, searching for the right words to say. Do I have to say something?

"You're thinking too much, Luna. I can hear your thoughts."

He takes me into his arms, crushing his mouth against mine.

This kiss is demanding, impatient, hungry. His hands slide down my sides and grab the edges of my sweatshirt and dress. He pulls them over my head. I am exposed except for my bra and panties. My body is almost bare, my heart is open, and my soul is visible. There's nothing I can use to cover myself. Seeing as he's almost in the same position as I am, I let myself flow within this moment. It's been so long since I've been with a man. It's been forever since I've cared for my partner. And I never have shown my vulnerability the way I do with Harrison. He's shown me the same openness. It's only fair to trust him with this too.

"Fuck, you're gorgeous," he mumbles against my lips, sliding his hands over my naked back toward my buttocks. He squeezes it before pushing my panties down. "I've wanted to squeeze your tight, beautiful ass since the morning you did that to me."

He kisses my skin as he lowers himself down my body. "It feels like it happened eons ago. We've been through so much that I feel like I've known you forever."

His warm hands spread and caress my legs as he disposes of the small article of clothing, slowly, tempting me, scattering pleasure along the way.

"But I still have so much to discover." He rises, staring at my almost naked body. He snaps my bra open from the front clasp. "Next time, I promise I'll take my time undressing you. But today . . . I need to feel that you're alive. To see you come alive when you scream my name."

I press my legs together, feeling the dampness between them. Each word he professes sends a tremor through my body.

"This moment is all I've thought about for the past twelve hours," he confesses, taking me into his arms, setting me down in the middle of the bed.

He plants kisses along my bare skin. Each one flutters through me. "I am dying to taste you, to feast on you. To burn from the inside out as I bury myself deep inside you."

Harrison undoes his jeans, pushing them down. I take my time staring at his gorgeous body. The ripped abs, lean torso, and broad shoulders I've seen before, but I've never had a chance to appreciate them. I lift my hand, wanting to touch him, to trace every ripple, learn each dent and kiss every corner.

He positions himself over my body. "Are you okay with this happening between us?"

Goose bumps clothe my bare skin as his hands stroke my arms.

"Isn't it a little late to be asking?"

"It's never too late." He traces a line close to my breasts, but he doesn't touch them. "Fuck, I imagined them being two beauties. They are perfect, like you." He runs his finger along my jaw. "I would never go through with it if you decided this isn't what you want, never."

"I want it." I draw a breath in a stuttered gasp as his lips brush against the base of my neck. "I need you to fill me, to fire me up like a star."

I float with elation as his lips touch mine. If I could ask for an unlimited supply of something, it'd be his kisses. All of them. My heart skips several beats when his long fingers trace my body. My hands slide up and down his torso, learning every sharp line of those perfectly cut muscles. His hard erection presses against my stomach. The spark is back, this time igniting the center of my core.

He nibbles my skin, caressing every inch his lips have touched. I shiver as his tongue runs down my belly and he separates my thighs. I cover my face with my hands as I scream when the tip of his tongue touches my core.

"Your sweetness is addictive." He dips his face against my pussy. His tongue flicks my swollen clit.

I grip the covers of the bed as he inserts a finger inside me and his mouth continues making love to me. A force like none I've ever felt builds inside my body concentrating right where Harrison's mouth is. I push myself harder against him, seeking release. The warmth he creates flows effortlessly in an endless stream of pleasure. He licks me, kisses me, and thrusts his fingers faster. My head is about to explode. I'm becoming stardust in his universe as I moan his name over and over.

He moves up. His eyes find mine. "Watching you fall apart is one of the best miracles I've ever witnessed, Luna. You're the most beautiful woman I've ever seen in my life."

The tip of his cock is right at my entrance. I hold my breath as the magnitude of what's about to happen is bigger than I anticipated. The lines are gone. We don't have rules, only a demand for one another that's greater than our fears. He slides inside me leisurely, pushing his ample length so deep we fuse into one.

He thrusts in and out.

Filling me.

Filling us.

Every second that passes, the bond between us strengthens. It happens with every slow, loving, and tender thrust. This buildup is different from anything I've ever experienced in my entire life. It feels as if this is the first time I've ever been with anyone. His tender hands caress my body. Mine mirror his movements. During this life-changing moment, no words are spoken, yet everything is said between us as we build a fire as pure and blue as his eyes. The raging flames flicker between us, blazing our bodies, igniting our souls.

And when I feel like I can't take anymore, he changes the rhythm. It's faster, frantic. Slow and easy is off the table, the pressure inside me begins to build up again as he pumps into me deeper. I arch as I reach my climax, my walls milking his throbbing cock. The entire universe is crumbling as we both moan. He buries himself deeper as his body shudders a couple of times before it stills. I cling onto him screaming his name as we both come together.

"Luna." My name sounds like a prayer.

He remains silent, then kisses my neck. "You just brought me back to life," he says gruffly.

I caress his face. My arms and legs feel heavy, just like my eyes. The orgasms have taken away the last strand of energy that I had left. All those hours of work come crashing down on me, and I finally close my eyes.

EPILOGUE

Luna

I filed my first report with HIB. They gave me a badge, and credentials to sign in to the computer system which has more security protocols than the Pentagon. Those were Mason's words. I received a laptop and a big payment. As of today, my checking account balance is at its highest ever. That was only for this week's job. I have money. Not that I didn't have any before, but my salary with the FBI is nothing compared to what HIB offered to pay if I accepted the job.

Mason and Harrison gave me a tour of the corporate offices, the gun range, the training installation, and the cafeteria. I had a meeting, and they updated me on Esteban's condition. He's out of the hospital and at home with his parents. He doesn't remember much of the events. The job offer came after the good news.

"If I accept, what am I going to do with the current case?" I asked because the change of scenery is tempting.

"You can leave it for the FBI to work on it, or . . ." Mason tapped his hand on the glass table. "You could solve it while you work for us. You'll have all the recourses from HIB available twenty-four seven.

Once you've gathered enough intelligence and if we as a team decide that it's enough to bring him down, we will support you."

"Mr. Medina is considered one of the biggest human traffickers in South America," I informed them.

"Our team has gathered enough information to prove that there are bigger fishes to trap," Mason added. "He's strong, but there are names that the FBI doesn't pay attention to because they aren't affecting this country . . . yet."

"What does that mean?"

"It means that you can be privy to more information once you are part of our team, not before," Mason stated with a firm voice.

"I need a little more time to assimilate what happened during the past couple of days," I countered.

☆ ☆ ☆

"How does this work?"

I can't take her seriously. Her hair is all the colors of the rainbow, she has butterfly tattoos on her arms and wears the most beautiful dress I've ever seen. And she wants to talk about my case instead of chatting about the heart-shaped crystal pendant she wears. *Can we be best friends?*

"We discuss your last assignment." She looks at her path and then at me. "You're new to the team."

"No, it was a consulting job. I work for the FBI."

"Oh, then you have to report to them, don't you?"

I shake my head. "They don't know I'm here. Actually, I don't think they know where I am. They think I'm working undercover in New York."

"But you're not?"

"I've collected data, made a few contacts. It's a long-term operation . . . but I'm going back next week and quitting. I am a better fit at HIB."

She scratches the tip of her nose lightly. "Why is that?"

I give her a brief history of what's been happening with my job.

The rocky relationship I have with my boss. The reasons I left Alexandria, and how I went from missing my family to finding a home.

"It's not only him but his brothers and the Beesley girls who are like his sisters," I continue. "Then, there's this mission. And the job offer. They took my ideas and actually let me be the one leading. Mason was supportive and helped, but he let me do most of the work."

She gives me a knowing smile. Her look encourages me to continue.

"Though, I feel that by leaving the FBI I'm letting them win."

"What are they winning?"

I sigh, thinking about what they'll win if I go.

"What are you losing with this new job?"

I toy with my bracelets, missing the four that I had to use on Wilson. The pay is better, the opportunities to do what I love are right in the palm of my hand, and I will be working with Tiago. My brother. Lucas is thinking about the offer too. "I win. Is it bad that I don't feel any remorse after killing one guy?"

"Did you have to?" Her question is simple, but weighing the answer isn't just that simple.

"To save my brother," I respond, nodding, then pulling my chopstick and showing it to her. She tries to hide the smile. "I'm not saying it felt good, but I was relieved that he's okay and that this guy wouldn't kidnap another kid."

She nods.

"If you have to do it again?"

"I would do it, but I hope I don't have to . . . I just don't know how my father is going to feel about me leaving the FBI and moving out of the house. Though I shouldn't care. He lied to me for years."

The timer goes off while I'm telling her about my mother and everything that happened to her.

"As parents, we make mistakes," she says, turning off the alarm. "But it's because we love our children. With time, you can work things out with him. Even if you are away from home."

She clears her throat.

"I feel like you can go out in the field today if you wanted to. But, if you want to talk more, here is my number. My Skype information and my email address—they aren't the same." She hands me a card. "We can also discuss your father and how you adjust to all the changes you're experiencing. Seems like you're doing all right but it's always good to have an outsider listen to you."

"Thank you." I've never liked going to counseling while working for the bureau. It felt like I was being judged and if I said the wrong thing I might lose my job. Here, well I have nothing to lose.

"I hope this helped."

I put the card inside my wallet. "It did, and I might call you soon."

*

A year later

"Are you alone tonight, sweetheart?" Joe, the bartender asks. I shrug, winking at him. He's an old friend of mine. I grab the glass, looking around the dim, crowded bar for a place to sit. In the corner, I find an empty table. It's busier than I expected for a Thursday night. Looking at the flat screen as all the patrons grunt, I understand. The Rangers are playing the Bruins. I consider myself lucky that I grabbed the last table. Lifting my glass, I swallow my cold, cherry-lime flavored drink. I don't enjoy the taste, but the Shirley Temple will have to do it for now. If I had a choice, I'd be drinking whiskey. Looking at my clothes, I remind myself to stay in character.

"Is this seat taken?" My gaze drifts to the man who's speaking in a low voice and has clear blue, captivating eyes. He wears a fitted black shirt and a pair of jeans.

Straightening my back, I flash a wide smile at him. "I'm waiting for a friend."

"A friend?" He arches a brow, lifting his hand and snapping his fingers. "What are you drinking?"

"I'm good, thank you," I say with the sweetest voice I can manage. Would a librarian sound like that? No, maybe she should be somber. Hmm, I didn't do much research for tonight. I smooth my plaid mini skirt, straightening my back.

He glances at the table, taking my drink. Smoothly he places it in his firm, sexy lips, sips it and spits.

"Fuck, Luna what are you drinking?"

I bat my eyelashes at him. "Shirley Temple, I didn't think you'd drink it." Glaring at him, I give him my best upset librarian look—I think. "You don't just go and take food from other people's tables."

"You're not a stranger," he defends himself.

Gah!

This is going downhill.

"What happened to lonely librarian meets dangerous outlaw?" I glare at the man who just ruined our fantasy night.

One corner of his mouth lifts, then he glances at me. "He saw his girlfriend wearing a tiny skirt that barely covers her tanned legs and gorgeous ass." He serves me with a smirk and a gaze filled with naughty thoughts. "What if tonight we forget about my birthday present voucher and focus on you?"

"I'm counting tonight as one of your fantasies, Everhart." I rise from my seat, placing my arms behind his neck. His arms wrap my body, one hand resting on my butt. "Five all-time sexual fantasies, this is number three. I don't care what you think."

A lopsided grin stretches across his smooth lips. He takes off my fake glasses, placing them on the table and pulls the pens holding my hair up, letting my wavy dark hair fall on my shoulders. "Having you is my all-time favorite fantasy, Luna." His filthy-naughty-bedroom voice makes my gut clench. Leaning closer, he brushes his lips against my ear. "There are a few surfaces that we haven't explored yet in our new place. Do you want to . . . come?"

I lean closer, rising on my tiptoes. His woodsy, amber scent welcomes me as I place a kiss on his jaw. My hands slide down his strong chest, traveling to his stomach, and stopping right on the waistband of his jeans. "You're all hard," I say, my fingers gliding to his crotch and palming his semi-hard length.

"Luna," he growls, taking my hands and kissing them. "I don't plan on walking three blocks with a hard-on."

"Oh, but you will." I tilt my head, smiling at him, and sauntering away in the direction of the door.

"I'll make you pay for this," he mumbles into my ear once he catches up with me. And I hope he comes through with that threat.

We walk the short distance from the bar to our place. Stepping in the elevator, he puts me in front of him. I wiggle my ass as I feel the ridge of his erection. Resting my head on his chest, I look up and find his gaze.

He places a sweet kiss on my forehead, the mischievous smile appearing right away. "I love that you try, but I guess pretending isn't something I love to have between us."

I get it. Part of our job is to be undercover for missions. As fun as it is to pretend to be Wonder Woman or that I'm a tourist, he prefers to be with me.

Just me.

Once inside our place, he shuts the door and arms the security system. Then, he presses me firmly against the wall.

"You know what my fantasy is for tonight?"

He lifts my hands, holding my wrists together, and placing them above my head. His lips trail down my face, my jaw, my collarbone, and across my breasts where he lingers for a couple of breaths.

"You know what my fantasy is, baby?" He releases me, taking a step back.

The foyer is illuminated by candles and flowers. Vivaldi's Autumn piece begins to play in the background. He takes my hands, kisses them and smiles.

Pulling a red velvet box out of his pocket, he drops on one knee and opens it.

Inside there's a rose gold solitaire ring.

"Harry," I whisper, covering my mouth lightly.

My heart thunders inside my ribcage as I hold the happy tears threatening to cascade down my cheeks.

"Luna, you came into my life unexpectedly. I had no idea how much you'd change my life. You shook my entire world, showed me true love and have remained by my side during my best and my worst times. Every day with you is a new challenge and a new adventure. Whether we are at home, on vacations, or working on a mission, I want to spend the rest of my life with you."

He takes a deep breath. "I love you. You're my life—the best part of me. Please, fulfill my ultimate fantasy. Would you be my wife?"

"Yes, yes!"

I take his face with both hands, feathering kisses on it. "Of course, I'll be your wife. Have I told you yet that you bring happiness into my life? You mean the world to me, Harry. You're the best thing that has ever happened to me. I can't imagine life without you." I lean forward, hugging him tightly. "I love you forever."

His arms go around my back, our lips brush, then press together. I moan as his tongue parts my lips. We kiss hard, long and fully as we exchange new promises without words and ignite that fire that never stops consuming us.

"You're all I need, Luna. My only fantasy. My entire world. I love you for always."

Dear Reader,

Thank you for reading Fervent. Ever since I wrote Unsurprisingly Complicated, I wanted to write the stories about the men who worked with Mason Bradley. As I reader I enjoy most kinds of genres, except horror. And one of my favorite authors and a woman who I've admired for many years is JD Robb (Nora Roberts). Her, Agatha Christy and James Patterson are some of my favorite suspense/mystery/thriller authors. The Women's Murder Club is among my favorite series. Writing this book was a new challenge, also, the beginning of a new series. I'm planning on bringing Mason and his crew back together.

There are many cases that need to be solved, and Luna had just started to dig into the FBI case. Her and her new boyfriend are ready to leap and take the world by storm.

In case you're wondering, here are my next projects.

2018 projects:

Found January/February 2018 (Keep reading for an unedited excerpt of this must read story)

Untitled (Fitz book) April 2018

Untitled (Harrison & Luna) June 2018

Untitled (Tucker duet) September 2018

After finishing the book, and if you enjoyed it. Please do me a favor and leave a review on any or all the retailers where it's sold. Spread the word telling others about it. Don't forget that I love to hear from you, my readers, so please don't hesitate to email me.

Thank for your continuous support.

Sending you all my love and lots of hugs.

Claudia xo

ACKNOWLEDGMENTS

I am so grateful to so many people. First and foremost, to all my readers. You're the power that pushes this engine. I am grateful to have you. Thank you for reading my words, and for supporting my books. Thank you so much for those emails and notes, they mean so much to me.

My husband for his continuous love and support, not sure where I'll be without you, babe.

To the amazing group of editors that helped me shape Fervent. Paulina, Ellie, Virginia, Marla, and Mo Stysma.

Stephie Walls who was writing but still made time to go through the manuscript and helped me polished it. I'm so thankful for everything that you do for me.

Thank you to Debra and Drue who help continuously help me pushing my books and my brand.

My beta readers, Yolanda, Colleen, Christine, Melissa and Patricia. Thank you for reading the first draft of Fervent and helping me with the Everhart boys who are proving to be amazing and challenging.

To Hang Le. I'm thankful for her patience, her talent and her friendship. I love you so much.

To my Chicas, you're the best fans in the universe. I love you from here to the moon.

Thank you to Give Me books. To all the bloggers, and event organizers. Your effort and energy are what makes my releases such a success. Thank you so much for everything you do for them, I appreciate every single one of you.

Claudia is an award-winning, *USA Today* bestselling author. She writes alluring, thrilling stories about complicated women and the men who take their breath away. She lives in Denver, Colorado with her husband and her youngest two children. She has a sweet Bichon, Macey, who thinks she's the ruler of the house. She's only partially right.

When Claudia is not writing, you can find her reading, knitting, or just hanging out with her family. At night, I like to binge-watch shows with his equal geek husband.

To find more about Claudia:
www.claudiaburgoa.com

ALSO BY CLAUDIA BURGOA

Unlike Any Other

Decker the Halls

Made in the USA
Columbia, SC
14 March 2020

89188963R00135